THE DISTANCE FROM HOME

DANIEL JACOBS

THE DISTANCE FROM HOME

DANIEL JACOBS

International Psychoanalytic Books (IPBooks)
New York • IPBooks.net

International Psychoanalytic Books (IPBooks)
Queens, New York
Online at: www.IPBooks.net

Book design by Dan Williams

ISBN: 978-1-949093-09-4

Printed in the United States of America

for Sue

Always keep Ithaca fixed in your mind.
To arrive there is your ultimate goal.
But do not hurry the voyage at all.
It is better to let it last for long years;
and even to anchor at the isle when you are old,
rich with all that you have gained on the way,
not expecting that Ithaca will offer you riches.

—C. P. Cavafy (trans. Rae Dalven), *Ithaca*

CHAPTER ONE
DEPARTURES

The dead never look as good as they should or as happy as they might. George Albright lying in a coffin didn't look as though he'd agreed to die, even though death had come at his own hand. His jaw was clenched and his lips drawn down in disgust.

"It was ghastly," Pru, his wife and my best friend, said over the phone. George hanging in a closet, a Countess Mara tied around his neck. His face bloated and blue, his swollen tongue sticking out at her. He must have known Pru would be the one to find him.

"Don't blame yourself," I said. She said she didn't. He'd made his own bed.

The news came as a surprise, of course, but I can't say I was shocked. My mother died when I was nine. No death shocks you after that. Her passing was one of two events that changed my life. The second took place in 1972, when George included me in his travel scheme.

Looking back, it seems strange that all of us should have agreed to go. Only George knew precisely where Gokyo was or what it would take to get there. Least prepared of all for such a trip—Hannah Avery. That was me, age thirty-seven, a woman who never left her bed unmade or a library book unreturned, an unlikely candidate to trade the comforts of a Manhattan two-bedroom, rent-stabilized apartment for a mountain tent and sleeping bag. Unlikely to take sudden leave of the Musée Baudry, where I was a curator, to change the course of my life by trekking.

Now, twenty-two years after our trek, the Frank E. Campbell Funeral Chapel was seeing George Albright out, as they had so many since 1898. Jews mourned at the Riverside Memorial Chapel on Amsterdam Avenue. Catholics and Episcopalians had their churches scattered throughout the city. Campbell's, on the corner of Eighty-First and Madison, concentrated on wealthy East Siders with tenuous connections to religion. Paul Levin and his wife, Miriam, were at the service. Miriam and I went back a long way, and Bobby, her son, was one I would have liked for myself. He arrived on the red-eye from Stanford, where he was teaching linguistics and hoping for tenure. He must have come right from the plane. His face was unshaven and his suit crumpled. Ever since the trek, he had been very fond of George. There were tears in his eyes as he came toward me. "There's no way we can all go to Gokyo again," he said, hugging me tightly.

I freed myself from him and straightened his tie. He could go on his own now, I said. George wouldn't mind. He began to cry and said George never liked being left behind. He was right about that. George always wanted to be at the center of things, as he was this morning.

There wasn't a lot for Pru to arrange. George had left specific instructions—where, when, who to invite. He had decided on the chapel's famous "white-glove service," which calls for soft lighting, polished pews and recordings of your choice. George Albright had been director of cosmetic surgery at Lenox Hill Hospital for thirty years, past president of the New York Medical Society as well as the American Society of Plastic Surgeons.

Medical colleagues arrived for the funeral in somber Armani suits and Sulka ties, which the Duke of Windsor was known to favor. Surgical residents hurried in straight from the OR, jackets thrown carelessly over blue scrubs. Many grateful patients came: those for whom he had provided altered breasts, tucked tummies, reshaped thighs, and reconfigured noses. There were a few actresses in the crowd. One, I think, starred in a film I never saw. Another was a face I'd seen on a daytime serial when I was down with the flu. In the front row, George's grown sons sat silent, heads erect and eyes forward, trying, I suppose, to remain composed while they waited for their mother to arrive. Waiting was something they had been used to. As youngsters, they had often waited for their father to come home and waited for their mother to laugh instead of shout. They took the opportunity to avoid their parents' quarrels by claiming a "need to study" instead of going with them to Nepal.

The meeting to discuss the trek began modestly enough. "So you've decided! You took your time about it," George said, ushering me into the living room, where the others had already gathered.

Pru came and kissed me. Libby and Howard Kramer gave a small wave. They were both in their forties and deep into law: Howard newly appointed to the bench of Second Circuit Court of Appeals, Libby a busy divorce attorney. When they were profiled in *New York* magazine five years earlier and described as "up and coming," Pru recognized Libby from high school and they renewed an old friendship. The two couples had seen a lot of each other since then, with me sometimes tagging along. Howard and Libby lived near Lincoln Center. They would offer to pick me up and take me home if we were all going to one of the boisterous parties that the Albrights gave.

That evening of the meeting about Nepal, in 1972, was very different and hardly a celebration. It was a warm summer night and the windows of the Albrights' Fifth Avenue apartment had been opened to let in a breeze from the park. Only a handful of people had been invited beside Libby and Howard. Paul Levin and Bobby, then thirteen, were there. They sat side by side on folding chairs. The boy gave me a hug and Paul a tired smile. The presence of Leon Kaminsky was a surprise and not an entirely pleasant one. The Albrights, for good reason, hadn't told me he would be traveling with us. I'm always awkward meeting former lovers: finding myself vertical instead of horizontal, talking because there is nothing else for us to do. Leon looked at me and grinned, motioning me to a seat beside him. There was nowhere else to sit.

George began by telling us how he had always wanted to trek in Nepal and how glad he was that we were all accompanying him. "It's a fabulous country," he said, unfolding a map that showed a small green smudge between the yellow of India and red of China.

The little I knew about Nepal came from visiting an Asia Society exhibit, *Reign and Ritual.* One room was filled with religious statuary fierce bronze Durgas and graceful Shivas. Its walls were cluttered with ancient scroll paintings depicting the life of the Buddha. Another room was devoted to a short history of the mountain kingdom: stiff, unsatisfying oils of bejeweled rulers interspersed with black-and-white photos of impoverished subjects. I thought Nepal was an ancient country, but learned it was unified only in 1769. The rulers' history of corruption, assassination and vile court intrigue made the Medici look like schoolchildren. I gave up following their family wrangling when I learned that the nineteenth-century hereditary prime minister, Jang Bahadur, had fathered a hundred children, many contenders for his power. Birendra, myopic and with an unnervingly blank expression, had only recently ascended the throne at the time of the Albright meeting. He ruled a desperately poor country of twelve million. Eight million were illiterate and 45 percent hadn't enough to eat. It hardly seemed a country worth ruling over or, I thought, visiting.

"It's going to be a totally different experience than any you've ever had," George told us. Roughly one hundred and twenty miles wide and five hundred and fifty miles long, Nepal hosted over one hundred mother tongues, many without a written counterpart. A nation with eight of the world's tallest mountains, including Everest, and a life expectancy of 45.

"We'll be trekking for a little more than a month, with some days in Kathmandu on either end. There'll be porters to carry our stuff."

George warned against our drinking the water or eating anything uncooked. He held up a bottle of Lugol's iodine solution that we were to put into any liquid we drank. Shots for tetanus, cholera, typhoid, smallpox, and polio were needed, plus gamma globulin to protect against hepatitis. Then there were the clothes we had to bring: T-shirts because the sun was hot during the day, sweaters and long johns because the nights were cold. Gloves and wool hats would be necessary as we climbed higher. We would need insect repellent and sunscreen. And we were to watch out for leeches that could get into your boots and suck blood from between your toes. George began to sound like the warnings that came with my diet pills—the ones it's best not to read. If others were having doubts about the trip, they weren't admitting them.

I wondered how I would explain to Harrington, the director of Musée Baudry, that I was taking a long vacation on short notice. "The paintings will still be on the wall when you get back" was all he said.

That was one of the museum's problems. The funds for new acquisitions were very small. Marcel Baudry, for whom the institution was named, had died in 1954 at ninety-two. He had cornered the egg market in France at the turn of the century. He sold his chicken business and moved to Manhattan with his French wife in 1912, investing his money in Brooklyn tenements. He made enough to buy a mansion on Seventy-Eighth, just off Fifth Avenue, and began collecting art. When he died, his two daughters in Paris and a son in London had no interest in returning home. They turned his residence and its contents into the Musée Baudry in exchange for tax exemptions and a promise not to sell its holdings. The Baudry is dwarfed by its neighbor, the Metropolitan, and looked down upon by its nearby rival, the Frick. Marcel had been considered *nouveau,* "still smelling of the chicken coop," according to Elsa Maxwell. He had been eclectic in his tastes, filling his home with art from every century: a potpourri of interesting and valuable works, among them a few eggs by Fabergé and a small head of Christ attributed to Verrocchio. The museum was best known, however, for its two El Grecos, its library of illuminated manuscripts and the small collection of Dutch still lifes that I oversaw. The Baudry boasted of a pocket-sized rose garden and a café with the best mille-feuille in town.

What had been hardest to leave behind were my tulips. I live in an apartment on Riverside Drive without a view of the Hudson. It goes without saying I have no garden. A window box jutting from my ninth floor would be an invitation to calamity. Besides, I have no green thumb. When, as a child, I started a garden, tomatoes rarely ripened and broccoli grew lanky. So I wasn't leaving real grow-out-of-the-ground tulips, but illustrations of them. Two original watercolor-and-gouache illustrations from an unidentified tulip catalogue, one done by Bartholomeus Assteyn, the other by Ambrosius Bosschaert the younger. Painted in Holland in the seventeenth century for people like me who didn't want to bother with or couldn't afford the real thing. Or for wealthy buyers who wanted to see the bloom before they bought the bulb. There's the advantage of their blooming year-round. The illustrations are museum quality; the Bosschaert is a single white *Speramondi* with four leaves and touches of red at the edges of its petals; the Assteyn depicts a striated yellow-and-red *Schoon Sollfer* with a beetle beside it.

I am considered an authority on Dutch flower painting, though the book I wrote, *Seventeenth Century Dutch Garden Design,* which first got me a job at the Musée Baudry, is long out of print. There aren't many of us devoted to garden design. We meet, when museum budgets permit, in dreary airport hotels near London, Istanbul or Amsterdam. Of course, much of the talk is about the tulip and its journey to Europe from Turkey as early as the sixteenth century. There are the expected papers on the tulipomania that gripped Holland from 1634–1637. Buying bulbs was like purchasing stocks then: fortunes were made and lost on which bulbs bloomed most beautifully. Possession of a rare tulip was the ultimate status symbol, the Lamborghini of its time. One bulb could be worth a bricklayer's monthly wage. And what if you had bought hundreds of them?

I will leave the tulips to my daughter, May, who never really liked them, though she understands their value. I told her she could sell them and make her old age more comfortable. There are now roughly 120 species of tulips catalogued into endless sub-types and groupings, but none of them equal the blossoms on my wall. I can't afford to insure them so I worry about them when I go away.

Of course, there were other things I was more than happy to leave. Nineteen seventy-two, the year of the trek, was a bad year. The wheels were coming off the Vietnam War. Ho Chi Minh's troops had crossed the DMZ. The United States was withdrawing ground troops while increasing its air attacks. Still, the body counts kept coming: boys fresh out of high school sent back in bags. Westmoreland gave glowing accounts of Pyrrhic victories. The peace talks in Paris seemed stalled. Back home, the maxi dress was in and the miniskirt out, and leisure suits were the rage. There were Betty Crocker Easy-Bake Ovens for kids and Linda Lovelace's *Deep Throat* for adults. It was the year eleven Israeli athletes were murdered in Munich and a coal slurry in West Virginia killed 118 (with seven missing) after a dam failed. I marched to stop the war a few times, sent letters to Washington now and then, gave money when I could. I was too caught up in my own life with Frank to do much more.

Frank Hobart was an autodidact who could talk about everything from Australian cattle dogs to the best way to make guacamole. Tall and thin, with horn-rimmed glasses when he could find them, he bore a slight resemblance to Arthur Miller before Marilyn.

His conversation was of full of surprises—words thrown in from German or Latin, puns, double entendres and bits of poetry. I often thought his mind was like the Met or the Louvre, where you never knew what you might come upon. Yet there was nothing showy in his manner. He accepted that he was thought brilliant and tried not to disappoint. When I asked him once what he saw in me, he answered, "Your beauty, intelligence. *Quoi d'autre?* Your need for order, respite for a restless mind."

"Is that the same as love?" I asked. He smiled and kissed me, saying, "It's as close as I get."

That was close enough for me. I knew he had given me more of himself than he had to any woman. He had welcomed me into his literary world and his personal history. Frank always had ideas about what to do. He admired Racine and his twelve-syllable alexandrine rhyme scheme. He insisted I brush up on my college French so we could read *Phedre* aloud. We did crosswords together, and on snowy evenings he taught me how to win at Scrabble. We went out often, as Frank loved theater and opera and had a subscription to the New York Philharmonic. He was a very good cook, but not much on housecleaning. Forty-one and never married, with no interest in children.

"They are like sponges soaking up time," he would say.

He always kept a place of his own, though he was with me almost every night. The celebrated author of three books of poetry and a collection of essays, *Culture and Crisis: America's Way in the World* (Knopf), Frank was forever reading or on the phone arranging to meet someone famous. He had drinks, more than once, with Harold Pinter when the playwright was in town. At the opening of Gordone's *No Place to Be Somebody,* we sat with Joseph Papp. I liked the play, but Frank had his reservations.

"A bit polemical, don't you think? In line for a Pulitzer, no doubt. Who's going to vote against a decent play about race relations?"

In bed that next night, before turning out the light, he read what he'd written about it for the *Village Voice.* "What do you think?" he asked. I had learned by then he wasn't looking for my opinion, only my admiration.

Frank was more interested in my work than I was. Made me teach him all about Rembrandt's etchings, several of which we had at the Baudry, *The Three Trees* being the prize. He tracked down the ownership of each of the still extant eighty-two original copperplates and corresponded with the owners about their condition and provenance. He read every book he could find on Rembrandt and soon knew as much as I.

"Maybe we can pop over to Madrid one day and see his *Judith at the Banquet,*" he said.

We planned to go the following spring—Madrid and the Prado, the Roman ruins in Valencia, maybe the beach at Alicante. In the meantime, he decided to interview my boss for a piece on the Baudry family. Harrington was delighted and, for a while, he smiled on me. "Quite the man, your Frank. He'll do our place some good. Hang on to him." I did, for two more years.

During that time, my neighbor Mrs. Olsen lost a grandson in a Vietcong rocket attack on the Da Nang air base. She lived in apartment 9C, I in 9D. We had become friends waiting for the self-service elevator and then managed a dinner every few weeks. She was a widow with one divorced daughter on the Grand Concourse and one beloved grandson, Sam, that I heard all about. It took awhile for the boy's body to be delivered home. I would sit with her in her apartment, a jungle of upholstered chairs, dying plants and fading silver-framed photos while she waited. She told me about her grandson and I told her about Frank.

I told her how uneasy Frank was with me and time. He didn't understand that you had to look at a painting for hours before it revealed itself. And then you had to find just the right place for it. It drove him crazy that I still hadn't decided where in the museum to hang a recent donation, a painting of dead poultry by van Utrecht. He trusted his first impressions, whether it was about a book, play or painting. There wasn't a minute he would waste. His watch as big as a hand. A paperback stuck in his jacket pocket for the subway. He hated having to wait while I reapplied lipstick or touched up my hair.

"Ready yet? They won't hold our reservation," he'd call querulously from the living room.

"In a minute," I'd reply, flustered by his tone.

At dinner, he was looking for the check before I'd finished dessert. Frank called me "slowpoke." When I objected, he became sarcastic. "At your pace, the world needs thirty-six hours in a day."

Mrs. Olsen listened and nodded sympathetically, saying that her experience had been different. Her husband had been a very patient man. She thought selling insurance made him that way.

There was a final fight with Frank. We were late for a meeting with one of his friends. I had taken a quick shower and was slipping into a dress. I could hear him pacing in the other room.

"In a minute," I called.

"That's it!" he shouted, and began storming around the apartment, throwing his things into a suitcase, piling his books by the door. I caught up with him at the elevator, the back of my dress unzipped.

"That's what?"

It was over, he told me. He'd come for his things in the morning.

After he left, I would have agreed to go anywhere except back to my apartment. George had proposed the trip to Nepal earlier but I had declined. Frank hadn't been interested. Now it suddenly seemed like a good idea.

"It will do us all good to get out of here," George said that evening we met to discuss the trek. Everyone in the hiking party was a friend of mine or, at least, an acquaintance when we began.

It was different afterward. George, for instance, never quite understood why I never visited Nepal again. He didn't understand how hard it would be to go back.

Now he was dead and 1994 wasn't 1972, no matter how much I might like it to be. Today it was Clinton, not Nixon. Hillary instead of Pat. Massacres in Rwanda and Sarajevo. And in America, O. J. Simpson was charged with murdering his wife, and it was the "Year of the Family."

Family had never been George's strong suit. Everyone knew he couldn't keep it in his pants. When his most recent infidelity went public because of a patient's lawsuit a few months ago, Pru couldn't take it any longer. George had broken his promise to stop once too often.

"He wasn't a spring chicken anymore; you'd think he could give it up," she'd told me over the phone.

And then a week ago he'd been asked to resign the chairmanship of cosmetic surgery. He called Pru, his voice shaking. "They wanted a younger face," he said. "It's all about marketing now."

What he'd been marketing, Pru told me, was his pecker. "Maybe because I lost interest in it awhile ago, knowing it had been other places."

She made a dramatic entrance at Campbell's. Just as the organ music stopped and the Unitarian minister rose, she hurried down the center aisle to a seat in front with her children. Louise, her latest lover, had her arm around Pru the entire time. Pru looked terrible. Short red hair like a soiled woolen cap that should have been given to Goodwill long ago, a long black skirt bought on sale last year, and a wrinkled silk blouse. I suppose some who didn't know her might think her appearance was due to unmitigated grief, but, in fact, she had looked that way for years. Even before Nepal, she'd stopped caring about clothes. Never wore jewelry. No makeup. Her pale, round face with its snub nose and large teeth gave her the look of an angry chipmunk. She had, by her appearance, quite consciously become a sharpened pin aimed precisely at her husband's work and swollen pride.

"What's the use?" she'd told me. "Men are always after something they don't have. Women are different, some at least. Carrying a baby makes you love what you have."

Only May, our daughter, was missing. Dear May. I imagined her beside me. Her body taut, hands clasped in her lap as she stared straight ahead. She would be looking in disbelief at George's smooth, gunmetal-gray coffin, as sleek and as large as the Buick he drove; its massive surface relieved only by ornate brass handles, three to a side. I could almost hear May whisper, "They'll never use those. It's all done on wheels and there's a machine that lowers coffins into the grave."

A lovely girl. A fount of mind-chilling information. A child

I've never fully understood. That easy familiarity and empathic attunement that comes with being female together? Well, it never fully happened. I think I was afraid to let it happen. Could it have been different? Could it change if she returned? Somehow, I doubt it. Being an only child in a single parent family isn't very much fun, for mother or daughter. It's always a struggle to find the right amount of closeness and distance. May is the name her father and I agreed upon, though she was born in August.

"She was created in the springtime of our love," her father wrote me.

An easy child: no tantrums, no eating disorder or wild adolescent mood swings. Even as an infant she had an unnerving calmness about her, almost a secretiveness. She did well in school, went to parties and gave some. Had boyfriends who were polite. One of the best things I did for her was to start piano lessons young. She would play for hours at a time. I loved our apartment when it was filled with her practicing. I would stop what I was doing, stand at the living room door and listen. Simple exercises at first, then more complex compositions. The music, whatever it was, wound around us like a huge downy quilt under which we nestled. She did extremely well with Bach but also had the gentle, precise touch necessary for Mozart. Her teacher encouraged her to apply to Juilliard. When I asked her how serious she was about the piano, whether she wanted to try to make a career of it, she smiled and looked me full in the face. "No" was all she said, and went back to playing.

She was very attached to George and Pru, who took her skiing every winter and to Sag Harbor for a week in the summer. There were always books we both liked and plays and wonderful concerts in Europe: Beethoven's late quartets at Wigmore Hall, Verdi's *Requiem* at Amsterdam's Concertgebouw, *Tosca* in Berlin. She kept all the programs in a scrapbook with notes about the performances. There were other things she loved: the markets in Provence and the gardens of the Alhambra, the cherry blossoms at the Brooklyn Botanic Garden. One time, never to be repeated, we went to Indonesia together. She thought my work was "cool" and helped now and then with research. She often asked George and Pru about her father. It was easier than asking me. She'd come back with odd bits of information.

"He wasn't very tall, was he?"

"Still isn't," I replied.

"You loved him, right?"

"Still do."

"You were just very different, right?"

"Yes."

"That's why you don't want to go back?"

"He has his own family now and I have mine."

She is staying with her father now until she finds a place of her own. She will attend graduate school at Tribhuvan University in Kirtipur in the fall, some five kilometers from Kathmandu, where her father lives. Founded in 1959, it is Nepal's first university and its largest. The photographs of the campus are not impressive—modern architecture of the 60s and 70s; large, square cement buildings, painted brightly, but bland and without decoration. Her going there makes sense. She thinks she wants to live in Nepal for a while and is interested in engineering, something her father and I know little about. I called them when I heard about George's suicide, leaving a message on the answering machine. They responded with a telegram delivered directly to the funeral home. "Subha-yatra, George" was all it said.

May being with her father means I am alone again. It takes some getting used to after twenty-two years of child-rearing, of answering questions about her father, about how old he was and when she could see him. He sent her letters and photos of Nepal, and then, when she was eight, pictures of his new wife and later of their newborn daughter. May wanted to meet her half sister, but she was too young to fly alone and I did not have the heart to go back. Her father always asked about May's progress, wanting a report on her grades and her health. I'd written him that the local public school wasn't an option. She'd be home by three without much homework. I told him I wanted her in a private school with lots of clubs that would keep her late. He said he'd send what money he could, which wasn't much.

My father helped. He had been kind when I told him of the pregnancy. I think he liked the role that an absent father allowed. I took May on the subway to the Bank Street School every morning when she was young. Dad picked her up every afternoon and stayed with her until I came home. The three of us ate together most evenings. She went to Ethical Culture after eighth grade, where she tried out dance and won a seat on the student council. My father was proud of her and, on weekends, often took her out to lunch and shopping for dresses. His stroke and hemiplegia two years ago put an end to that kind of fun and changed her in subtle ways. Her sorrow was more private than mine, but I noticed her generosity toward me became greater after his stroke. Though she seemed happy enough, I often caught her staring into space.

"Is something bothering you?" I would ask.

She'd just say that she'd been thinking.

"About what?"

She was wondering, she said, how other people lived and why they died. It was in her sophomore year that she took her first long trip to see her father, begging me to come with her, asking more than once how I felt about her going. When she returned, she said very little about the visit, only that it was very different and that her half sister was very sweet. She told George and Pru she'd wished her father had a piano.

May said she wanted to go again and did, the summer before attending Yale. She chose to major in physics, a subject I knew as much about as I did about her social life. I knew she had good friends in college. When I asked about boyfriends, she said, "Some."

"Serious about any of them?"

"Only serious enough to sleep with."

Then she'd tell me about classes she was taking. A mystery, my child. She did her best to bear the burdens of being an only child, trying to make her mother feel less alone while, at the same time, trying to find her own footing. I knew from living as a child with my father what a difficult task that was. I'm busy enough without May—my work and friends and men. Yes, men, but no man. At my age, finding someone seems less important. I fill empty hours remembering companions and lovers, thinking of my mother long dead, and of paintings in museums that I'll never again visit.

When I was a little girl, my father took me fishing. We would drive to the public beach early in the morning and drag an aluminum rowboat from the top of the car to the water. Casting our lines into the dark lake, we would watch the mist rise above the trees and melt against the brightening sky. Then a sudden tug, and splashing on the surface as I would reel in. Dad, always ready with the net and tape measure. "I think it's a keeper!" he'd cry. But it rarely was. Never quite measuring up. Thrown back. When I wasn't a girl anymore, I began to wonder whether it was chance or choice that kept me single.

There was one time in my life when I stopped thinking about such things. A time when I lived only in the moment, watching for a short time my loneliness, like mist, disappear above me. And in a strange way, I owe that time to George and to Pru as well, still my dearest friend. It's clear to me now that from the moment I agreed to go to Gokyo with them, I began another life.

CHAPTER TWO
BEGINNING

From the start, I was afraid of breathing deeply. In Delhi, where our group first landed, I covered my face against the warm wind's sweet malignant scent. Like a giant wave, that wind carried with it the flotsam and jetsam of its travels. There was the smell of wild herbs and dung, of chickens and the damp hide of horses. The wind mixed in startling and varied combinations the sweat of work and lovemaking, the juices of muskmelon and mango, smoke from burning cow dung and incense from temples. When the wind stopped, only an exhausting heat remained. It mercilessly drank from the land and the people on it, leaving them shrunken and thirsty. It cracked my lips and burnt my skin and sent me, chastened, back to my air-conditioned hotel room to bathe and drink bottled water.

Even though the heat was intense, Paul Levin was determined to sightsee and begged me to go with him.

"Bobby's glued to the TV. I told him we were only in Delhi for a day, but he won't budge. He said I should go, but it won't be as much fun alone. Come with me."

Paul hired a cab that took us along streets where a rainbow of saris disappeared behind explosions of exhaust from buses and trucks. Bicycles and motorbikes crowded us off the road or suddenly sprinted in front of us; drivers pressed their horns and yelled out windows. We passed hump-necked oxen pulling wagons, boys pushing carts piled high with fabric, men unloading furniture in the middle of the street. Where there were traffic lights, people ignored them.

The streets were lined with vendors selling everything that Woolworths used to offer: thread, scissors, knives, fabric, candy and candles, cheap jewelry, pink and white cotton undergarments next to polyester sport shirts. Barbers squatted beside their customers, who offered their stretched necks to straight razors. The noise was incessant—the low rumble of vans, the piercing sound of bicycle bells, the clamor of car horns; hawkers shouting and children crying.

Our first stop was the massive India Gate, a huge arch designed by Lutyens to commemorate the thousands of Indian soldiers who died fighting for Britain in World War I. The ponderous structure was solid, imperious and unimaginative: the very essence of British oppression, mocking the human vulnerability it honored. The heat was stifling. The only shade was directly under the giant arch, already crowded with perspiring tourists drinking from plastic bottles and regarding with caution the eternal flame burning there.

Then, at Paul's insistence, we toured the 254 acres of the gigantic Red Fort, where Mughal rulers had lived for two hundred years. We walked from one palace to another, went up and down steps, stared at painted walls and at ceilings crowded with tiny mirrors. I was drenched in sweat, exhausted and irritable. We headed for a park in search of shade and came upon a zoo. The small stinking cages were covered with heavy black mesh. It was hard to see into their dark recesses, where panting leopards and mangy lions lay gaunt and listless. Even the birds looked bedraggled, beaks dull from pecking cement, yellow skin exposed where feathers were lost. Paul peered into the cages and grimaced.

"Locked up for life," he said. "Let's get out of here and go for a swim at the Oberoi." I hesitated, reluctant to desert the lonely beasts. "Come on, you can join the ASPCA later," he said, and went into the street to fetch a cab.

Having a drink at the pool, Paul resumed the conversation. "Nothing wants to be caged."

Miriam, Paul's wife, was a friend of mine. I knew a lot about their marriage, at least from her perspective. More than once Miriam and I had talked about Paul's self-pity and petty resentments, his feeling that Miriam's insistence on more family life was interfering with his career. And then there was Bobby, Miriam's son from a previous marriage. Miriam hadn't thought of going on the trek, insisting Paul and Bobby do the "male bonding thing" without her. "And besides," she had said, "who's going to take care of our daughter?"

Zoe, now three, was the child they'd had together, even though Paul hadn't been "ready." He loved his daughter, and at Miriam's suggestion, took her to Central Park on weekends. He read to her the nights he was home. There weren't that many. He was considered "promising" at the New York Psychoanalytic. Retaining that status meant attending evening meetings and volunteering for work. Recently graduated, he was already serving the membership and program committees and was asked to record the minutes of the admissions committee. He had been "tapped" to be the discussant for a presentation by Arthur Valenstein, a prominent Boston analyst who was the closest thing to a son-in-law Anna Freud had. Paul's own paper, "The Candidate's Transference to His Supervisor," had been published, after numerous revisions, in *The Psychoanalytic Quarterly.*

"Trying hard to escape your keepers, is that it?" I asked. Paul lay beside me in a plastic lounge chair.

"Moving toward them, maybe. Miriam says I always take a circuitous route."

"Beyond East Seventy-Third?"

"I'm on Seventy-Sixth, Hannah. My office is, anyway." Paul stared at me with dark unsmiling eyes. He leaned forward, grasping my hands. "I need your help."

"With what?"

"I'll explain on tomorrow's flight." He rose and dove into the pool. He was still swimming laps when I left.

"Follow the river until it turns to ice. Follow the ice until it turns to rock. Follow the rock until it turns to sky. Then we will be there."

Paul was reading to me as the forty-passenger turbo-prop sailed over the white teeth of Gurja Himal and Dhaulagiri. I looked down at that small portion of the fifteen hundred miles of Himalayan peaks that extend through six countries.

"We'll be where?" I asked.

"We'll see, won't we?"

I asked how it had gone for him and Bobby in Delhi. Paul explained that Bobby was doing what adolescents do: "Trying to break my balls." But that didn't mean Paul had to like it.

"Poor you. He's really dear, you know."

"Sometimes," Paul conceded. He went on to tell me how the boy was his mother's "dear" all the time. If Bobby got sick or injured on the trek, Miriam would never forgive Paul. He looked out the window, where dark clouds hid the mountaintops. I squeezed his knee.

"He'll be fine. You know how much he's had to deal with."

After Bobby's father died, Miriam took to bed. Newspapers, candy wrappers, tissues, empty coffee cups piled up beside her where her husband had slept. She only got out of bed to cook supper for Bobby. Then she began to complain of something burning. Called the fire department so often that social services got involved. I had to take Bobby for a while. My father was sweet with him, telling Bobby he too had lost a father and that his mother would be all right.

"It took Miriam awhile to get a grip," I remarked, patting his arm.

"Get a grip on herself or me?" Paul put his head on my shoulder and stared into space. "I'm sorry, Hannah. That was unkind. But you can see how all that history makes it much harder."

I was an only child, so there was no chance to be someone's sibling or aunt. Bobby was the closest substitute for a nephew I had. Miriam understood that and let Bobby stay with me when she was in a particularly bad way. When he was little, we packed lunch, grabbed some towels and took the subway to Coney Island, bathing suits under our clothes. That was until he got too embarrassed to take off his wet suit behind a towel. After that, it was a Broadway matinee before a treat at Howard Johnson's where, if it didn't always have all twenty-eight flavors, still managed enough of them for a decent banana split. When Paul came on the scene, he was more than glad to have me take Bobby. "Sometimes, three's a crowd," he'd say.

I shifted position and Paul lifted his head.

"Then why come all this way with him?" I asked.

Paul, looking like a scolded schoolboy, sat up straighter. He stared out the window for a moment. "Not doing well in school, hanging out with the wrong kind of kids. Miriam said he needed more of me."

He picked up *Nepal in a Nutshell* and continued to read: *"October is the ideal time for trekking. The monsoon has passed and the days are cool, bright, and cloudless."*

Of course, it wasn't like that at all. The Kathmandu valley, at forty-six hundred feet above sea level, appeared a soggy tangle of green fields and mud. We "deplaned," as they say, into a downpour, the last gasp of a dying monsoon.

The ride into town was unrevealing. The city seemed empty except for a few inhabitants scurrying toward shelter. The speed of the bus made the wooden houses, leaning one against the other, hard to see. Our hotel, the Bodnath, was one of the more luxurious in Kathmandu. Three stories of poured concrete with lots of plateglass and an ill-furnished lobby. Windows at the rear faced an outdoor swimming pool. The rain beat hard against the plastic flowered cushions on the white metal chairs around it. Rough winds had driven the leaves from a chinaberry tree so that only its hard poisonous yellow fruit remained.

George Albright was clearly exasperated. "Jesus! Rain! How did this happen?"

I suggested he not take it personally, but of course he did. Everything in life was measured by how it made him feel. He was immediately on the phone to the Sherpa cooperative that was providing our porters and guides. We sorted out our equipment on cramped hotel-room floors, leaving George to change the weather, which he seemed to have every intention of doing.

CHAPTER THREE
KATHMANDU

At breakfast the next morning, I found Bobby and his stepfather huddled over a map of the city.

"May I join you?"

"Sure," Bobby said, smiling. He was a muscular boy, shorter than Paul by a head, with thick brown hair that hung to his shoulders. On his upper lip, the traces of a mustache seemed a dirty smudge of charcoal. He tried to make up for the deficiencies of being thirteen with a silver ring in his right ear and a swagger. Miriam and Paul were upset by this sudden tilt toward adolescence, but I didn't mind. The Baudry was full of portraits of young men with earrings and mustaches.

"What's your plan?" I asked them.

"The Asian hole," Bobby replied with a sly smile.

Paul looked glum, but I laughed. I knew Bobby meant Asan Tole—the very center of town, the site of numerous temples and a famous bazaar that sat beside the ancient India-Tibet trade route. The great square was filled with mountains of fruit rising from uneven paving stones—rough lemons and bead plums, wood apple and watermelon, mango and bananas. Green limes fought for space amidst blood-red pomegranates and muddy yellow apricots. Oceans of rice, white and brown, flooded the blue plastic sheets spread beneath them. It would be easy to become lost amidst the rows of spice merchants sitting cross-legged behind their wares: bins of brown, red and yellow powders giving off strange and alluring scents. Or to spend too much time and money in the small jewelry shops that lined the streets where owners scurried to fetch yet another lapis necklace, each one bluer than the last. The steady beat of a frame drum and the high pitch of a bamboo flute vied with the hawking shouts of vendors selling saris, along with matching glass and plastic bracelets.

"Asan Tole's an excellent choice," I told Bobby.

"You can help me buy stuff." Bobby was half out of his chair, eager to get started. I put my hand on his arm.

"Thank you, that's very sweet." I looked at Paul, who nodded encouragingly.

I told Bobby that since it was raining, I thought I'd stay in and catch up on some correspondence.

"You're going to write letters?" The boy looked at me with genuine amazement. He told me I could do that at home.

"But I wouldn't. I'd pick up the phone instead." I told Bobby that letter-writing was a lost art. When he was sure I wasn't making fun of him, he smiled and came around to hug me.

"Sure, Hannah, and you're the one to find it. Cool!"

Kissing him good-bye, I told him to pick out some postcards for me. Then I went back to my room and wrote a number of letters to friends who never received them. I also sent a note to my director, Mr. Harrington, outlining how we could find the money to clean our El Greco cardinal. A fund-raiser for the old man might have considerable appeal. He was looking more jaundiced each day, his red robe turning orange. Of course, there was the danger of him being taken off the wall "for restoration" and left in the basement so that the money raised could be spent elsewhere. Not on art, that much was certain. Maybe for renovations of the gift shop instead.

A director was only as good as the money he raised. Museum studies, in which Harrington had a degree, taught you how to flatter rich dowagers with the hint of a new gallery in their name. Or funds might go for paraphernalia in Harrington's office: custom-built bookcases for art books he never read; a Bokhara carpet, essential for any first-time museum director. One of his more modest purchases was a nineteenth-century cast-iron-tiger doorstop that kept his office door ajar. He enjoyed hearing the phone ring and listening to his secretary say, "Office of the director. Whom shall I say is calling?" I keep telling her it's "who," but it doesn't sink in. Harrington doesn't care about grammar any more than he does about the El Greco. He wants to make it big—the Louvre, the Pergamon or the Met. The way to get there is to increase the endowment of your museum through galas that make the society page or special exhibits that garner critical attention. El Greco's priest was small potatoes in Harrington's scheme of things. Yet I felt I owed it to the old boy to try to do what I could for him.

I began a letter to Frank, then thought better of it. What more could we say to one another? And even if he wanted to respond, where could he find me? I tore up the sheet of stationery and looked out on a drab day. A dense curtain of gray was drawn across the mountains. The narrow street below was deserted, except for a few luckless souls scurrying through the rain. They clearly had something in mind. More than I did. I felt lost, like a traveler who doesn't recognize the photograph on her own passport. Then came the whining jangle of my phone. I almost didn't answer.

"Hello, Hannah. You there? It's Leon. How about joining me in the bar? Not too early for a Bloody Mary."

"That's one way to beat the rain," I said. He answered that there was only one way better. I laughed and told him I'd see him in twenty minutes.

I wondered why I wanted to keep Leon waiting. I had nothing to do before meeting him. But, then again, there was no sense in meeting him at all. I had no real interest in him now, not after Frank. I supposed there was no harm in being friendly. As we were thrown together for a while, I might as well make the best of it. But what did he want? Maybe nothing more than company. The rain wasn't letting up any more than my strange sense of uncertainty about Leon's call.

I lay on my bed wondering if I should have come to Nepal at all. The small room was tasteless, with cheap furnishings and badly framed floral prints. My new hiking gear sat on the thin green carpet like unexpected guests. The clutter reminded me of Leon's walk-up on Mott, off Canal Street. All that ugly used furniture he refused to part with—a tattered couch covered in ghastly pink brocade, pine bookcases carelessly stained, and a desk so wobbly that I was afraid to set anything on it. He yelled at me for washing the windows. "Next there'll be curtains," he exclaimed. He didn't want to live like we were in "the 'burbs." I shouldn't "mess with the place."

It was hard not to. His clothes were piled on the floor until I bought him a dresser. I had to tidy up just to find a corner to read in. The few small closets were crammed with junk: wooden tennis rackets, a rusting catcher's mask, a typewriter with missing keys, cracked mirrors, frames without pictures. The bathroom was even worse. No shower curtain or bath mat until I bought them. Everywhere a jumble of old toothbrushes, mangled tubes of toothpaste whose caps had long disappeared, natural laxatives of every variety, and the perfume bottles of former lovers—all of which I threw out. Leon didn't like it. And he resented the fact that I was salaried while he lived hand to mouth.

"The Baudry is not just your workplace, it's the way you want to live," he said.

When I brought home a set of dishes from the restaurant supply store around the corner, he stared at their plain white surfaces and then at me.

"The soul of a curator. Always wanting to improve the collection."

He never used them, sticking to his chipped Salvation Army china. Leon stored his own paintings in a haphazard fashion under the double bed, which had a bent metal headboard he had rescued from someone's trash. "Gallery Sous Lit" he called it. I had to get a flashlight and quite literally crawl under there to rescue them. He, of course, was more interested in my being in his bed than under it. But where we did it didn't really matter to him. It was the frequency that was important, and the element of surprise. On the kitchen floor while dinner got cold, in the bathtub hardly large enough for one, once late at night on the landing outside our apartment door. Never, interestingly enough, in his studio.

"Private space. My own personal hell."

I asked him if there wasn't just a little corner for me—a place for me to sit and be with him. He said it was not a place for two. Not even for one most of the time. It was "a hateful place" and I should "stay away from it." I had no choice. He'd enter the large room that served as his studio and lock the door behind him. And when he emerged hours, sometimes even a day later, he locked the door after him, as though I might steal something. I'll admit I tried to force an entry more than once.

But when he'd finished a painting or, at least, felt he could finish it, he'd show it to me: bright colors hurtling into one another and then plunging into a surprising darkness, rearing again, and scattering. The canvas could hardly contain them. The paintings were far better than his lovemaking, which had that urgent, grabby quality some men never learn to control. It was the paintings and his troubled intensity I stayed for. He struggled to give shape and color to a private anguish, to transform personal pain into something public and visible. I kept looking for that kind of transformation in our love; wanting the white bed sheets I'd bought to become the canvas on which we could record a rare and intimate connection. In the end, I showed him how he might get a one-man show at Julia Krent's 57th Street Gallery and he, in turn, showed me the door. Or, rather, I found it. It wasn't an affair behind my back, like with Frank. Just a phrase he'd written.

I'd come home early from the museum one day. Leon wasn't there. A pounding headache—the parting gift of an afternoon's staff meeting—made me head for bed. The mail, some of it unopened, lay on it. I was used to that. Leon always read his mail in bed, if he read it at all. He rarely opened bills until the phone went dead or the lights were shut off. Then he would suggest one of us run to the bank with a payment. There was a plain white envelope on the bed, open but with a stamp affixed, ready to be addressed. Inside it was a sheet of paper. I took it out and immediately recognized the handwriting: Leon's father. There was no salutation, just these words: *How could you do such a thing to your mother? Living with a shiksa.* No signature. And below, in Leon's hand, a reply: *Papa. Don't worry. It's not serious.*

I lay there for a while, hoping Leon wouldn't return until I could figure out what to do. Then I packed my bags and left. For a while, Leon tried to convince me that it was just a lie to get his father off his back. But I knew he would never fully give himself to me.

I continued to follow his career over the next few years, watching him progress from Julia's to the more prestigious Forum Gallery, then on to a small group show at MOMA. Through me, George Albright got interested in his work and bought several paintings. As Leon's fame grew, so did the value of George's purchases. He boasted of his acquisitions to every guest in a way only Cosimo de' Medici could have bested. But Pru never liked them.

"There's no way out," she'd say. "He traps you with his colors, spins you around, pushes and pulls you here and there. It's exhausting. Nothing's centered. I can't imagine how you lived with him as long as you did."

Three years didn't seem so long. After our affair ended, we would run into each other at various art openings and charity benefits. He'd make the tiresome, predictable moves some men feel obliged to carry out. A drink later? A movie sometime? See me home? But there was no real passion in the proposals and I learned to shut them down pretty quickly.

There was one opening, however, at which he seemed more serious. His father, like Grandma Moses, began painting late in life, after his son had become prominent. It galled Leon to have his father get in on the act. Abe Kaminsky's show was a small one at a little known gallery on Avenue D. I had no intention of going. I hadn't talked to Abe since Leon and I had split up. I never answered the old man's letter telling me he had nothing against me personally, that I couldn't help being who I was, and that, in the end, I would be happier with my own kind. But Leon had been insistent on my attending.

"Please, I need you there," he said. "You're the only one who might understand."

There was the usual collection: girls in boots and velvet nail polish, bearded men sporting T-shirts and graying ponytails, wealthy Park Avenue types lured by the promise of a "find," and a handful of critics attracted by the Kaminsky name. What was unusual was the sad clump of thick-ankled refugees who refused to take off their heavy wool coats. They clung to one another and whispered in Yiddish as they stood stoically before each painting, shaking their heads in sad recognition. The old man's work wasn't bad. Darker than his son's, but more direct—the pain more obvious in the pitiful, desperate figures that filled his canvases. Paint had been heavily applied and then unevenly scraped away, giving forlorn faces a startling dignity all their own. And his night scenes of the camps matched van Gogh in intensity if not skill. Leon, however, wasn't having any of it.

"It's dirty linen hung in public," he said, emptying the white wine from his plastic cup with one gulp.

"Some of them are quite good, you know." I turned to point out one I particularly liked.

"Think so?"

Did everyone have to know his father was in Auschwitz? For Leon it was like pulling down one's pants in public, being the victim again.

"What about what he did to me? I've told you how he was."

He went for a refill on the Chablis. He returned and said accusingly, "So, you like his work?" I told him again that I did and had told his father so. Leon replied that he could see my review in *ARTnews* already: "*Haunting and provocative. In the tradition of Kollwitz.*" Right. I said I wasn't there to write a review.

"But you have opinions. You always did." I recognized the belligerent tone of a man halfway to a hangover. "You didn't see him pacing in the middle of the night in his underwear, that damn number tattooed on his arm. You know, he never covered it up. Had his shirtsleeve shortened, I think, so it would show. A survivor, that's him. Yelling and using his fists. The camp he tried to escape from? The beatings and the torture? Only part of it's in his paintings. We got the rest. Afraid every night of how he would be. Not telling anyone about the bruises. Just you."

I squeezed his hand, told him I felt sad for him and kissed him on the cheek. He gazed at me. He said he thought that painting was just his father's hobby. He'd never thought he'd show them. They were barbed wire with shreds of his childhood hanging from them.

"We all have ghosts haunting us," I said. When I went to get my coat, he followed me, wanting to go home with me.

"I don't want to be one of your ghosts. Make me flesh and blood again," he said.

I must admit I was tempted. Curious, I guess, as to whether things could change. But I knew better. I asked him why the sudden urgency. He told me he'd made a mistake. He had been serious about me, but couldn't admit it. I took his hand again.

"I don't see it that way," I said. Anyway, if it was a mistake, he'd have to live with it. After that, he began to call, wanting to go to lunch or meet for a drink. More often than not I declined. Besides, Frank had begun taking up more of my time. After a while, Leon's calls were less frequent. I heard he was dating an art student. So I'd been surprised when I found out that he was going on our trip to Nepal.

The hotel bar was off in a corner of the lobby, far from the plate glass windows and swimming pool. It was large and dark, with heavy wooden chairs covered in red imitation leather. Though it was not yet noon, candles were already lit on small circular tables. There was the smell of furniture polish and stale beer. The room was deserted except for Leon. A Bloody Mary sat half-empty on the table in front of him. He rose to greet me, kissing me on the cheek.

"They don't quite have the knack of it. Not enough vodka and the juice tastes of the can. But it's good enough to get you through a rainy morning. What'll it be?"

I ordered a mimosa.

"I don't know about orange juice. They add water to a concentrate," he said. He reminded me about adding Lugol's. I'd forgotten the bottle and, rather than go back, said I'd take my chances. He held up his own, but I waved it away.

"It tastes bad," I said. He gave me a dubious look.

"Throwing caution to the winds? That's not like you." I told him if I were cautious, I wouldn't be here at all. Leon called to the bartender, who doubled as waiter. "Two mimosas for my friend."

"Two?"

"We're going to be here for a while, aren't we? You have to catch the bartender when you can. Takes lots of breaks. Must be a union man." Leon fished the ice out of the mimosas, which came in stout Coca-Cola glasses. "Better a little safer than sorry," he said.

The juice was thick and overly sweet, cut only a little by the slightly drier taste of a cheap champagne. There was no way I'd get through two. I took another sip and settled back in my chair. I hadn't really talked with him since we'd first arrived In Delhi. "Well, how's the trip been so far?" I asked.

"Should it have been something?"

"Of course." I reminded him of the twenty-two hours flying, the three movies and five meals. Two nights in Delhi at the Hotel Oberoi with a day for touring sandwiched between them.

He shifted uncomfortably in his chair. "I decided not to stay at the Oberoi. Went to a cheaper place. I got a massage there that almost killed me. Thought after the flight I could use it—an hour for only fifteen American dollars. Sounded pretty good. Called down to the desk. Fifteen minutes later, this huge Indian guy in a turban comes to my room with a table and tells me to undress. No towel or anything. Right away, I don't like him. Fingers like meat hooks. He begins to dig into my back. I told him 'Hey, go easy!' but he won't listen. When I begin to groan, he says it is a good sign. I was releasing the toxins accumulated from living in America and eating pigs. The guy was nuts, I'm telling you. I tried to get off the table. He holds me down. Swear to God! Said I'd get cancer if I interrupted the treatment. 'Treatment?' I said. 'I thought this was a massage! There's nothing wrong with me.' He doesn't answer. Tells me angrily to turn over. I'm not about to refuse. Starts working on my upper thighs, near my balls, and now I'm really scared. Meanwhile, the pain is intense. He starts talking about how America poisons the body and the mind. Then starts talking enemas with holy water from the Ganges. That's when I really freaked. Starts twisting my intestines with his hands. Says I need a high colonic if I'm ever to be well. I got him to stop by agreeing to it."

I stared at him. "You didn't!"

He leaned forward. "I only agreed to one. Evidently, it's better on an empty stomach. I tell him I've just had lunch, which wasn't true, but he could come in the morning before breakfast. He wanted to be paid in advance, the pervert. What could I say with his hands at my crotch? He finally lets me get dressed. Next morning I'm out by five o'clock. Take a cab to the railway station and go to see the Taj in Agra. Don't come back for my things till eleven that night. Afraid he might be outside my door with his enema bag and holy water if I were any earlier. Get to the Oberoi by midnight."

I asked Leon why he hadn't stayed there in the first place. He took a sip of his drink. The tomato juice left a small red line along his upper lip. He wiped it away with the back of his hand. "Yards of marble, fancy lighting. A garish mausoleum for people who don't know they're dead."

But he liked that there was a front desk and security, even if the rest of the hotel was "a warehouse for shit art" like some of the museums back home. I sipped my mimosa and hoped aloud he didn't have the Baudry in mind. Besides, he should be grateful for museums. I reminded him that MOMA had given him his own show.

"You think that was easy?" He was working himself up, twisting his paper napkin into a little red stick. "I had to fight to get things hung the way I wanted. Curators think they are artists and know better than you. You're different, of course."

He said no one could argue with illustrated manuscripts or a Hans Holbein. But that horrid Mondrian exhibit going on at MOMA at the same time as his? "Having to see all those little squares marching along like Nazi storm troopers and everyone making a fuss over them." He threw up his hands and bent his head in mock surrender. "Having to smile at the opening like some quisling. Yes, yes, it's great art. Now let me out of here!"

I reminded him that it was me he once had to get away from, how he'd lock himself in his studio after we'd argued.

"It wasn't you exactly but what you brought," he said.

He couldn't stand the smell of ARM & HAMMERed sheets, those white dishes, the shag rug—a home like the one he'd grown up in. His face lost its animation. "I'm ready to change, Hannah." He stared at me. "Are you?"

His question surprised me. It hadn't yet occurred to me that he might be here because of me. I was on my guard. "Do I need to?"

He didn't answer, but looked around for the waiter and a check. He said he had an umbrella, that the temples would be beautiful in the rain, and maybe we'd even get to see that little girl who's a goddess. "The one they keep locked up." I wondered what other girls he was interested in and asked if he was still seeing the art student. He was standing now. "You heard about her?" He studied the bill, so I couldn't see his face, and told me it hadn't been serious. He waited for me to stand and then took me by the hand as we crossed the lobby.

"For you or for her?" I asked.

He said she had wanted to move in. He held the door for me. It was only drizzling now. The air was warm and daylight a blessing after the dark bar. We walked down the hotel's circular driveway to the street. "We're in Kathmandu with a day to kill," he said, opening a green travel umbrella over our heads.

When I had lived with Leon, he scoffed at owning an umbrella. He refused to use either of mine, no matter how inclement the weather. Where had he gotten this one? Was it even his? Dark green with flowers: unlikely. No doubt left in his loft by a woman. He'd never have bothered to return it. Might not even see her again. There was so much about him I still didn't understand. Not that I was any clearer about myself. Only art clarifies things—for a moment anyway. Paintings at the Baudry: silent, wise and enduring. Never going anywhere. Content in their space like Cimabue's *Virgin Enthroned with Angels;* figures flattened, Mary staring out to a point beyond time.

"Jesus!" Leon said, suddenly squeezing my elbow. "Take a gander."

On both sides of the narrow street, naked figures carved on lintels copulated in every conceivable position. I felt Leon's hand squeeze mine. But I was thinking of Frank. The way he stopped breathing at night, then a gasp and restart. It scared me but he wouldn't see a doctor about it. His lovemaking was the same, full of gaps and hesitations, like a stalled car that bucks and then catches and begins to move forward, slowing for a bend in the road, then picking up steam, only to suddenly run out of gas with a sudden sputter. Afterward, we'd stand in bathrobes, cups of coffee warming our hands, and stare into the courtyard below.

Leon studied the erotic carvings as if to memorize them for future use. "Turn you on?" he asked.

"A little," I admitted, realizing how much I'd missed a man's touch. We walked through the tangle of people toward Durbar

Square—dodging speeding bicycles, bumping past women in saris carrying melons in straw shopping bags, sidestepping men in T-shirts and baseball caps who held aloft trays of marigolds that floated above them like orange clouds. Thin, tired-looking women struggled to push wooden carts piled high with bolts of patterned cloth through clogged streets. Vendors squatted on the sidewalks, their harvest piled in front of them. We picked our way through mountains of apples, fields of potatoes and carpets of rice. In shaky stalls, goats' heads dangled from giant hooks. Men wielding folded newspapers shooed away the crawling blanket of flies that made the goats' eyes dance and their tongues hum.

"Look there." He pointed across the street to an ornately carved doorway flanked by two huge wooden lions, yellow paint peeling from their loins.

"Out of a dream." I leaned against him. They were different from the photos I'd seen: not really ferocious, only trying to be. They guarded the living goddess Leon wanted to see. I told him she was kept indoors except for certain holy days, when she was carried out in a great chair. Her feet never touched the ground. He asked how I knew that.

"I read."

Leon smiled at me condescendingly. "Always prepared, Hannah. Things labeled and put in place. No room for confusion."

"Too much already. No sense adding to it," I answered.

He put his arm around me. "Like toothpaste squeezed from the middle. Or wet towels left on a chair."

I looked at him ruefully. "Dishes in the sink."

We stepped into the courtyard, where rows of latticed shutters faced us. I had brought binoculars and began studying the carvings on them—first the feathered neck of peacocks, then the tendrils of some unfamiliar vine, and, here and there, a lotus blossom traced with such delicacy, I could not take my eyes from it. Leon was growing restless and wanted to look. I handed him the glasses. He asked which window was hers.

"All of them, I suppose." I told him the goddess was a child. He wanted to know what kind of child. I said she was a young girl.

Once she menstruated would be replaced with another, younger girl. "You know something about that," I added jokingly.

Leon put down the glasses and stared at me. He hadn't shaved, so a dark shadow covered his face. It gave his long, thin nose even greater prominence. His eyebrows seemed a thick line of black paint across a canvas of white skin.

"It wasn't all on me. You had something to do with it and maybe with your last boyfriend's leaving as well."

I hated the way he could sting when I least expected it. My eyes began to water but I refused to cry. I didn't want to talk anymore. So I took a guidebook from my purse, found the section on the goddess and began to read to myself. Of course, Leon wouldn't let me be. "What does it say?" he asked, trying to look over my shoulder.

I read how the Kumari Devi is not born a goddess, but is chosen from among four- to five-year-olds from the gold- or silversmith class. They must have thirty-two specific characteristics, such as black eyes, unblemished skin and straight hair that curls to the right at its end. The guidebook described how the candidates are locked in a dark room where men in horrible painted masks try to scare them. They make terrifying noises and display severed animal heads. The girl who shows no fear is the real goddess and is installed until she reaches puberty. Leon was suddenly a child listening to a bedtime story, asking me what happens next. I told him once she has menstruated, she is allowed to live a regular life. But she may have a hard time finding a man, as her husband is destined to die young.

Leon studied the color photo of a latency-age girl swathed in colored silk, her face painted, a jeweled crown on her little head. He scanned the windows with the binoculars. "I want to see her," he exclaimed. He began calling, "Come out. Come out. Wherever you are."

I shushed him, hating that need men have to possess a woman, if only with their eyes. He went into a pantomime, his hands clasped in front of him. "All dressed up and nowhere to go." He made small jumps. "Feet never on the ground."

The rain had stopped, but it was still gray and getting colder, with the kind of dampness that creeps into your bones. While looking for a taxi, we ran into Paul and Bobby. There was a large green circle around the boy's mouth.

"I bought him a wooden flute. The paint came off in his mouth. Even his tongue is green."

"It's hardly his fault," I said. "It will wash off."

Bobby thought it was "kind of cool." He hoped they celebrated St. Patrick's Day in Nepal because he was ready, showing us his emerald tongue.

"Ready to get sick," Paul replied. "Between the paint and the pastry, you'll be lucky if you live till dinner." Paul put his arm around his stepson, as if to prevent him from darting away.

Bobby leaned in against him. "That's the doctor speaking. Thinks I've poisoned myself."

"Can you believe it? The kid's trying to get high. Before we even get to Asan Tole, he makes fun of the Hanuman monkey statue at the palace gate because its face is red. Then we go into a temple and he takes a marigold from someone's brass tray."

"I thought she was selling them, Dad! How was I supposed to know they were some kind of offering? Besides, I gave it back when she started yelling."

Paul ignored him. He described how Bobby had found a sweet shop and started eating pastries while Paul was busy looking at jewelry. "Stuff flies had been all over. He thinks it's the place where they put hash in the dough."

"I don't think it's the place, I know it is!" Bobby insisted.

I asked him how he knew.

"From school. The Holy Ganesh Bakery. Right down the street from the Taleju Temple. I wrote it down."

Bobby pulled out a crumpled scrap of paper and showed it to Leon. A classmate's father, he explained, had been there in the sixties. Bobby admitted to having eaten half a dozen pastries before Paul stopped him, but nothing had happened yet.

"Maybe they changed owners or something," he said, looking mystified.

Leon was holding on to my hand. Paul looked at me distrustfully.

"I thought you were going to stay in and write letters," he said.

I told him I'd written to almost everyone who I thought wanted to hear from me and a few who didn't. I asked the two of them to come with us. We were going to see the city from the temple hill and then, if the rain didn't start again, take a walk along the river.

"No thanks." Paul was acting hurt. "Four's a crowd."

"How about three, Bobby? You want to come?" I asked. The boy looked at Leon, whose face went suddenly blank.

"Uh, I don't think so, Hannah. Can't leave old Dad here. It's his one chance to wash my mouth out with soap." Bobby put his arm around his stepdad, who tried to shrug him off. But the boy held on to him and crooned in his ear, *"Beautiful, beautiful green mouth . . ."*

CHAPTER FOUR
THE MONKEY TEMPLE

"That's a match made in heaven!" Leon said as we climbed into a cab. He wondered what Miriam had been thinking when she unleashed them on one another. "They'll be at it all the way to Gokyo."

Bobby's mouth reminded me of the first time I wore lipstick. I was fourteen and going with my father to the Bensons' annual spring party. Dad had bought me my first black dress for the occasion, velvet with a scoop neck, long sleeves and rhinestone buttons running down the front. We'd found black shoes with the hint of a heel to go with it. The lipstick was my surprise for him, as was the bun in which I'd gathered my hair.

"Well, missy, you are growing up!" he said, setting down his highball unsteadily. He'd never overdone it when my mother was alive, but after she died, he drifted toward the bottle. Nothing terrible, I thought at the time, just a way of comforting himself when there was only me around. He eyed me up and down.

"People will be mistaking you for my girlfriend." He poured more scotch into his glass. "Better stick close, sweetheart, those Benson boys will be wanting to get you upstairs."

"Dad!" He'd turned my trying to please him into something dirty and disgusting. He found me sulking in my bedroom when he'd finished his drink. He held my coat in his hand.

"I'm sorry, honey," he said. "Let's forget it and have a good time."

Of course, no one at the party thought I was his girlfriend, because they knew he had one already, a small fact he hadn't bothered to share with me. I thought those nights he didn't come home until late had something to do with his business like he said, and the Saturday night invitations were because people felt sorry for him. When I'd asked to come along, he'd reply, "You'd be bored." I never knew about the women he had after Mom died. I've found out since that there were quite a few. And he never married any of them.

Our taxi was a small Suzuki with lumpy seats and a broken window. Leon somehow managed with sign language and a bit of yelling to negotiate a fare that satisfied him. He sat close to me, his arm tightening around my shoulder whenever the taxi suddenly sprang forward into a space vacated by the cyclists that bedeviled the narrow streets. We lurched along rutted streets where muddy children jumped in and out of puddles. I shut my eyes as our driver wrenched the wheel this way and that to avoid them.

Ten minutes later, when we turned a corner, Leon nudged me. At the top of a hill, Swayambhunath, the "monkey temple," floated in the air above us. The temple is a religious site for both Buddhists and Hindus, the spot where a lotus was said to have risen in the lake that covered the entire Kathmandu Valley eons ago. It was festooned with colorful prayer flags that, like a thousand birds' wings, seemed to carry it aloft.

I bent forward to look at it through the taxi's cracked windshield. The Buddha's giant blue eyes stared down at me without blinking. Giant, garish eyes. A clown's eyes. Sizing me up, weighing my worth.

Eyes I'd seen before. I am nine years old again, sneaking into what had been our dining room. Mother lay in a hospital bed, the bars raised between us so she couldn't fall out or I in. That metal fence always separating us. She had given up climbing stairs weeks before. There was no bathroom on the ground floor, so first there was a bedside commode and later bedpans. Women I didn't know came to empty them and to take care of her and me. She became so weak she had to be lifted onto the bedpan, her thin limbs dangling helplessly over the white uniforms of thick-armed Puerto Ricans. Soon even that was too much for her. The room began to reek of her loss of control. I stood there, hoping she would see me and say something. Father found me.

"Mommy's tired, sweetheart. She needs to rest."

Her stare was unwavering as I backed toward the door, my father gently tugging at my sleeve. She made no sound. Her eyes seemed to grow bigger and more frightening. They took over my dreams and my waking. I see them, every time I pass the Gentile da Fabriano in the Baudry. Mary is holding her baby stiffly in her lap, not looking at him, but into her own world of pain.

I shuddered and turned toward Leon. As he stared at the temple, his eyebrows were raised in mock awe.

"Jesus, get the Maybelline, Mamma!"

He was almost shouting. I laughed with relief and opened the guidebook, reading as best I could as we bumped our way over toward the shrine. *"The all-seeing eyes of Buddha never blink, never sleep. The eyes are found four times, facing in different directions."* I looked up. "Same two eyes on each side of the temple. And there's a third one on each forehead, for good measure."

The taxi deposited us at the foot of the monument and we began to climb the 365 steps to the temple. Monkeys, considered holy, darted up and down the central metal railing, giving out loud, assaultive screeches. Children, their skin the color of walnuts, tugged at our clothes. "Dollar, please! You give dollar." Several held out green lemons for us to buy. Others offered a wilted bouquet of marigolds. Leon waved them away.

"Don't be harsh. They're only children. Some of them won't even survive."

"Gonifs, is what they are. Used to be a dime, now it's a dollar."

"They could be homeless," I said, beckoning the children back. "Sleeping in doorways. Picking in rubbish. Dying of malnutrition or dysentery or God knows what."

Leon shrugged and moved ahead of me up the steps, the children running behind him. I glanced again at the temple eyes, neither old nor wise, now just blank and unfeeling. Leon was probably right. There was nothing to do about these children, about those caged animals in the zoo, about my mother's dying or the damned foul weather that refused to change.

"What?" Leon said when I reached him. "What do you want me to do?"

"I don't know. Nothing, I guess." My breath came hard after the long climb. Before us lay the vast Kathmandu Valley. The Bagmati River was a sliver of gray, winding through a soggy greensward. The distant foothills of the Himalayas seemed to rise reluctantly toward a dark cloud that filled the horizon. A chill wind had set the long lines of colored prayer flags dancing, each flap a useless offering to heaven. I felt Leon's warm hands on my arms, gently turning me to him.

"Look, Hannah. Charity begins at home. Letting yourself be loved." His look was tender and full of yearning. I put my head on his shoulder, words rising slowly like dough.

"Neither of us is much good at that." He kissed me lightly on the forehead and told me we could get better at it. When I told him there was a children's center on Amsterdam Avenue where I wanted to volunteer, he said he'd come too, that we could go together, live together, sleep in the same bed, do the same things we used to do. I wrapped my parka more tightly around me like a protective skin I hadn't yet grown into. A hermit crab in her borrowed shell. My mother alone in her rented hospital bed; father sleeping upstairs with the door open so he could hear her if she called. Next to his room, my own, too large and lonely for a little girl. I would get into his bed when he was downstairs and fall asleep under eiderdown, only to wake and find myself once again in my own room.

"I don't know. What would make it different? It's only the distance from home that makes it seem possible."

"Anything's possible, anywhere." He was holding me again. "You're cold. Let's go back to the hotel." His body was a large, soft cover I wanted to pull onto me. But the smell of turpentine reminded me of the closed studio door, of the endless household chores that had fallen to me, and of Leon's irritation at my doing them. The twisting cable knit of his sweater seemed like a chain-link fence forbidding access. Over his shoulder, the great blue eyes gazed at me without expression.

"It's too soon," I said. "Let's be together awhile."

We wandered around the chaotic jumble of small shrines and holy temples surrounding the giant stupa, the many gifts of merit-seeking kings and holy lamas since the seventh century. Women in saris and sandals, men in faded jeans, baseball caps and logo-laden T-shirts crowded the hilltop with offerings of rice and ghee. Some burned money as they prayed. Others were ringing bells or setting prayer wheels in motion. On the far side of the vast courtyard, in a corner, stood a gilt-roofed temple the size of a child's backyard playhouse.

Because so many women and children surrounded it, I knew it must be the one built for Hariti, the goddess who in my reading I'd come to like most. I told Leon about her, that she was a demoness who had five hundred children. She abducted the other children of the city and ate them. Grieving parents came to the Buddha asking for justice. So he stole Hariti's favorite son, hiding him under a rice bowl. Hariti, after searching the world for her son, came to the Buddha for help in finding him. He told her she had many children and was grieving the loss of one. He asked her to imagine the despair of parents when Hariti stole an only child from them.

"And?" Leon asked.

"The Buddha held out a pomegranate. Hariti repented, swearing that from then on she would no longer harm children, but eat only the fruit that had been offered to her."

Leon wanted to know if the Buddha gave Hariti back her son. I thought he had, being the Compassionate One, but Leon wasn't so sure. "Maybe not," he mused. "Maybe she had to live with loss."

I took his hand. History had abducted Leon's childhood and a death mine.

"Now Hariti is a goddess. She protects all children, born and unborn. Women pray to her to be fertile." I pointed at the line of mothers and children, waiting to make an offering. Leon looked peeved.

"That's the problem. No population control. Everyone has to have a kid in our country and half a dozen in most others. Otherwise there's something wrong with you. Nobody stops to think that maybe we're breeding ourselves out of existence. They should be praying to Margaret Sanger instead of this Harini."

"Hariti."

"Harini, Hariti. What's the difference?" He told me there should be condoms instead of prayer flags waving in the wind. Ones you could pick right off the line, go home and use. "The best protection for children is not having them."

The anger in his voice startled me. "I think we should go," I said.

We started down the same 365 steps, with the same or maybe different children surrounding us. One offered to show us a nearby temple, another to fetch us a cab. The crowd of children around us was growing, some touching our clothes, others jumping up and down and yelling to get attention. Small hands offered beads, limes, gum or tissues.

A little girl pushed her way to the front. She held up her hands filled with hard candies wrapped in shiny paper. I gave her a coin and took a few. The wind flew at her dress, revealing small brittle ribs and skinny legs with knobby knees. I knelt down in front of her while Leon held some of the others back.

"Namaste. Thank you," I said. She stared at me. "I'm Hannah. What is your name?" She didn't answer and backed away when I tried to stroke her hair. At the bottom of the steps the crowd thinned as the children ran up toward another tourist. A little boy grabbed my hand.

"Ciya? Ciya?" He pulled me into the street and pointed toward a small house with a hand-painted sign: CAFE VAJRA.

"He's right," Leon said. "We could use a cup of tea."

He took my arm. The boy accompanied us the half block to the restaurant, shooing away other children and repeating "*Ciya,* good." He began running ahead of us and back like a small dog off its leash. Leon sent him away with a few rupees as we entered a room crowded with rough wooden tables and benches without backs. The walls were covered with tattered psychedelic posters carrying messages about hugging one another and doing good.

Leon looked around in disbelief. "It's either we're back in the sixties or sometime in the future when saving the whales is a major concern for the Nepalese."

"Why shouldn't it be?"

"Priorities? National interest? You've heard of them?"

"You mean because you don't live near the sea and have never seen whales, you can't want to save them?"

Leon said these people should be trying to save their own asses.

That came first. Most make a few hundred dollars a year, if that.

"What's saving whales going to do for them?"

I looked away and began to thumb through the guidebook, looking up where we might go next. A waitress bowed and handed us each a menu.

"Just *ciya* for me," I said. But Leon was studying the choices intently. He asked about the chicken takari.

"Very tasted," the waitress replied, bowing again. He ordered it. When the waitress left, he asked me what she'd meant. Was it tasty or had it been tasted? I asked why he had ordered it if it was going to worry him. He said he'd rather worry about the chicken than the chick. "One minute liking me and then not."

I covered his hand with mine. "Should it be easy? Knowing what I want?" But touching him I realized how good a man's body could feel.

"We're talking who not what." He asked me if I still loved Frank.

"No. I think of him, of course." I spread my napkin in my lap and then looked back at Leon. I'd come to realize, I said, that Frank had a lot more ideas than feelings. Leon nodded and added that he had always thought Frank odd. He made like Groucho Marx with his eyebrows.

"How would you know? You never met him." The waitress came with a large bowl. Orange and yellow flowers made little islands of color in a muddy sea of gravy from which Leon began to pick out chicken parts. He held one up for closer inspection with his fork.

"Looks like they cooked the chicken along with the yard they found it in." He tucked his paper napkin under his chin. "Well, here goes."

"You never met him," I repeated, tasting the dark, salty tea. He reminded me he had twice, once at George's Christmas party and then at an opening for Myra Tessing, "the homely one with the collages." He couldn't stand how Myra had gone on about her work reflecting a fractured society. Meanwhile, her collages were "fifth grade all over again."

He continued between bites of chicken. "But odd is what he

seemed. Frank, I mean. Hey, this isn't bad," he said, pointing his fork toward his bowl. I agreed Frank could appear aloof.

"Not just aloof." After chewing for a few moments, Leon added, "But odd. You know, like in *oddball, odd duck, odd fellow, odd infinitum,* that was him." He chuckled to himself. "But real smart, I gather."

"And polite," I added. He smiled and said Frank was who I thought I needed after living with him on Mott Street. He said that Frank was like a Mondrian. He looked up from an almost empty bowl. "Form, color, but no real passion."

I pushed back my teacup and stared at him as he continued to eat. "I happen to like Mondrian."

He looked up at me and laughed. "More than me?"

He wiped his mouth with a paper napkin. He thought I wanted to close the distance between us but just didn't know how. Never had known, and he supposed Frank had been no help on that score. Leon ate quickly, gnawing at a bone and spooning up the leftover gravy. He rose, set some money on the table, and came around to hold my chair. As I got up, he hugged me from behind and whispered in my ear.

"I'm sorry about Frank, but let's go back now." His breath was warm, his body firm against my back.

He was right about me, Frank and maybe even Mondrian. But was what he offered any better? His style was familiar, different from Frank's, but no less dangerous. If I was going to make love to him, I wanted it to be different.

"Not till we've been to the river."

"Why is that?" he asked, still holding me.

"Because I want to see it. Don't you? Of course you do."

I took his hand and led him to the street.

CHAPTER FIVE
THE MEETING

Close up, the Bagmati River wasn't what it seemed from a distance. The thick green scum on its banks gave off a fetid odor. Great piles of refuse rose along the shore. Scavengers crawled over them like dung beetles, filling cloth bags with whatever they could use or resell. Beyond the garbage heap lay a holy ground where two corpses wrapped in silk were being cremated. Thick smoke, grayer than the day, rose from the pyres, blowing past mourners, rising toward the temple ghats where vultures perched on holy roofs. Large stone steps led gaunt and naked worshippers into the river, where they bathed in the ashes of ancestors and were purified.

It was unnerving, this intimacy between the living and the dead, purification and pollution. I was assaulted by acrid smells of burning flesh, panicked by the singsong prayers of a son poking the burning body of his parent with a pole. I closed my eyes, trying to restore through momentary blindness some sense of order. The sudden harsh clang of temple bells startled me. I watched as they set the dark, slow-winged vultures circling. I reached in my purse for a handkerchief and the guidebook.

Leon stopped me: "You've read me enough." He said the guidebook didn't really change anything we were seeing. There was still mystery behind any explanation of what we were witnessing. "Only art makes things clearer," he said, "and lovemaking can."

"Sometimes," I said, taking his hand. I felt a surprising relief in this simple connection, palm against palm, fingers intertwined. Around us, time circled on black wings, and the dark smoke of pyres obscured the naked limbs of bathers. The only thing protecting us from dying was the warmth of a hand, the tenderness of a smile. I remembered how, at the beginning of our love, Leon had swept away my fears, catching me up in his arms, floating me on the riptide of his talent and all the beauty and passion that flowed from it. He must have known what I was thinking because he asked, "You will come back to my room, won't you?"

I hesitated for a moment. "Only if you promise not to make too much of it."

We were making our way across the lobby when George darted out from the bar. His face was flushed and he had the urgent look of a conductor who's lost his score just before the concert. "Jesus! I've been looking all over for you. We're all in the bar with Nawang, our guide."

"We're really bushed," Leon said. He glanced at me. "Been to every temple in town. Saved ourselves at least a thousand reincarnations. Can you fill us in at dinner?"

"Shit! You don't seem to get it, Leon." They'd been waiting an hour for us to return so we could get the plans straight. "So, if your majesties don't mind joining us, maybe we can get this trek started."

I squeezed Leon's hand. "We'd better go."

He sighed and took my arm. "All those temples and the gods still aren't with me."

I told him it was because he had made fun of Hariti.

The group stared at us as we entered the bar, their faces as drained of welcome as the empty glasses on the table in front of them. I felt like that wayward teenager, coming home past curfew, the smell of Old Spice still on me. Father would glance up with a sad expression, nod and then continue staring at the TV. The next morning, standing at the refrigerator, drinking juice from a Tropicana bottle, he'd ask, "How'd the evening go?" I'd tell him about the party, the movie, the dance, or the boy I'd been with. His only response, "Next time, try to get in earlier."

I scanned the crowd. Everyone was there, looking upset. The Albrights. Libby Kramer and her husband, Howard, the tall, dignified federal court judge who'd been on the bench only a few months. One of Nixon's better appointments. When we arrived, Howard wore an expression he must have reserved for those in contempt of court. He and Libby had been reluctant to come in the first place: Howard unsure of leaving the bench so soon after his appointment; Libby, never one for exercise, wondering if her body would hold up. Besides, it meant taking leave of her busy law practice. Divorce was Libby's specialty. She was sought by women betrayed by their husbands and by men looking for a skirt to hide behind. Traveling for both meant the agony of rearranging court dates. They'd been back and forth about it, before George finally convinced Howard it was the trip of a lifetime. Libby wasn't so sure. Then she became eager, so as not to disappoint Howard, while he began to have doubts, fearful of his wife's discomfort on the trek. What finally decided them was never clear, although Pru claimed it was George's dogged insistence.

Bobby was slumped in one chair with his feet on another looking bored while Paul shot us a discourteous look. Standing in a corner was a short man with a broad face, flat nose and wide eyes. He resembled the photos of Tibetans I'd seen in a *National Geographic* while waiting for a teeth-cleaning. Hair a black lacquer bowl. With him, a taller, younger man, narrower of face and nose, hair dropping straight to his shoulders from under a woolen cap. He was a Holbein portrait, serious, dignified, with the hauteur of inexperienced youth. He might have been handsome had not his features been roughened by acne or some childhood disease.

Libby, worrying a scotch, smiled at me bleary-eyed as we took seats. It was a smile I knew well: crooked, sardonic, dangerous. She didn't drink all the time, just in those moments when the future seemed particularly uncertain, as when her brother in California fell ill and, at first, they thought it was cancer. I smiled back at her, but not too broadly. She looked like an unguided missile and I wanted to stay out of range. George was standing in front of the group, about to speak.

"Did you enjoy yourselves, you two?" Libby called in a stage whisper. There wasn't time for an answer, even if I'd had one to give. Albright began by introducing Nawang. The older man in the corner stepped forward, gave a little bow and immediately stepped back again. He may have been our guide, but George was running the show. He explained that Nawang's English wasn't good, but he knew the mountains. The situation was this: if we stayed and waited for a flight to Lukla as planned, we could wait a long time. The bad weather had delayed flights.

"Nawang says there are lots of expeditions ahead of us hoping to get out." The guide's face was blank, while his younger companion stared at the floor. No one knew when the planes would fly again. It depended on visibility. "They don't use radar," George explained, "so the pilot has to be able to see the landing field."

"I should hope so!" Libby said. Dark blue veins began to swell in her temple and her hand tightened around her glass.

"It's hard to know when the cloud cover will lift," said George. Libby asked if there was an alternative. She finished her drink and leaned forward to better concentrate through what was a growing alcohol haze.

Nawang had suggested we begin to hike from Lamosangu. It was a few hours by bus from Kathmandu. George warned us that starting there meant a lot more walking—a hundred and sixty miles of it—if we were to get to Gokyo. I took the bus across town to work and had taken strolls along Riverside Drive toward Grant's Tomb. I had, with Pru's encouragement, survived a long hike to the Village from Seventy-Second Street and Broadway. That was about it. One hundred and sixty miles seemed impossible. But when I calculated that we had twenty-five days or so to walk it, it came out to six or seven miles a day. That didn't sound bad. George said we'd have to change the date of our return flight, but it would all be worth it. We could pack our gear tonight and be ready to start in the morning.

"Getting to Gokyo is still the plan?" Libby asked, glancing at her husband, who was carefully shredding his napkin. Howard stopped long enough to give Libby a wan smile. George nodded and held up a map. It would be tough but we could do it if we hustled. George's finger traced a blue line. The first part of the trek would take us into the foothills, climbing steadily toward Jambesi. Nawang began whispering to his younger colleague, then raised his hand and waited for George to call on him. He stepped forward and said, almost fearfully, "Tomorrow, no good. Saturday."

George had familiarized himself with the diseases we could contract, the shots to be taken, and the latest rate of exchange. He'd even mastered a few important Nepali expressions like "Put it there" and "Thank you." But he hadn't much of a clue about religious beliefs. I spoke up and told him what I remembered from the Asia House exhibit.

"Days of the week have specific meanings attached to them," I explained. "Saturday is a bad day for any new undertaking."

Howard asked if that meant waiting another day. He was nervously gathering the napkin he'd shredded into a pile. Leon said we'd barely have enough time to get to Gokyo as it was.

"Pack your shit. I'll talk to Nawang," George commanded.

"You don't want to force him to do something against his religion," Libby protested. She looked around for support, but chairs were being pushed back and bills settled. George, with his arm around Nawang, whispered urgently in his ear. The guide listened, head bent, then shook his head and said something I didn't quite catch.

"Well, that's done," Leon said, taking my arm. "Now back to original plans."

It was beginning to sound better and better, away from crowded streets and strange smells, from the anxiety rising like a tide in all of us. I wanted to nestle in the small space of encircling arms and not have to think about anything or anyone, not even about the man whose arms would embrace me. I was going to keep my relationship with Leon simple—just the comfort of firm muscle and soft lips. We were leaving when Libby reeled toward us, her arms outstretched and her voice loud.

"Howdy, strangers." She hugged me hard, as much for balance as out of affection. "How about joining us for a drink?" She let go of me and steadied herself with a hand on Leon's shoulder. "It may be the last one you'll get." She began an off-key version of "On the Road to Mandalay," waving her thin arms like an orchestra conductor. She stopped long enough to tell Howard to order scotch and sodas. "Or just have him bring the bottle."

Howard took her arm and told her to sit down. He turned toward us. "Next she'll be doing a striptease."

"I'll stay for that," said Leon, motioning me to a chair. I was surprised and remained standing.

"Weren't we going?" I asked.

"In a minute." He had been the eager one all morning, but now I was the one left wanting. I gave him a quizzical look, but he just smiled benignly. A cat with the canary, I thought. I turned away and seated myself beside Libby. I took her hand, hoping to ease her earthward.

"You left out a few lines," I said. She promised to make them up to me and hugged me again. It was no use. She was well beyond recall. Leon took a seat next to me. The waiter brought scotches.

"Time is melting away like the ice cubes," I whispered to him, rattling my glass. Leon fished them out of our drinks. Paul was making his way toward us, a worried look on his face. Leon gave him a wave.

"The more the merrier." Leon motioned Paul to a seat. He squeezed my leg under the table. "Love's like wine, don't you think? The longer you wait, the better it is," he announced.

"That's profound!" Libby leaned toward us. "But is there a context, Leon? Am I missing something?" She looked at me unsteadily. "Of course, there's always the other argument: *Carpe diem.*" She lifted her glass. "The wine might be better tomorrow. But, will you? That's the question."

"What's the question?" asked Paul, who by now had pulled up a chair.

"What's better, today or tomorrow?" Libby said, staring at Paul with watery eyes.

"How about yesterday?" Paul asked. That got Libby singing about how love was such an easy game to play. It was clear she was harboring a particular worry, one she couldn't reveal sober for fear of ridicule. It wouldn't come out until she was good and tight, beyond being taken seriously. Then she could speak her anxious truths in ways only court fools and drunks are permitted. I wasn't eager to hear them just then, but Leon didn't budge.

"This fellow Nawang from the Sherpa cooperative?" Howard's manner of speaking was full of caution, as though he might skid on some legal black ice. "Do we know anything about him?"

Paul had found out that he was not Nepalese, but from Bhutan. He'd come to Kathmandu in search of a job. I asked him about the younger man. He was an assistant from around here. His name was Pemba. Paul reported that George was still talking with them.

"Making them his own, like he has us. Trying to change

Nawang's idea about Saturdays."

Paul had found out that Nawang had been leading treks for six years. In an arranged marriage for the last two. A woman from his village.

"Nothing like the girl next door," Leon said, draping his arm over the back of my chair.

Libby was eyeing my drink. "You don't mind, honey?" She poured most of it into her empty glass. "The only way you'll marry, Leon," she said, leaning in front of me so as to address him directly, "is if someone arranges it."

"With a shotgun," Howard added.

"I wouldn't be so sure," Leon said, winking at me. I felt both flattered and resentful. As though he were certain he could have me whenever and however he wanted. Libby asked if that was a proposal.

"Be careful, Hannah, honey. Remember last time. Make him show you the ring."

With that, I was ready to go. I tried to get up but Leon tightened his arm around me. Paul, meanwhile, was taking everything in but his drink. From his sullen look it was easy to gather he wasn't happy with what he saw. I asked him if something was bothering him. He just stared at me as though I'd broken a promise. Ignoring my question, he went on with his story.

Nawang had brought his wife back to Kathmandu after the wedding. She didn't know anyone here. Now she was pregnant and he was away most of the time.

The scotch tasted flat. Without a warm finish, it went nowhere, just left me expecting something more. "That's awful," I said, not sure whether I was referring to the liquor or the story.

"She'll go back to Bhutan soon to give birth," Howard said in a tone that didn't argue with fate. He'd heard such separations were common. An informal understanding between husband and wife to go their own way. "They don't take marital fidelity seriously. Neither partner has to be faithful," he said.

Paul was shifting nervously in his chair.

"When in Rome. Here's to marital infidelity," Libby said. She lifted her glass and waved it front of us.

"It's something you know about?" Howard asked with mock concern.

"Not firsthand," she admitted, explaining she heard about it all the time from her clients. She leaned toward her husband, who sat opposite her. "You don't leave me alone long enough. If you did, I might consider it."

"Welcome it, even," Leon put in.

It's easy to joke about serious things, I thought. Even if left in her village, Nawang's wife would still be a married woman and mother. It was a respectability of sorts that eluded me. The consciousness-raising groups I'd attended with Miriam hadn't changed my status or my attitude. I felt still beyond the pale, burdened with a mysterious defect that women pitied and men tried to take advantage of. I looked at the sapphire ring on my right hand. That ring, two brooches and a set of small diamond earrings were all my mother left me. The cool blue stone eyed me with suspicion. No husband. No child. Not even an illegal abortion to try to hide.

"Sad story, isn't it?" I murmured to no one in particular.

Leon pressed his hands against the edge of the table until his chair tilted dangerously back. He had the knack of knowing my thoughts.

"Nawang's wife's or your own?" he asked softly.

"Mine?" I said, embarrassed. I told him there was no comparison. I had no family or village to return to and I certainly wasn't pregnant. I intentionally turned away from Leon toward Libby and Howard. "But I do have friends."

Leon brought his chair upright. He took my hand, saying gently that we didn't really know anything about Nawang or his wife or their relationship. He touched my arm. "But I know I am your friend."

I knew he was and leaned my head on his shoulder and closed my eyes. I felt his lips on my forehead, a sweet attempt to separate me from sadness. Libby, eyeing us, suddenly took up the argument.

"Women get shafted everywhere. Gone is gone in any language." She drained her glass. "Left with a bun in the oven, or several already served up. Women trying to store up enough potatoes to feed their kids. Do you know how many single mothers are in that position?"

She saw them in her office every day. Husbands going off, stiffing them on support. It would have been all right if Libby had stopped there, but booze clouded her judgment.

"Take Leon here. Wandering off with all sorts of women, then wanting to come back when it's convenient. Ask to see the ring, Hannah!"

I knew "Libby loose lips" is what she'd been called in high school. Saying out loud what everyone was keeping to themselves. Asking Beth Noonan in the lunchroom, so everyone could hear, if it was true that she'd passed algebra by letting Mr. Bertram feel her tits. Thirty years later she was still at it. She turned to me and gestured toward Paul.

"Why did he leave her at home?" she asked. "Miriam should be here with him, or maybe instead of him." She brought her face so close to mine that I couldn't see anything else.

"There's Zoe," I said, but she ignored me, saying it was the same old story for Miriam and lots of others too.

"Their Paul's gone, whatever the reason." She turned to Paul across the table, gazing at him unsteadily. She reminded him it was what Frank had done too. "Left Hannah. Took up with Ursula someone or other." It was too old for words, she said. "Ulysses wanders around like a bachelor, Aeneas leaves Dido." She paused to drain her already empty glass.

I didn't want to listen any longer. I tried to catch Leon's eye, but he was leaning behind me to tap Libby on the shoulder.

"And who appointed you the Greek chorus?" he asked. Libby rose unsteadily to her feet and turned toward Leon.

"Not some man, that's for sure. I'm self-appointed." Leaning on the table, she nodded toward her husband. "Now, take Howard. He was happy to leave his wife. His first wife, I mean. The one before me."

Howard reached across the table. "That's enough."

"Who says?" She pushed his hand away. "When things get serious, they try to shut you up. Want you to just march in step. But go along or not, they're likely to leave you. I mean, if you can leave one wife, you can leave another. Right?" She sat down again.

Howard stood up. "It's time to go."

Libby looked up at him as though she hadn't understood what he'd said. She continued a torrent of slurred words about her life before she met Howard. How men said they'd call and didn't and how you have to protect yourself.

"With booze," Howard said wearily.

"With the truth," I said, suddenly feeling sorry for her. It was hard to be like Libby with a mouth as big as your heart.

"Right! With the truth! I don't usually drink, do I, honey?" She motioned Howard toward his seat. "Oh, a scotch before dinner or maybe a martini. I'm drunk now. Know why?" She lowered her voice to a stage whisper. "Because I'm scared. Scared for all of us. We shouldn't start on a day Nawang doesn't like."

"What else are you scared of?" Leon asked.

Libby leaned across the table, suddenly beckoning Paul toward her. "Whether I can make it. See?" She thought it was going to be tough enough, even if we'd flown to Lukla. Now it was going to be a lot harder. A hundred and sixty miles or more, up and down, getting steeper, air getting thinner. Her knees could get bad. And she didn't like the cold. Maybe she hadn't brought enough warm things. Wasn't hypothermia a possibility?

"I'm older than all of you, except him." She jerked a thumb toward Howard. "He's been looking forward to it for so long." What if she couldn't make it? What if she ruined the trip for him? She began to cry, rubbing her tears from her cheeks with her sleeve.

"You'll be fine, honey," Howard said, reaching to put a consoling hand on her arm. Libby shrugged him off. "But what if I'm not? You'll go on without me."

"Of course I won't. You're my wife."

"Wives don't seem to count for much." She shuddered and

suddenly looked sick. I wanted to tell her that things would be all right, but I wasn't so sure myself. I put my hand on hers as much to comfort myself as her.

"This weather's gotten everyone down. You'll feel better by morning."

Howard, agreeing, helped his wife to her feet. They left with Libby leaning hard against him.

"Well, she covered all the bases," I said gloomily.

"A rough outline, I'd say." Leon's arm encircled me, pulling me toward him. "It's for us to fill in the colors." He rose, taking my hand, and asked Paul to excuse us.

"Let you go, yes. Excuse you? No," Paul said.

Leon was digging in his pocket for money. But Paul raised his hand in protest, saying the drinks were on him. He eyed me sullenly and warned against Greeks bearing gifts. I went around behind him, my hands on his shoulders.

"What am I supposed do? Tell me."

He shrugged. We left him looking for the waiter.

CHAPTER SIX
TOGETHER

"What's with him?" Leon asked as we crossed the lobby.

"Missing Miriam, I guess."

"Not missing her enough." Leon turned and stopped in front of me, hands on my shoulders. "Let's not miss our chance. It can work, can't it?" He kept them there until I answered.

"Caveat emptor."

He asked what I meant. "No guarantees. No warrantees. No refunds." He gave an exasperated laugh. "I'll take my chances."

"Even though the item's already been used and returned?" His eyes were half-closed, his jaw clenched, the sure sign I'd gone too far.

"Don't be hard. You don't do either of us justice."

Suddenly I was embarrassed by my self-deprecating remarks, afraid that I'd persuaded him not to try with me after all.

"Let's go," I said. "Only don't expect too much."

"Oh no, Hannah. I expect a lot." He squeezed my hand hard. And he got a lot. More than I knew I could give. It started tenderly, his kissing my eyes and nose as one might a sleeping child. He traced my lips with the tip of finger and parted them with his tongue. Slow, solemn, patient, he waited until I spiraled toward him, reaching for him, wanting him, making him gasp with pleasure. Then his mouth explored the tender places of my body. At last, he placed me on him and I rode us where we needed to go.

Then as soon as Leon was able, we started all over again, bringing with it his continued tenderness as well as my growing confusion. Once had been clear. What were we beginning in this second time, or maybe ending? Naked in this tiny room in a strange city: my clothes tangled in the cheap sheets. The overhead light on and the bed creaking so loudly I was sure we had everyone in the place listening. Leon's familiar body doing new and surprising things I wasn't used to and wasn't sure I liked.

"You've changed," I whispered.

"I don't think so."

"Oh yes. That art student taught you a thing or two."

He stopped what he'd been doing and lay on his back. Why had I brought her into it, he asked. Did I always need to spoil things?

"I'm with you, where I want to be," he said. I waited a long time for him to say more.

When he didn't, I began, "I'm sorry. I just . . ."

He faced me abruptly. "Don't explain. Don't," he commanded. He kissed me hard and placed his knee between my legs. "Besides, you're right. I'm changing. Feel it?"

I did, but was uncertain.

"Are you sure?"

"It's not the time for questions." He was in me before I was ready. My lack of excitement made him all the more determined. He tried to imprint himself on me, to become the definition of my desire. He was on top of me, pushing himself into me again and again, squeezing my breasts, kissing me hard and telling me to fuck him blind. As though I hadn't been doing just that.

"Give it to me, baby. Everything!" He was moving fast in me and all I felt was upset. I wanted to join him, but he'd gone on his own journey, searching me, probing for some unspeakable solace, using me for some private end I couldn't fathom. The sweat of his neck where I tried to kiss him filled my mouth with a sharp, salty taste. My hands wandered aimlessly over his body. What had started out a honey blend of tenderness and caring had become this: each of us alone, trying to find some way home. It wasn't Leon's eyes anymore, but the garish eyes of the Buddha that floated above me, watching me with strange detachment. Those eyes became mine and I saw just another man and woman in a seemingly endless animal embrace.

There was an end to it sometime before morning. Leon was finally sated or just plain tired. He kissed me, rolled over on his stomach with his arm across my abdomen and fell asleep. And then, of course, I couldn't. Leon's sprawl left me almost no room, and his arm was like a sick animal come to die on my stomach. Could he ignore my feelings as he had and still say he loved me? What was love anyway but a way of getting from someone what you wanted? I lay there angry and imagining Libby fast asleep, her cares temporarily sunk in sodden dreams. Howard had gone along with her preference for twin beds.

I pushed Leon's arm from my stomach. He rolled onto his back.

"You okay, honey?"

I didn't answer, afraid he would start with me again. I put on the shirt he'd discarded, shut off the light, and pulled the covers over me. I prefer making love in the dark, in a place of half shadows and uncertain images. I suppose it's because I hate the fat cells puckering on my thighs, the skin loosening around my belly. Frank hadn't seemed to mind, any more than he minded the paunch of his own belly or the hair graying on his chest. He wasn't much into looking, in any case. Leon, of course, had to see everything. Touching wasn't enough either. He had to look and talk too. "How's this? As good as last time? . . . Ah, that's sweet!"

I wished I were with Frank again, a man who never said a word, never seemed to want too much, sometimes just gave a low moan or grunt of satisfaction in the end. When he couldn't get it up, which happened more and more often, I reassured him that it was because he'd been working too hard. "It won't last," I said.

It did. We didn't. At first his sudden departure confused me. But when a mutual friend told me that he thought Ursula Bowitch might be giving Frank more than books, it began to make sense. She owned the bookstore on Broadway and Seventy-Eighth we'd frequented. Frank had stopped by to find a present for me. That's how it began. She wasn't particularly pretty: pale, unhealthy-looking skin, curly close-cropped hair, too yellow to be natural. Lots of silver rings on bony fingers that ended in stubby unvarnished nails. After I learned about her, I phoned the Albrights to tell them I was going with them.

"Well, this is a surprise," Pru had said when I called. "I hope it doesn't mean trouble at home."

Trouble? I adjusted my pillow and pulled the sheet around me, trying to separate myself from Leon and the new trouble in my bed. I closed my eyes, willing myself away from Leon, back to Frank, from the fire to the frying pan.

Copake Lake, a year ago. July. Two weeks in a rental by the water. The sky bright and cloud-filled like Thomas Girtin's painting of the Lake District, which he'd never visited. I was away from worrying whether the van Gogh still life in Gallery One was a fake, as a curator visiting from London had suggested. I knew it wasn't, but everyone in our field knows the story of Otto Wacker. He claimed the paintings he was marketing at the Cassirer Gallery in Berlin were genuine van Goghs. He concocted a story about their Russian owner needing to remain anonymous. The van Gogh scholar de la Faille was fooled into thinking them authentic. But Wacker's fraud was exposed and he spent nineteen months in jail. Whenever we met, Harrington, terrified of scandal, kept returning to the story of Wacker even though it was forty years old. I assured him our van Gogh was authentic, but he wanted me to go over its provenance and the previous assessment and submit a report. He insisted von Stein be brought from Utrecht to affirm its authenticity. His unnecessary trip came out of my budget.

The hotel room was hot and Leon had begun to snore. I took off his shirt and moved as far from him as I could. Copake Lake kept coming back to mind: Frank stripped and already in the water.

"Come on," he hooted.

I was folding my clothes on the far side of a rock, where Frank couldn't see me. Naked, I waded in, moving gingerly on the slippery stones. Frank came around to help. I dove into the pond before he could, surfacing to tell him how cold the water was.

"You'll get used to it. But I don't know if I'll ever get used to you. Those tits. How did you come by them?"

"A yard sale. Cheap," I answered, pushing my hair from my eyes. Then the sound of a great blue heron rising from the water. I pointed to it, glad to change Frank's focus. He squinted. Without his glasses, everything was a blurred canvas.

"Beautiful," he said uncertainly. He put his arms around me and gave me a slurry kiss. I was the bird he had his eye on he said. I gently undid his embrace saying I couldn't stay afloat with him on me. I drifted on my back, the sky blue as a Matisse wall. The sun high and dazzling created sudden sparks of shifting light on the water's surface. Then, a sudden stirring beneath me, as though a huge fish had swum by. I righted myself as Frank's head popped out of the water.

"You're great from below." He said the water magnified my derriere, making it "as round and white as a full moon."

It had been a tough two weeks with Frank after my watery "full moon" had turned him on. What he wanted most was anal sex. I kept putting him off. He had a lot of fancy explanations for his interest. Frank's vocabulary always dressed up his desires. David Levine had got Frank right for the *New York Review of Books*—all head and hair. I liked that so many people told me they'd seen it. Reflected glory, after all, is what a curator thrives on. I'd lived off Rembrandt and cozied up to Vermeer all my adult life. As long as they were the genuine article.

Frank, with all his might, tried to be that. And he *was* truly smart, a serious scholar and public intellectual. His ideas were debated; his company sought. But none of it came easy for him, despite what people imagined. He was always afraid his carefully constructed cover, his private witness-protection program, might be blown; that his sordid history would catch up and embarrass him. He was ashamed of the cramped, hardscrabble farm of his South Dakota childhood and dismissive of his God-fearing parents. He was still haunted by the suicide of a high school friend he felt he could have helped and frightened by the approaches of a priest he'd liked and had to run from. And there was Carl, his quarrelsome alcoholic brother who inherited the farm, drove it into the ground, and kept asking for money. The books Frank wrote, the reviews, the lectures were his cover. He'd indicted his past, found it guilty as charged and locked it away for life. In the end, he'd found Ursula, a woman like him—one who was all print and no pictures.

George understood the situation immediately. He had gone to the bookstore to see Ursula for himself. "If her tits were any smaller, she'd pass for a man. Fucking her, he's in both worlds," he'd told me at dinner one night. "Or neither," Pru had added. Cold comfort when you're alone.

I looked at Leon, his mouth partly open, lips moving lightly with each breath. At least, there wasn't any doubt he wanted a woman. He just didn't know what a woman wanted. Could I blame him when I wasn't certain myself? Perhaps it was enough being on my own, being a curator, saving the old cardinal from a slow demise, and knowing the van Gogh was genuine and that nothing would ever change that.

CHAPTER SEVEN
GETTING READY

We were first to breakfast. After I'd deflected Leon's early morning attentions, there was really nothing else to do. We took turns in my shower that, amidst groans, sporadically sent out gushes of cold water. We dried each other as best we could with towels that could only have been meant for dishes. Leon borrowed my toothbrush. After a fruitless search for my hairbrush, I used a broken comb that he dug out of his jeans. While he dressed, I checked my face and neck for any signs of the night's activity.

At breakfast, Leon was solicitous, asking me what I wanted to eat. I ordered a poached egg and dry toast. He smiled, expressing surprise I wasn't hungrier. I didn't respond. He pulled me closer, seeking reassurance I wasn't interested in giving. I wanted to focus on the day ahead. I glanced at my watch. It was seven-thirty. I knew George would want us on the bus soon so that we could start trekking later in the day. We'd have to be ready by nine, the latest. All the things that should have been done last night, left to the morning. The room a mess, everything out of place, and where had my hairbrush gone anyway? Searching for it in my mind, I didn't notice Howard.

"May I?" He stood politely until Leon pulled a chair out for him. He told us Libby was still sleeping and he hadn't wanted to wake her.

"I'll bet you couldn't if you tried," Leon said, stirring hot milk into his coffee. "She packs a wallop, that woman."

Howard said she'd been embarrassed about bringing up Frank. "It's old news," I replied, handing him a menu. I asked if we should order something for Libby, as we would be leaving soon.

"Not till this afternoon." Pru had told him that for a sum Nawang had tempered his views. He and George had been haggling over the price. They had both driven a hard bargain and, according to Pru, seemed to respect one another for it. They'd agreed upon an undisclosed amount of rupees, for which we would all be taxed. Now Nawang was willing to take us as far as Lamosangu today. But the trek, the "new undertaking," would not begin until tomorrow. Howard smoothed the napkin on his lap.

"This way, everyone gets something—George, Nawang, even the gods," he said.

I nodded. "And Libby gets to sleep in. Lucky her."

"And lucky me," Howard said brightly. "No more reassurances until she wakes." Leon wondered if the gods were so easily fooled.

"It seems like chutzpah," he insisted.

Howard leaned forward conspiratorially. "It means you have another morning together." The waiter brought me a scrambled egg and buttered toast.

Back in my room, Leon showed no signs of leaving. He shoved the water bottle and fanny pack from the room's only chair onto the floor and sat down. He stretched out his legs and clasped his hands behind his head.

"You did enjoy last night, didn't you? It was certainly better than the last time." In the silence that followed, I made the bed and began to pick up things from the floor. He waited until I said I didn't remember the last time. He didn't blame me. It was not one of his stellar performances. He reminded me it was after we'd already split. We'd gone to a movie and were thinking maybe we should try again. He flung his head back and looked at the ceiling.

"It's not important," he said. I could feel him looking at me again. "What's important is our sense of last night."

"Sense?" I stared at him for a moment, then began to fold a sweater I'd knitted for Frank but kept for myself. I told him there was no "sense" to it, no meaning other than we had once been in love.

"Touring old sites is sometimes better than seeing new ones," I said, placing a pillow back on the bed. He protested that he wasn't the "old Leon" anymore. I'd even said he'd changed.

"Some," I agreed. "But I haven't."

I was working on the turtlenecks now, folding them one on top of the other. He hadn't moved from the chair.

"Frank still on your mind?"

I stopped what I was doing, trying to find an answer. Was it

Frank? Was it having given Leon another chance and the knowledge that we had come up short again? Or was it that I was ruining what was worth working on?

It took some time before I answered. "It's me. A beastly longing for something that nobody can satisfy." I felt embarrassed by what I'd said and frightened by its truth. He rose and came to hug me.

"That's okay, baby."

I leaned against him. The warmth of his body seeped into me like sun through a window. He kissed me gently and held me very close. But then his hands began to wander.

"That's your idea of helping?" I tried to pull away. "Don't you have your own business to take care of?"

"I'm packed. Never unpacked. Just a few things to throw in the duffel. Don't worry, we'll hunt down that elusive wildebeest."

He released his grip and set about helping in earnest. Found my wool socks. Stuffed my sleeping bag so it fit more tightly in its sack. He put all the things I needed for the bus trip in my fanny pack—tissues, sunglasses, Life Savers, and water bottle. He held up the guidebook.

"You'll want this." Then he turned his attention to my odd assortment of paper, stamps and pens. "You'll need plastic bags for these. I'll get some from my room, though I doubt you'll find a mailbox in the mountains."

When he returned, I asked him why he was doing all this. "Because it's what you want." He was folding my poncho into a neat square. I put my hand on his back.

"Thank you for helping. But it confuses me. Last night did too. Loving is so messy." He covered my hand with his own.

"It's the other way around. Love orders things." We packed my duffel. Leon checked the bathroom cabinet and looked under the bed for stray items. Then he set my things by the door. The room seemed sparse and uninviting. A space that had been strewn with objects of every size and color was now dully neat and unprepossessing. I wanted to get out of this soulless box that I'd emptied of dream or desire.

"I'm ready. Now I'll help you," I said.

Leon repeated there was nothing to do.

"I'll come and help anyway." His room was only a little larger than my own, with paint peeling from a corner of the ceiling near the bathroom. The same cheap furniture and same shiny fabric on the bedspread and curtains. I asked where his things were. He had taken them to the lobby when he went for the ziplocks.

"So there really *is* nothing to do," I said. He disappeared into the bathroom and reemerged with two glasses and half a bottle of brandy.

"Isn't it early to be starting?" I asked.

He handed me a glass and filled it halfway. He sat in the chair and I on the edge of his bed. He took a large sip, held it in his mouth to warm it, then released it into his throat. "Good stuff." When he got up, I thought it was to move closer, but he went into the bathroom and stared at himself in the mirror. He wondered if he'd gotten a tan even though it had been cloudy. He turned toward me, smiling. "Or is it the beginning of jaundice?"

"Let me see." I beckoned to him. He came toward me and sat at my feet, his face peering up at me, childlike. I told him he looked the same, always dark, even when he shaved. I bent forward and kissed the top of his head.

"In the dark is where you keep me," he said.

I patted the bed beside me. "Why don't you come up here into the light?"

He took another sip of brandy and then rose slowly to sit beside me. I put my hand on his knee and told him he was sweet and I did love him, but didn't know in what way.

"Let me know when you've figured it out."

He lay on the bed and closed his eyes. He looked tired, but not unhappy. It was as though he'd reached some conclusion about us; some knowledge of me that I didn't yet possess. Looking at him half-asleep, I wondered what to do. He wasn't the same person I'd lived with five years ago. Success had mellowed him. He didn't, like Frank, pretend to be someone he wasn't. I lay down beside him and kissed his closed eyelids. Maybe it could get better, all of it.

"That's nice," he said without moving. I kissed his mouth and then his chin. He remained motionless. I rubbed his chest though his shirt.

"You good?" I asked him.

"Keep it coming," he said, pushing my hand to the edge of his pants.

My warm feelings drained like water down a sink. I sat up. Still lying on the bed, he smiled and squeezed my hand. "Okay. You don't have to sit beside me on the bus. I'll take a seat in the back."

"That's what you want now?"

"No." He got up and emptied the brandy glasses into the sink. "Not exactly. But you're not sure whether you want any more of me." He had rinsed a glass and was drying it with the edge of his shirt. "Liking it and then not."

"Do I seem that type to you? Someone who buys a dress, wears it to a party and then returns it?"

Leon shrugged, set the glasses on the bathroom shelf and turned toward me.

"You're not dishonest. Some women truly like the dress when they buy it, but really dislike it afterward. Since you can't exactly take me back today, why not keep me in the closet for a while. See how I look a little later."

His air of condescension angered me. I asked what had he expected. I reminded him that I had been the one left hanging when he'd told his father he wasn't serious about me. And he still hadn't said he loved me, only that he "wanted to be" with me.

"What does that mean?" I asked. I told him I couldn't trust him and only half wanted to. He looked at me and smiled.

"I think you're the pot talking to the kettle."

Leon came toward me. "Don't!" I cried. I felt caught by him as well as some tangled thing in myself. I was the moth I'd seen under a hotel table fluttering in a web. Or maybe the brown spider that sat in a corner, clinging to the rocking web, slowly immobilizing the moth before killing it. When I finally looked up from the deadly drama, I saw a mother reading while her daughter splashed in the blue-tiled pool. I wanted to tell them what I'd witnessed, but was afraid of sounding odd. Why should they be concerned about a moth's murder?

"I'll see you downstairs," Leon whispered.

He closed the door behind him. After a while I stopped crying and I lay on his bed staring at water stains on the ceiling. I felt small and alone in the double bed. There were sounds of footsteps in a room overhead and somewhere a toilet flushed. I thought I might never leave that room. Never see Leon or Libby or any of them again. I felt an inexorable disappearance of self, like a terminal anorexic.

I dozed into a dream.

I am a girl of seven or eight running down a long hall. Perhaps in a hospital or school. Doors on either side. Some of them open. I seem to be looking for something or someone, but there is no one about. I push open a door and enter a room where I see a bed with someone lying in it. The body is covered with a sheet as if it were a corpse. I pull back the sheet and Leon smiles up at me. I scream and run away. I look behind and it is not Leon but my father who is chasing me.

I'd dreamt it before, many times. Sometimes the faces changed. Frank instead of Leon. Leon instead of my father. And even though I've told versions of it to friends and more than one shrink, the reason it keeps returning still eludes me. Dr. Grossbart, the best of them, told me it was my own passion that I was running from, that I was Frank and Leon and my father, as well as the frightened girl. It makes a kind of sense. But neither the doctor nor I understood, at the time, that it was him and his treatment that I was running from. I don't know that my understanding of the dream has changed anything very much. I still don't like it and I still keep dreaming it.

A knock on the door. "Hannah. It's almost noon. We're beginning to load the bus." Leon held out a cup of coffee and asked if I was all right.

"I suppose I am. Except for a dream." He told me not to think about it, to wake up to a new adventure. "We're starting for Gokyo."

"And you'll sit beside me on the bus?" I asked.

He smiled a smile that was different from the one in the dream. "If you really want me to."

CHAPTER EIGHT
BUS RIDE

An old yellow school bus was parked at the hotel entrance. Its engine coughed loudly under a dusty hood that boulders had used for target practice. There was a headlight missing and the windshield was scratched. The tailpipe muttered, giving off suffocating gusts of dark exhaust. I put a handkerchief to my nose as I waited to board. Beside the bus, our gear lay in a disorderly mound that Pemba was sorting. He wore a faded T-shirt that was a size too small. It rode up on him, showing muscles that danced around his spine. He was piling the tents in one spot and duffels in another under a steady barrage of commands from Nawang, who was crouched on the roof of the bus waiting to be handed the baggage.

George was at the front door with a clipboard, as cranky as an eighth-grade teacher assigned to cafeteria duty.

"Pru, where the hell's our map?" he barked.

She told him he had been looking at it last night and must have put it someplace. He insisted that he'd given it to her.

"For God's sake!" She was almost shouting as she unzipped the backpack at his feet. "Look, it's right here. Use your head once in a while." George ignored her without taking the map she offered. "Nawang, make sure it's all tied tight." Then yelled to the driver, "Cut the engine, will you?"

Libby was trying to get out of the bus while the rest of us were climbing in. She pushed past me.

"I hope they haven't cleaned my room. I left something in the dresser drawer." Her face was flushed and she looked worried.

"Not your passport!" I said.

"No," she whispered. "My diaphragm!"

She was running toward the lobby when I took a seat behind the bus driver, who, sipping a Coke, seemed unperturbed by the hubbub around him. I told Paul the seat was saved, but he plopped down beside me anyway.

"Just till Leon comes," I cautioned.

"Okay, but I need to talk." He stowed his fanny pack under

the seat and settled back.

Libby came running back. "Jesus, you'll never guess where it was." She was pointing down toward herself. "In the old safety deposit box where I left it."

A few minutes later, Leon passed down the aisle. He nodded to me, but that was all. I turned to see him take a seat next to Bobby a few rows back.

"What is it you need to talk about?" I asked Paul. He put his hands behind his head and looked past me out the window.

"The clouds have finally lifted. We're in for better weather."

In the distance, the mountains that I'd known were there, but never fully seen, rose and stretched themselves with frightening clarity. I sat there wondering why Leon hadn't said anything to me as he passed. Did he think I'd somehow arranged to exclude him? I looked back again, trying to catch his eye, but his head was bent, studying something Bobby was showing him. When I turned back, Paul was eyeing me.

"You've gone down that road before. Take care."

I was too angry to answer. I gathered my stuff and pushed past his knees before he could get up. "I need time to myself," I said. I settled myself at the opposite window and put my pack on the seat beside me, making it clear just how much I didn't want his company. I was hoping Leon might join me. But when I looked back, he was gazing out the window and smiling to himself.

In all the years I'd known Paul, he'd never been happy. And if there wasn't a real problem, he'd make one up. He worried about money when everyone knew he was doing well. Years before, he'd been worried about being accepted for training at the New York Psychoanalytic Institute; made it sound as if he were trying out for the Olympics. Of course, they'd welcomed him with open arms. Since graduating five years ago at thirty-three, he was becoming a bright star in an ever-darkening sky.

One of his friends was a Russian-born obstetrician from Odessa. I met Igor at a dinner party Paul and Miriam gave. A small man with sour breath and sallow skin who recited Pushkin whenever the opportunity arose. At dinner, he pushed himself toward me as he spoke, forcing me against my chair. He told me, thanks to Paul, he'd read Freud and felt bad that so few in his country had the opportunity to do the same. Hoping he'd back off, I said that Russians might have other things on their minds. He sat up and shook a soupspoon in my direction.

"You mean like harvest. You picture us like Pavlovian dogs, salivating at thought of food." He said Russians were no longer peasants like American propaganda portrayed them.

"Long live Freud and Brezhnev," I said, returning to my cream of leek. But, of course, Igor couldn't let me alone. He pursued me into the salad course. He had heard I worked at the Baudry and imagined it was like the Hermitage, only smaller, of course. All museums, though necessary, were the product of ill-gotten gains. He thought Marcel Baudry had only collected art to satisfy his "new American ego." I said I loved collectors, that I'd be out of a job without them, forced into factory work or prostitution.

"For you they the same," Igor replied. He thought prostitution a good idea and said he would come visit me.

I smiled back. "Cash on the line. No credit cards and no rubles."

For reasons hard to fathom, Paul liked him. Maybe it was because Igor had referred him a few patients with postpartum depression or maybe it was the black caviar Igor brought back from Brighton Beach.

I looked over at Paul. His eyes were closed and he had that sad pensive look that psychiatrists learn to cultivate. Was there trouble between him and Miriam I didn't know about? She had complained at times, but what wife doesn't? I couldn't imagine serious trouble, but you never know what really goes on between couples. After all, lots of people were shocked when Frank and I broke up. There was no use going down that road. I dug the guidebook out of my fanny pack and began to read about Nepal. The passage described the climate as very cold and national character as "stamped with perfidy and mendacities." It went on to quote from the diary of a traveler to Nepal who, in 647AD, described the people as having "a severe and savage inclination to which neither good faith nor justice nor good literature appealed." I closed the book.

The bus was leaving the hotel. A deafening sound made it clear that the muffler had rusted out or been knocked off by a rock in the road. The acrid smell of exhaust seeped through the floorboards. I lay back and closed my eyes, hoping to avoid a headache. If the Nepalese hadn't changed their ways since 647, we were in for a hell of a time. Good literature didn't appeal to them? What was the writer thinking? Most people who lived in the seventh century couldn't read. I picked up the guidebook again, turning to a different chapter. There was a section on Buddhism and the "four noble truths." I only got as far as the first.

To live is to suffer: In man's life everything is suffering, his birth, separation from loved ones, getting old, getting sick and finally death.

I looked out the window. In the distance the sun had turned to fire the gold roof of a temple. Beyond it, in shadow, brooding mountains. We passed a long line of women, each with a huge basket of kindling strapped to her back. They wore long black skirts set off by colorful striped aprons and blouses of magenta and gold. A few pregnant girls, their pace slow and ungainly, brought up the rear. Mountain forests were disappearing onto the backs of women carrying them to market and to the campfires of trekkers. A long day of walking in bare feet for a few small coins. A life that might kill you before you're forty, if childbirth didn't do it sooner. I'd heard that in the mountains, when women have their periods, they are "unclean" and are made to stay alone in unheated, often unventilated huts regardless of the weather. Women become ill or freeze to death in those places, women who are mothers. In the villages, women dig potatoes or plant wheat. In the city, they peddle moonshine, work as domestics or sell vegetables on the street. The lucky ones who can read and write find low-level jobs in government. When a Nepali woman dies, her consciousness leaves her body to wander for a while. If she, in that altered state, can realize that the demons and deities she meets are nothing but products of her own mind, she achieves enlightenment. If she takes her visions to be real and flees from them, she will seek refuge in a womb and be born again into the miserable state of human existence. A mother's womb, the beginning of trouble.

We were moving steadily into the country. There were long flat green fields of rice planted along the banks of a slow-moving river. Water buffalo lowered their heads to drink the murky water. Clusters of small stucco houses appeared suddenly and then were left behind before I could take them in. I turned back to get a better look, but they had disappeared into clouds of black exhaust. Oxen were working the drier land. Chickens in small pens listlessly pecked at bare earth. I remember closing my eyes. Then a dream:

I am looking at my hands. One unblinking blue eye appears in each palm. I bring my hands to my face, eyes to eyes. The eyes in my hand shut and I cannot see.

I awoke with a start.

Paul was studying me. "Are you awake? Can we talk now?"

"We have to talk about you, not me," I said, wiping my hands with a tissue.

He put my things in the aisle and slid in beside me. I asked him what was bothering him.

"Miriam. Miss her, but relieved to be away. Go figure."

"Go figure? You're the psychiatrist, remember?"

"I've been trying to think what's wrong." He brought his foot to the edge of the seat to retie his boot, creating a wall of flesh between us. His shorts rode up his leg, revealing the curve of his muscled thigh. Rivers of dark hair made eddies and swirls as it cascaded over his white skin, until it petered out high on his leg. Paul was concentrating hard on his laces as he spoke.

"I find myself thinking a lot about this one patient. She gets angry about weekend breaks. Won't talk on Monday. Just shows me the tiny cuts on her arms." He looked up at me, gauging my reaction. "Forgets to sign the checks she gives me. Calls me a lot."

"Sounds like a honey."

He went on to tell me how good-looking she was; that she was divorced without children and rich. His voice was matter-of-fact and clinical.

"Ex-husband settled a fortune on her so he could marry his accountant." His voice changed, colored by anxiety. "I can't seem to get her out of my mind." He thought she might kill herself while he was away. Maybe she already had.

"Believe me, Paul. That kind doesn't go easily."

I thought of Ursula's shop around the corner from me. There was a rumor that her landlord wanted to rent her space to a restaurant, but she'd resisted leaving. She was still there, a bad virus that just hangs on.

"She's messed up and kind of impulsive, but she's funny and smart. And knows she's good-looking. On the board of the Philharmonic and half a dozen charities. Invites me to go places with her. I refuse and she's back the next day with another invitation and another little scratch. Saying how much she would do for me if I let her. Wants me to fuck her." He hesitated. "Sometimes it's arousing. I know it's crazy, but I think about being with her." He looked away for a moment. He said that if she wasn't already dead, she might show up in Kathmandu. It'd be like her, once she got the idea in her head.

"She knows you're here?"

He blushed. "Yeah, in case she really needed to talk."

He was clearly out of his mind. Had she called him? I asked. There'd been a few hang-ups but he didn't know if it was her or "just the screwed-up phone system."

I didn't want to look at the excitement in his face. I turned to the window instead. The sun was setting. A great shadow was advancing from the mountain peaks, spreading itself over the valley. Why was it always so hard? Things like love that should be easy. I was sure he loved Miriam. And I knew, for all her complaints about his working too much and not having enough time for family, she loved him. But love wasn't always enough. Never was, in fact. It certainly hadn't been for Frank and me, if love is what we ever had. Maybe it wouldn't be for Paul and Miriam.

I glanced at the cover of the guidebook, where a brown-skinned girl with marigolds in her hair smiled up at me. A smile so out of keeping with the growing darkness that it frightened me. I turned toward Paul.

"It's a fantasy, that's all. A sign that something needs fixing."

He nodded. "I know." He attempted a smile and tried to take my hand, but I didn't let him.

"So, what's going on with you and Miriam?" I asked.

He told me in some detail. A long list of complaints followed by an even longer list of hurt feelings. In brief: he married too quickly, before he really knew what he wanted—or what he might be capable of having. He hadn't realized how hard it would be to raise a son that wasn't his own. And Zoe, only three, was still coming into their room at night. Sure, he loved Miriam, but it wasn't easy being with her. There was never enough time to do all he needed: see patients, take notes, go to the gym and try to write. She didn't understand that there were meetings at the Institute he had to attend. At home, all Miriam talked about was the kids.

"And she thinks I've had enough analysis." Not easy to satisfy in bed either. "For Miriam, detumescence is not part of her sexual vocabulary." And though she never said anything, he knew she compared him with her first husband, and he wasn't coming out the winner.

"Who can compete with that Dying Gaul?" he complained. "Perpetual strength and beauty preserved like marble in her memory."

I told him he was talking nonsense, that Miriam adored him. He was alive, flesh and blood, and had given her a child.

He smiled. "There's nothing like Zoe in this whole wide world."

I asked what Shapiro thought about all this. I was out of ideas of my own and hoping Paul's second analyst could help me out.

He shrugged. "He won't answer. Just keeps mentioning Odysseus. I've read *The Odyssey* three times since my analysis began and I still don't get it. 'What are you trying to tell me?' I ask. You know what he says? 'When you've answered that question, you'll be home.' Everyone says he's the best. My first analyst was nice, a good woman, but limited. I think maybe I married Miriam because I couldn't marry her. But she wasn't rigorous. Gave advice instead of interpretations. I don't know how she got as far as she did."

I told him there was nothing wrong with advice. People need it.

"But not when you're in analysis," he said. Shapiro was much better, though a lot more opaque. He wrote papers on Fairbairn that Paul read and thought he understood. "Lifts weights between patients. I know because he keeps a set of barbells under the couch. But with him, it's like being married a second time. If it isn't working and you leave again, it's clear there's something wrong with you." He grabbed my hand. "You'll keep all this to yourself, won't you?"

CHAPTER NINE
ARRIVAL

The bus began to slow as it made its way through Lamosangu, a place of no particular beauty. All I can remember of it is a narrow, dusty street with small, shuttered houses, a few shops lit by dim kerosene lamps. It was twilight when we pulled up to a huge banyan tree in the center of town. A crowd was already gathering, mostly barefoot boys in dirty shorts and no shirts. In the fast-approaching darkness, their faces turned the color of dust.

"We're here," George sang out from the rear of the bus. "From now on, no more wheels. Watch your stuff. Things can disappear pretty quick."

We huddled around the bus, clutching our possessions and gawking at the huge gnarled tree where spirits were thought to live.

"The banyan is the temple in these villages. It is a sacred spot," said Howard *sotto voce.*

The tree's twisted branches seemed ominous, the many arms of Durga reaching out, trying to encircle us.

"Its seeds cling to the leaves of other plants, feeding off their host, strangling it," Howard continued. The pale light of a rising moon played hide-and-seek in the twists and turns of the ancient tree. I was reaching for one of its large green leathery leaves, said to be a resting place of the gods, when Pemba came up and gently touched my arm.

"No good to do. Disturb spirits."

I apologized, saying I had a lot to learn about Nepal. He nodded, looking at the ground. Leon came up to me and put his arm around my shoulder and asked if I'd enjoyed the ride. I told him it would have been better had I been with him but that Paul had needed to talk.

"About his patient?" Leon said he'd been through that already with Paul. "There's no doubt, he's edging toward it."

He brought his mouth close to my ear while he increased the pressure on my shoulder. I stared at the tree as he talked. I said there was no way we were sleeping together on the trek. There would be no privacy. The tents were thin, everything could be heard. "We could ask them to set ours apart," he replied.

The group was beginning to move toward a field a short distance away where Nawang, with the help of Pemba and local men, were setting up camp. Some were separating out luggage while others were bringing firewood. The forests were being destroyed, farms depleted as topsoil was swept into rivers because of the national dependence on firewood for fuel. I bent down to get my backpack, forcing Leon to let go of me.

"Let's just be together. If it's good between us, then it can wait. I don't want to make a spectacle and separate us from the others. Don't be glum. We can still have a fine time."

The first night alone was hard. Village children surrounded us, giggling and pointing, peering into open tent flaps, sometimes putting a hand inside. I set my flashlight down for a moment and it was gone. When I lay on my back, the top of my tent almost touched my nose. Outside, only darkness, strangers and a foreign landscape. I thought of all of us—Pru and George, Leon, Howard, Bobby, Libby, Paul—lined up, head and feet in the same direction, as though laid out for burial. I thought of the deadly war going on in Vietnam. Nixon buried alive by his own strategies, trying to claw his way out with promises of eventual peace. And me, on a trip whose purpose was as murky as our politics. I pictured George dreaming of Nawang and the trail awaiting us. And Libby dreaming of calamity. I thought of Paul alone with his troubles in the tent beside me and of Frank, who was oceans away and in whose embrace I had found a temporary respite from uncertainty. Like colored glass in a kaleidoscope, my mind spilled me from one scene to another. My body in a sleeping bag became a larva enclosed by a chrysalis, hanging somewhere in space, hoping to grow wings. I thought of the girl I'd seen at a country fair lying in an iron lung, unable to breath on her own, waiting for a cure that would never come.

CHAPTER TEN
TREKKING

At first, it was easy, walking along the dikes that separated terraced fields of rice. The stalks were a foot high and not yet ready for harvesting. Nawang explained in English that was hard to understand, with Pemba sometimes helping, that the fields had been plowed by water buffalo, fertilized with dung and night soil, then smoothed by logs rolled over them. Dikes had been built so that when the monsoon came, the fields would flood. The rice saplings were planted in the muddy water by hundreds of hands. Six months after planting, the fields were drained and the crop harvested.

We were heading toward Jiri, a small town sixty-three hundred feet above sea level. It had been called the "Gateway to Everest" ever since Sir Edmund Hillary and Tenzing Norgay had passed though it in 1953. The fields folded one upon the other like piles of soft green velvet. Men and women in broad straw hats and pants rolled up to the knees waded through ankle-deep water. The villages they lived in were as small and spare as thumbtacks. The sun shone off the water with intensity that blinded me, even with sunglasses. I had to put my head down to recover my sight.

Ten days later, higher up along the east bank of the Dudh Kosi, the air was thinner and the climb steeper. The nights grew colder and forced me into my sleeping bag right after dinner. There were forests of cedar and maple where silver-gray langur monkeys shrieked in the trees above. Near Sagar we camped in an empty schoolyard. The town consisted of a dozen two-story mud houses with red-tiled roofs and no chimneys. The smoke of cooking fires rose though crevices in the tiles, creating a gray cloud over each hut.

"I envy them," Paul had said to me as he watched men urging bullocks into the first-floor barns. "I so need a home-cooked meal."

I told him I'd been thinking about M&M's all day. It's funny where your mind goes with eight hours a day of trekking. It begins to drift amongst the clouds or wander in the ruts of the trail. Logic vanishes like mist; only scattered images remain randomly torn from memory's album. Thoughts of the foods we couldn't have dogged us as we lugged our bodies uphill. Paul said he had been thinking of "mac and cheese" and of home. I asked if he really knew where home was.

"Somewhere I'm not," he said, poking his walking stick into the ground. "I am trying hard to be here in the moment. Nawang says there are rhododendron forests ahead."

He thought they wouldn't bloom this time of year. He was right. The giant trees, when we reached them, were gnarled arthritic hands that held no flowers. Lichens the color of blood were scattered over their skins. It was as though some great battle had taken place and only remnants of the dead remained. I told Paul it wasn't what I expected.

"People are always expecting more than they get. If they got what they wanted, I'd be out of business." I told him his wasn't a business, but a profession. "Tell that to Dr. Shapiro. He just raised his fee. Sixty dollars an hour to hear myself talk. And then he starts again with his Odysseus shit."

Once over the Languor ridge, we descended through fragrant pine forests to Jambesi. A short deep sleep in the town and then up again to face the long tedious climb toward Chamiang. Morning blended into morning, the sun never let up, the hard stones of the path remained unyielding. Evenings and mornings grew colder, afternoons hotter. We left behind any knowledge of the day or the date.

Each dawn began the same way. George made no effort to lower his voice, which rang through the camp like a burglar alarm. *Where the heck's Nawang?* summoned us from sleep. He ordered the porters around like they were nurses back home. He had mastered a few basic phrases, but none of the Sherpas seemed to understand him and he had to resort to tapping on his watch or pointing. The frigid air made white puffs of my breath as I dressed. I pulled on the same heavy sweater. Then Pemba's face peered at me through the tent flap.

"Hot water," he said as he produced a large metal bowl and set it on the ground in front of my tent.

"Thank you," I replied, and pulled it inside.

The basin of hot water made me yearn for more of it, a whole bathtub full. The chill morning cooled the water quickly; I could only wash my hands and face before it turned tepid. As I placed the basin outside the tent, Pemba came toward me smiling. *"Ciya?"* He held a tin cup of tea and a plate of sugar wafers. The warm metal felt good in my hands. Before I could thank him, he was off giving tea to George and Pru from a tray carried behind him by a porter.

Libby remarked that the service was good even if the hour was ungodly. Only her face protruded from her round tent, making her into a huge talking snail. She asked if I'd slept well.

"Strange dreams I don't remember."

"I've stopped dreaming. Being awake is strange enough for me." She disappeared inside the tent, where I heard her trying to wake Howard. It reminded me of my father waking me when I was a girl. Tickling my toes, blowing in my ear, and then finally reaching under the covers to grab a leg and pull me off the bed while I, screaming, clutched the blankets around me. Mother clucking over what a mess we'd made. Later, when she was sick, he'd just find my knee, squeeze it hard, and I'd get up.

Standing in front of my tent, I drank the tea slowly, taking in the scant yellow light that rose over the mountaintops. The sun had a way to go before it would reach us. Around me, the porters were taking down the tents and loading their baskets with our gear. The place was becoming just a green field again in which we, like dew, had collected for the night. With the sun, we would disappear without trace. I took up my fanny pack and walking stick and headed for the trail.

"Namaste," Nawang murmured as I approached him. He stood like a lieutenant reviewing his troops as we passed onto the trail. George was beside him, nodding to everyone.

"Cool now, but it's going to be a hot one. If anyone feels in need of salt tablets, let me know."

"George has thought of everything," said Pru as she stepped into stride beside me.

"We all depend on him for that," I responded. The trail was

rutted and rock hard. It led upward, beside fields of green spear grass dotted with huge white pines and barberry. Pru quickened her pace as she talked.

"Always surrounded by acolytes, isn't he? Nawang. Pemba, some of us. *Acolytes* is the right word, isn't it? Not sycophants or sybarites."

"You don't sound happy." I glanced at her. Her face was immobile, her gaze focused on the trail ahead. We were passing lavender-and-blue blossoms on an orchid tree, blooms so numerous and fluttery that they looked like little winged birds that might carry the whole tree into the sky.

"Why shouldn't I be? Beautiful country. The tour organized to a T by my efficient husband. And the company's superb." She took my elbow. "Speaking of which, I see you've found company of your own."

I laughed and told her Leon and I were friends wondering if we could be more than that. It was her turn to laugh.

"I thought it the other way round. That you were already more than that, trying like the devil to be friends. Now, that's something I know about."

I knew what she meant. Her marriage to George was far from ideal, but both of them hung on, like boulders on a mountainside. They were good to me in the weeks after Frank left. I dined with them four nights out of seven. Went with them to their place in Sag Harbor every weekend for a month. Pru was full of hugs and kisses and insulting gossip about Ursula; George, always sympathetic and properly disgusted with Frank. He even offered to go and talk with him. And if the man didn't come to his senses, George would rearrange his face for him. "I'm an expert at that," he reminded me.

Three years rooming together at Vassar had led to a lifelong friendship with Pru. She was never really attractive even then. Thickly built and short in the leg. But her hair had been nicely cut and her clothes stylish. It was her energy and intelligence that George, I knew, had found most appealing—qualities that matched his own. To me, Pru remains the most attractive and compelling of women, even though she has stopped trying to appeal. Her frankness never ceases to surprise me. I hadn't been raised by women who spoke their minds. My mother was too sick and her mother in New Hampshire too sad to talk much above a whisper.

There was green all around us—small emerald meadows where cattle grazed and fields of winter wheat rose in infinite terraces. Giant pines studded the landscape like dark exclamation marks. I spotted a macaque scurrying through the high grass. The trail turned into a silver river of stone as we headed higher. We walked in silence for a while. Except for our breathing, there was no sound. The sky was cloudless and the rising sun was making rapid advances on the mountains' shadows.

Pru took the hill we were climbing with an even, steady stride. It was as though she were saying to the hills what she said to her children when they wanted another ice cream. *There's no use arguing. I'm not giving in.* A will as hard as any of the stones we were stepping on. It was bred in the bone. She was a direct descendant of Anne Hutchinson, who had rebelled against Puritan Boston and left with a few followers for Rhode Island, where she could worship her own way. Pru's grandmother was an early suffragette and a leader of the Philadelphia women's temperance movement. Her mother became Yale's first tenured woman professor of mathematics. The men in her family had been competent businessmen, socially drab and willing to take a backseat to their talented and ambitious wives. Pru's father had no idea of how to be more than polite to his daughter. He hadn't tried to protect her from her mother's icy criticisms and intellectual hauteur. In response, Pru had developed a confused but steely will to be different from both parents, to submit to neither ambition nor passivity. Her choice of a husband helped forge the stubborn wedge she wanted between herself and her family. George wasn't going to be second fiddle to anybody, including Pru's mother, and he wasn't always nice to the old lady.

We stopped to rest against a stone wall built low so that weary porters could easily set their baskets on it. We had been climbing up, and now, at a turn, the trail descended. Pru found her water bottle and handed it to me. She could see I was already sweating under a sun that had begun to hint at its fury. I dug in my pack for a bandanna and sunglasses.

"Downhill's the hardest," Pru explained. She stared out over the green hills. A look of sadness settled about her face. "Like with relationships." She glanced at me thoughtfully. "Shall we plod on?"

I laughed and asked if we had a choice.

"There's always choices as long as one's alive. You don't always have to go on."

I asked if she was all right.

"I'm not suicidal, if that's what you're getting at." She looked indignant. "You ought to know me by now. Murder, maybe; suicide, never."

We continued to descend and then climb again. The valley narrowed and the path grew steeper. We entered a small village and then exited, seeing no one. Row on row of spiky plants without a name, like dwarf soldiers, paraded by. I asked who she was thinking of "offing."

"Oh, any number. George. Leon. Paul. Take your pick."

I asked if she knew about Paul.

"Who doesn't? Swears everyone to secrecy, of course, while he makes a spectacle of himself."

Pru was a few steps ahead of me, picking her way over the ruts and sharp stones of the trail, not slowing down as she talked. "I mean, of course, Leon's a port in your storm and why not? But you can't convince me you're serious about him." She stopped and turned to face me. "You'll be locked into his way of doing things. You'll grow resentful like you did before. Once he realizes that you want more from him, he'll push back with criticisms and complaints."

I said he was trying to change. She turned toward me. "Don't believe it. It's a man we're talking about."

Were she and George okay, ". . . besides the usual arguments, I mean?" I reminded her of the meetings at their place. It was their excitement about the trek that had made it possible for me to even consider it. "And now what?" I asked.

"Oh, I won't let you down. Don't worry about that. Our excitement was genuine, as was our desperate need for company. It would have impossible to go without friends." Most of their travels, she said, had dwindled to surgical conferences: lectures during the day for George, bookstores or galleries for her. Dinner with the same doctors in different cities. "Coming here alone? Can you imagine us together all day, day after day?"

"But why Nepal?" I asked.

"It's as far from home as we could get."

We spied a small farmhouse ahead. In front of it, a large black dog strained at a chain that was fastened to a metal stake. He was already lunging toward us, snarling, baring his yellowed teeth. Pru picked up a large stone and handed it to me.

"If he gets loose, hit him with it."

I felt light-headed as we cautiously approached. I'd never much cared for dogs of any kind. Even those on a leash in Central Park made me uneasy. One of the things I dreaded most about the trek was the thought of encountering a rabid dog. There were many loose in the mountains. It was one of the reasons for always carrying a sturdy walking stick with you. But no one had warned me about fierce guard dogs. The beast, its fur matted and muddy, grew more and more agitated as we approached. It gave a low, ominous growl that turned into a ferocious bark as it lunged toward us, chain rattling with the force of its fury.

"What if I miss?"

"Use your stick and start yelling. Maybe the owner's about."

Pru picked up another stone as we slowly approached the angry mastiff. "He smells our fear," Pru said. "It only makes him more determined to get at us."

"Maybe we should wait," I said.

"For what? There are lots of dogs like this." She moved up the trail toward the beast. "They chain them up during the day and set them loose at night."

There was a low wall on the side of the trail opposite the house. Beyond it, the land fell away precipitously. I followed Pru as we edged ourselves along the path, the angry beast less than a foot away. As it lunged toward us again, Pru gave it a clout with her walking stick.

"Don't!" I cried, fearful its fury would give it the strength to break its bonds. She was about to hit it again, but I pushed her along the trail and we began to run. Our breath came hard, and we stopped as soon as we were sure the dog wasn't following us. "How do you train an animal to be so vicious?" I was panting, bent over with my hands on my knees.

"Men do it."

I looked up at her. Her face seemed as stony as the trail we walked. I straightened up and put my arm around her shoulders. "There's something more bothering you."

She shrugged me off. "Don't get near it."

We didn't. We walked on together, past bullocks threshing stalks of rice, next to bright green fields where red poppies startled the eye, then alongside the dark stubble of old wheat fields lying fallow. There were fig trees in which brown birds perched, fat with fruit. Once, we spotted a mountain hawk gliding high in the cool air. We talked of school days, the weekend escapes from the dreary confines of Vassar to anywhere we could wangle an invitation—a friend's New York apartment, a football weekend in New Haven or Boston. We remembered hotels and country houses where boys tried to seduce us, a few of them getting their way. We recalled outdoor summer concerts. Music and the night all around us. A moon rising to meet our dreams.

"Whatever happened to Herman?" I asked. "The one from Brown who visited you one weekend? I think you went to see him once in Providence."

"Peter, you mean?"

"Tall with glasses?"

"Peter Lawrence. Herman was the nickname I gave him. Short for hermeneutics. A philosophy major, very serious. He's a professor somewhere now. If he isn't, he should be. Nose always in a book, when it wasn't between my legs."

I couldn't believe she'd slept with Herman.

"One didn't exactly sleep with Herman. Under him or on top of him, but never with him, really."

Why hadn't she told me?

"Hardly worth mentioning."

It had been a brief failed experiment in trying to love an intellectual. "You were always better with that kind," she said. I told her she hadn't exactly married a dummy.

Pru agreed George was smart. Knew lots of things and wielded them like a club. "So different from the Hermans of this world who haven't a clue."

"You sound almost remorseful," I said.

She admitted to thinking of Herman sometimes, wondering if he could have grown full-blooded if she'd been more patient and sympathetic. I laughed and told her those qualities were not her strong suit.

"They are two of the seven deadly womanly virtues," Pru retorted.

Before she could enumerate the other five, we'd arrived at a field where Pemba and a few of the porters were standing around a fire. He smiled, beckoning us.

"Eat?" he asked, bringing his hand to his mouth. Tea and biscuits had been doled out at dawn; breakfast was always after a few hours of hiking. Pru answered that we'd find a place to sit, and asked for tea. George and Leon were already seated on stones a few feet apart. All scent and sound had been distilled from the air. Untainted by the smell of a single flower or the noise of the simplest tool, we were folded into the sheerest envelope of heaven. Pru chose a spot far from her husband. We sat in silence, gazing at the mountains floating green and brown around us. No one was willing to spoil this paradise with words.

I do not know how long I sat there before I heard Pemba's voice. *"Ciya?"* He held out a cup to me, smiling. "And eat?" He offered me a bowl of oatmeal and a large slice of naan. He set down jars beside me—one, peanut butter; the other, jam. He seemed almost handsome. He could not have been more than twenty-three or -four. Even though his face was scarred, there was warmth in the dark of his eyes and grace in his strong brown body.

"Thank you," I said, touching his hand in gratitude. Not just for the tea, but for the beauty of the morning and the mountains that seemed, at that moment, his gift to us. He smiled back and returned to the campfire for more plates.

We ate in silence. The oatmeal was lumpy and the naan heavy and thick. But I was hungry. When Pemba returned with another plateful of bread, I smeared a second piece with jam and washed it down with copious amounts of tea. By now the others had joined us, spreading themselves out wherever they could find a stone to sit on. Pemba tended to them all, moving from one to another, filling cups, bringing plates.

"Not bad, this life," Leon said, moving from his stone to lie in the tough grass. He pulled the brim of his white sailor's cap over his eyes. I agreed, saying he and George would never find the time back home to walk together. George looked at his watch and said he'd be through a nose job, face-lift and tummy tuck by now.

"My husband is a great believer in messing with Mother Nature," Pru said, smearing peanut butter on a large piece of naan. I tried to head off trouble by saying we all messed with her somehow, not really knowing what I meant.

Leon spoke up from under his hat. "Yeah, that's what most painting's about, putting a nose job on nature, making it look the way we wish it were."

Whatever Pru had contained in her talk with me was coming loose: "There's no fun in just fucking women, it's fucking with them that counts. Isn't that right, George?"

He stared at her. "I just do what they ask me to," he said without emotion.

"He's never one to turn down a lady's request," she said, turning toward me. "Give her what she wants where she wants it."

It was a sure sign George had begun another affair. It was a chronic state with him and everyone knew it. When Pru first discovered his goings-on years ago, she hit the roof, called the woman up, terrified her, then threatened to divorce George. She stayed with me for a week and a half, going home before the children awoke, leaving after they went to bed. That way of dealing couldn't last. It became clear that George wasn't going to let her go easily. He was damned if he was going to pay alimony, child support and give away 30 percent of his future earnings to a woman who hadn't worked a day in her life. He hired a legal attack dog who claimed Pru's staying with me constituted desertion, urging George to sue for custody of the boys. George might not have won in court, but he looked ready for an ugly and expensive battle. I argued against her returning too soon and encouraged her to wait until they could find a therapist, but Pru was determined.

"I don't want to drag the children into this. And I don't favor long-range missiles. If we're going to fight, it has to be hand-to-hand combat. Besides, I'm not interested in finding another man."

While waiting for the doorman to fetch her a taxi home, she'd hugged me with one arm while holding her suitcase with the other. "Women are a lot easier to live with. You've been wonderful. Maybe we should marry," she said as a cab pulled up.

It was clear Pru had come to Nepal with that affair on her mind. "And they don't have to ask him twice," she said, referring to George's remark about his providing women with what they want. Her mouth was stuffed with naan as she spoke.

Leon sat up and pushed his hat back. "Time to get moving. Hannah, you want to walk with me?"

George stood up too, wondering where Nawang was. I reached for Pru's hand, but she pulled it back. "Don't," she said. "Don't try to make it better."

She grabbed her walking stick and stood up. Digging about in her fanny pack, she refused to look at me. So I said yes to Leon's invitation.

CHAPTER ELEVEN
THE NECKLACE

We walked slowly, slower than I imagine Leon wanted to, but he was kind about it. Breakfast was making noise in my gut and I felt stiff after sitting. I was feeling breathless and needed to stop often. We spent a long time admiring the rustic construction of a vertical corncrib beside a hut. By the edge of a small stream, Leon traced his fingers over the Buddhist prayer chiseled into a mani stone. Pemba had explained that people carved *Oṃ maṇi padme hūṃ* into large boulders on the trail and by river crossings. *Behold the jewel in the lotus.* I took out my guidebook and read how the lotus rises clean and fragrant from a lake's dark bottom. The jewel in its midst represents the teachings of the Buddha, which can allow us to bloom. I read aloud, *"By seeking enlightenment, we rise above what's dark and muddy in our lives."*

Leon was not in a meditative mood and was anxious to move on. We circled around the stone's left side as Pemba said was the custom and started up the trail again. An hour later we paused to gaze at the narrow valley that we had traversed. Leaning on our walking sticks, we took turns sipping a bottle of Gatorade that Leon had carried from the States. "The next to last one," he said.

He began focusing on a small stone hut with a thatched roof built a few yards off the trail. It stood silent, almost lifeless, in the bright sun. A garden wedged by the side of the house had gone to seed. There were no chickens rooting in the dirt, no dog barking. The only sign of life was the small chain of red peppers hanging from a corner of the low roof. Just as we were taking up our walking sticks, a woman, toothless and dirty, appeared in the doorway. It was hard to tell her age because her skin was dark and leathery. Her feet were bare. Her thin body was hidden in a loose black dress. She wore a tight black bandanna that accentuated the hollows of her cheeks and the formless, quivering cave of a mouth. She began cackling and gesturing at us, demanding, it seemed, a response.

"Namaste," Leon kept repeating, holding his hands together in front of him like a church penitent.

She didn't acknowledge his greeting, but continued instead to screech a jumble of vowels and consonants that must have formed a question.

"Gokyo," Leon said, pointing up the trail. Uninterested, she kept up a barrage of noises from which it seemed impossible to walk away. Suddenly the old woman, if she was old, disappeared into the hut.

"Maybe she doesn't like us getting so near her house," I said.

"Maybe she doesn't know how to be friendly."

The woman reemerged and beckoned us with one hand while in the other she held up large orange beads strung on a leather strap. Pemba had caught up with us now, along with Libby and Pru.

"She want you buy them," Pemba said. "She say they from Tibet."

Libby asked if it was true. Pemba shrugged. "She poor woman. Maybe lie because need money. Maybe not."

The woman pushed the necklace toward Leon's face. He backed up a step and asked, "How much?"

Pemba inquired, then said, "One hundred rupees." Leon asked if the beads were worth it? Pemba didn't respond. Libby wondered who he was going to give them to. Without answering, Leon pulled some crumpled bills from his shorts, carefully smoothed them out and counted them. He pushed several toward the woman.

"Tell her it is a deal for forty."

Pemba looked uncomfortable. "She poor."

"Fifty, then." Leon added a bill.

Pemba spoke quickly to the crone, who answered in an avalanche of thunderous and piercing noises that descended like boulders from a mountain, crashing one against the other as they rolled over us.

"She say no," Pemba reported.

Leon wasn't having it. "All that to say no? What else did she say?"

Pemba looked at the mountains. "That beads from Tibet and old."

"Do they look old to you?" Leon asked. Pemba shrugged again and looked at his feet.

"Jesus, Leon, make up your mind. My legs are getting stiff from standing," Libby said.

"Then move!" Leon retorted, his voice rising. "You don't have to stay. I just don't want to taken for a sucker."

"The difference is only a few dollars," I said quietly. Leon replied that it was about principle. Libby and Pru said they were leaving and wished him luck. Pemba was standing beside Libby, looking eager to go.

Leon turned toward the sunken, beaten face of the woman. She pushed the necklace closer to his nose. The beads were rough irregular squares, their bright orange color dulled by a layer of grime. It was hard to tell whether the dark spots on them were dirt or defects in the glaze. Without Pemba's help, Leon tried to make himself understood by raising his voice.

"Too much! I'll give you sixty-five, that's all." She did not answer, but shoved the beads even closer to his face in quick darting movements that seemed like jabs. He backed away but she moved in after him.

"Where in Tibet?" he yelled, trying to create distance between them with a wall of sound and broken grammar. "How you get them? Sixty-five, that's all!"

The woman paid no attention. She brought her face closer to his to better look into his eyes. She held the miserable orange chain in both hands, forming a frame through which they stared at one another. Two teens and an older man appeared from the dark recesses of the hut and eyed us ominously. I wanted to run, but was too frightened to move. The woman grabbed Leon's hand and shoved the beads into it. She tightened her hold, moving even closer, beginning to cackle. I could see her spittle on his face. The man began to walk toward us.

"Here, take this!" Leon cried, reaching into his pocket and thrusting a wad of bills at her without counting them. She snatched them, letting go of his hand, in which the beads lay like small leeches. "Let's get out of here," he said.

He took my arm and then turned again, this time toward the man. He bowed nervously and then pulled me up the trail with him. He turned several times to make sure we weren't followed. At a safe distance, he examined his purchase.

"What do you think?" he asked as he rubbed the dirt from them. I lied and said they were pretty. Pru had backtracked to examine the beads.

"Who on earth would wear these?"

Leon grabbed them back. "They're from Tibet. I'm going to show them to Nawang."

After Leon left, I asked Pru, "Why did you want to embarrass him?"

"I don't know. Because he hurt you with the letter you found?"

I told her that was long ago and not anyone's business.

Pru shrugged. "You ready to beat off a few more dogs with me or shall we find other partners till lunch?"

I said I was game. I put my hand on her shoulder. She didn't pull away, but bent to tighten the laces of her boot. Then she put her arm around my waist as we began to walk toward the trail. "I'm sorry for being so unpleasant. It's just more of the same. Charming doctor, smitten patient—a match to tinder."

I asked if it was someone to worry about.

"The fire just starts up and then it goes out. One after another. The *who* doesn't matter anymore to him or to me. I don't have to do anything, really, but wait. I do, however, like pissing on his parade when I can."

I told her she was pissing into the wind. But Pru insisted it got to him. She enjoyed being the grain of sand in his oyster: that irritating reminder that his life wasn't entirely pretty.

"He's stuck with me refusing to become a pearl."

Over the years, I had been growing more forgiving of George's infidelities. It just seemed a part of him that wasn't going to go away. It didn't mean he was bad any more than a drug addict is "bad." They were habits neither could control. And when George was good, he was very good: sweet, concerned, generous. If Pru could have seen his sexual behavior, as I had, as a kind of congenital deformity, a persistent malformation of self-regard, she might have understood that his behavior had nothing to do with whether he loved her or not. That his stunted ego development took the form of a constant need for reassurance that no honest marriage could provide was sad, as was the moral dwarfism that grew from it. I had felt for him in a way a wife could not. Addicts may not be bad people, but the way they continually disappoint is extremely hard to take. It was easier to come to terms with when it was someone else's husband. I hadn't forgiven Frank, never would.

"I know how it's hardened you, Pru."

"That's the difference between us. Your disappointments just seem to make you want to try again."

"While yours build character?" I smiled to cover a surge of anger. "Pru, you were born tough."

She asked me if that was why George had other women. I told her we'd been over that a million times, that whatever was happening was never because of her. It would have happened with anyone he married.

"Sometimes you have to take the good with the bad." I reminded her of how much he'd been concerned about Steven, their housekeeper's autistic son, and how he'd paid for the special school he attended. And he'd been so available when Pru's father died.

"And he gave you two good boys. They have his looks and drive and their own way of being kind." I recalled what a comfort George had been when Frank left. "You both were. It's just that in this one particular area, he's a compulsive shit."

"The old sex addict bit. Give it a rest, Hannah." Pru jabbed at the ground with her walking stick.

"Maybe it's true," I said.

"What if it is? Would you settle for it? You know, we still make love sometimes. Do the same things we always did and maybe a few new things he's learned from his outings. But it's all meaningless."

"Why do you do it, then?"

Pru looked straight ahead. "God knows. Everyone needs it sometimes. The next day I'll go out and spend George's money as though he'd left it on the dresser in a brothel."

Maybe she'd have the courage to leave one day, Pru said. But she wasn't interested in getting involved with another man, ever. They weren't worth the trouble. She wasn't willing to take "the good with the bad" like I was trying to do with Leon.

"What are you hoping for, then?" I asked.

"For one of us to just go away forever." She pointed to a nearby tree. "Look there."

A yellow-throated marten had settled on the branch of an alder. It was a male, preening his bright feathers and cocking his head one way and then the other for a better view of his world. On the ground around him a few daisies bloomed. With binoculars I could see the gray-brown heads of lavender asters that had once flowered. Somewhere a woodpecker etched tattoos on the trunk of a helpless tree. We walked in silence for a while. What more was there to say? Maybe there was no "right person." I knew it would never work as I wanted it to with Leon, There would be some good times, but also lots of fighting, and then a truce interrupted by sniper fire. Maybe that's all any of us could hope for either at home or abroad. Uncertainty, again and again. No matter how far I walked, I couldn't get away from the fact that things can turn on a dime—a conversation end in argument, a smile become a scream. A bullet might pierce a soldier's heart, a woman's love be dashed by the sudden slamming of a door. Life could be ended by a visit to the doctor.

It was getting hot now and the trail grew steeper. My breath came in short, hard gasps and my heart began a rapid banging in my chest. The sun that had warmed us in the early morning was now a source of real discomfort. It beat down without surcease. I looked for shade along the trail, but the shrubs and small trees offered scant protection. I reached for my water bottle, stopped, and took a swig. Instead of helping, the liquid, with its unpleasant taste of Lugol's, made me nauseated. There was a cramp in my left calf and disturbing rumblings in my stomach. I sat down on the side of the trail.

"I need to rest, Pru."

She said there was no need to push and sat down beside me. But after a few minutes she began a restless poking at the side of the trail with her stick.

"They say there are snakes in these grasses," she remarked.

I asked if she was trying to scare me into moving. She denied it, saying the snakes were harmless. "Most of them, anyway."

I smiled, feeling too tired to care. Pru stood up and asked me if I would be all right if she moved on. She just wasn't up to talking to anyone else. I told her the others weren't far behind and to get going. I'd wait till they came. She bent down and gave me a quick kiss on the top of my head.

"You're a peach," she said.

CHAPTER TWELVE
BEGINNING OF A BAD DREAM

Pru strode off and I lay back, pulling the brim of my straw hat over my eyes. I was perspiring and my breath came in short hard bursts. The earth was gaining speed beneath me. I gripped the grass, afraid I could be peeled off it. Pru's bitterness had unnerved me, and my nausea, along with a headache, was beginning to frighten me. I closed my eyes, wishing myself back home, safe behind curtained windows where the intricately patterned living room rug was all I knew of the Far East.

I must have fallen asleep: a building was burning. A child screamed. A woman leaned from the ninth-floor window. Firemen hauled beer and marshmallows toward the fire. I yelled at them to do something. They looked at me, puzzled.

I woke in a panic, looking for the fire, but saw only mountains. I felt like an old woman who one day no longer knows what's happening. The table she sat at for years is unfamiliar; her bed unrecognizable. I stared at my boots, trying to make out where I was. I struggled to sit up. Somewhere a child was screaming, a house was on fire. I felt dizzy and afraid of trying to stand. When I saw George and Pemba coming up the trail, pieces fell into place—the trek, the journey to Gokyo. I waved at them, glad for familiar faces.

"What are you doing here, all by your lonesome?" George peered down at me. I told him Pru had gone ahead and I was resting and feeling a little sick. He was kneeling now. "What kind of sick?" One hand was on my forehead, the other on my wrist, searching for my pulse.

"Just a little queasiness."

He checked my lower legs for any sign of swelling. "No cough? Nothing bite you?" I shook my head. He stood up, saying I seemed warm. I said it was the sun.

"Maybe." He had that noncommittal tone that doctors use when they're thinking the worst. He dug into his fanny pack and gave me a salt pill and told me he'd take my temperature at lunch. I swallowed the large white tablet without telling him how hard it was to keep it down. George extended his hand and pulled me gently to my feet.

"Okay?"

I nodded. "One foot in front of the other. We'll go slow."

Pemba pointed to my fanny pack. "I take it." Embarrassed, I said I could manage. He planted himself in front of me and pointed again. His body was lean and firm, without excess of any kind except for the ruts on his face and hair that fell to his shoulders. He was muscular in that wiry way, yet his hair and his height, only about five-seven, gave him a slightly feminine air. His look told me I had no choice. In handing him the pack, I felt relieved, yet oddly hesitant. I said I might need something.

"Then, I give you."

I shrugged, saying it meant being stuck with me for a while. Pemba smiled. George was studying my face.

"Better get started. It's a long way to lunch and even longer to camp."

We walked slowly to the crest of the mountain—three hours steady uphill—and started down the other side, picking our way along the steep, stony path. The descent was harder than climbing. Each step jarred my knees and upset stomach. The nausea grew worse. I began to have an occasional abdominal cramp that momentarily stopped me in my tracks. All George's talents as a doctor were now focused on me. He started on a complete medical history, from croup when I was two to my last attempt at losing weight. He didn't think diet pills a good idea. His determination to take a complete "review of systems" wasn't adding to my comfort.

Pemba noted my distress. "You okay?"

"Good enough," I answered, though I wasn't at all sure. Whatever I had, George joked, it wasn't sahib's knee. I asked what that was, trying to keep up my end of the conversation. Talking about sahib's knee might, at least, divert his attention from my need to stop again. He told me more than I wanted to know about inflammation of joints caused by the stress of hiking. He spoke as if he were instructing residents on rounds. To be polite, I asked what could be done for it.

"Elevation of the leg, rest, aspirin."

I suggested amputation might be quicker. George looked irritated. Pemba was a few steps behind us. The mention of amputation loosened his tongue.

"They cut off my uncle's foot. He get frostbite on Sagarmatha. No work anymore."

He began telling us what had happened. His English, at first hard to follow, became easier to decipher after a while. From what I could understand, the winds had suddenly grown worse while his uncle was climbing Everest with an American tourist. He had repeatedly asked his client to turn back, but the American refused, saying he had paid a lot for the trip. Other Sherpa guides were following their progress by walkie-talkie from base camp. They urged Pemba's uncle to turn back, even if it meant leaving his stubborn customer. But Pemba's uncle stayed at his job. The pair continued the slow, exhausting ascent, eventually reaching the summit by midafternoon. They were way behind schedule, with an arduous descent now ahead of them. The weather grew worse on the way down. Icy wind blew snow up all around them as darkness fell. Their oxygen masks and goggles were completely frozen. Blind, exhausted, increasingly uncertain of their location, they stopped trying to reach base camp and dug in for the night. Pemba's uncle was lucky to be found still alive the next morning.

"American dead," Pemba concluded. I was speechless, but George took it in stride.

"Everest can be a real bitch at times," George said.

I turned to face Pemba, shaking my head in disbelief at his story. He gave a sad smile, saying, "When Sagarmatha angry, bad thing happen."

George shifted his weight and gazed up the trail. He had a look of impatience that doctors have when patients are taking too much of their time.

"Just keep going and stick with her, Pemba," he instructed. He went off, digging his stick into the hard ground as he walked.

"What makes the mountain angry?" I asked.

"Wanting only, no giving," Pemba answered. He told me how on another expedition in 1963, nine hundred porters had hauled more than half a ton of gear from Kathmandu to Everest for fifteen rupees a day.

"Climbers in a hurry. Porters have no time stop and pray to goddess for good weather." The foreigners had come with too much pride and Sagarmatha had taught them a lesson. One climber died on the expedition. Guides had been badly injured.

"Everyone suffer," he said sadly.

"Wanting causes it?"

He nodded. "Cause much pain."

Wanting what? Needless conquest? Medals for taking stupid chances? For taking Hill 881 in Vietnam? Youth dying on hills that had no names, only numbers. Those soldiers still intact, scared shitless, ready to kill anyone who frightened them by their language or their looks. And back home, truth was dying too, not in a hail of bullets or rocket fire, but in the daily briefings of generals who could not admit failure. After a while, it didn't matter to me which side the dead were on. It only mattered that people were dying. And those lucky enough to survive would never be the same.

I asked what his uncle did now.

"Feed chickens," he replied. His aunt worked as a porter. "Twenty rupees for ten hours going up and down mountain carrying rich people things. Have only rice and lentils. Have to pay for food and place to sleep. Eat maybe once a day."

What was there to say? Could I offer sympathy for people who, at this very moment, we were exploiting? I had no words and Pemba offered none in return. Finally, I said, "Your English isn't bad. Did you learn it in school?"

He shook his head. His mother had worked for a wealthy English couple in Kathmandu before she married. She learned English from them and taught him. I asked if she worked now.

"She dead. Now study English on my own. Learn words from guidebook."

Silence again. Ten minutes of it, while the sun beat down on us and we picked our way down the mountain.

"She get tired, legs swell. Then need sit up to sleep. English couple take her to Bir Hospital. Ask her how to contact me and father. We have no phone. Send messenger to us. The doctor at Bir look at her, tell her to wait. A minister's mother in accident coming to hospital. Staff told to take care of important woman. My mother sit long time. We walk from village two days. When we come, she dead already."

"How terrible!"

"Die waiting" was all he said.

A parade of villagers rose from the valley floor from behind us: men herding goats, others prodding bulky yaks into a slow trot, women with live chickens in baskets, children and dogs running along beside. They were singing and laughing, greeting us as they passed with smiles that showed the gold in their teeth.

"Big holiday come. Mani Rimdu. They go to Namche."

I'd been told that Nepal had more holidays than any other country, but never knew much about of any of them.

"This about how Buddha defeat buffalo-head god who rule here." He took an English guidebook from his backpack and began to read the English haltingly.

For nineteen days demons are conquered by dance and song and the pious are rewarded. Monks as well as the People pray for the welfare of the world.

I had to explain what *pious* and *populace* meant. He, in turn, told me the date of the holiday is based on the phases of the moon and that the head lama of the Tangboche monastery announces the dates each year.

"Monks dance, tell story of life of Buddha. They bless many red pills and give them to people."

I asked what the pills were for. He smiled and said they came from the Buddha. "Make people kind and live long life."

He searched the book for more information. I wanted to take the book from him and read it myself, but I worried about offending him. So I listened while he haltingly read how kindness emanates from the center of a great colored sand mandala that is built for the celebration over many days.

What I was experiencing at the moment wasn't good. I felt weak and my head hurt. The nausea remained and I had begun to cramp again. "God knows what's happening to me," I muttered.

"You talking to self."

"Am I?" I looked at Pemba's rutted face, the scarred flesh, a map of poverty and childhood illness. Only his dark eyes were beautiful, like sudden pools of shade in a dry desert landscape. We rested against the gatepost of a small farmhouse.

"How much farther before we stop?"

"Just behind village. Maybe one hour."

"I can manage that."

But, in fact, I wasn't sure. To distract myself I asked Pemba about his father. He shifted his gaze to the ground.

"He go away after mother die."

And did Pemba have siblings?

"Sister live in Delhi now."

People always escaping, I thought, going elsewhere. Leon into his studio. Frank into a bookstore. Me, here. For the Nepalese, into India, rarely China.

"We're left alone," I said. And for the first time I really looked at Pemba as I might any man whose sorrows I could feel but never fully comprehend.

I thought of my father at his wife's funeral, separated from me by his own particular grief. He was bent over, head in his hands. I sat close with my arm around him. He smelled of the aftershave my mother had given him more than a year before. I'd known even then it wasn't the kind he liked. It remained unused until the funeral. In a dark suit, black shoes shined to a buff, hair newly cut for the occasion, he was someone unfamiliar. No longer my father, but a young man who had been a young woman's husband and sometimes friend, now burying with her all the secrets of their frustrated, ambivalent love. Secrets he would never share with me.

"We need walk," Pemba said gently. "Don't be afraid," he murmured. "I help you."

We made our way slowly down the mountain, Pemba taking me by the arm when the trail became particularly rough or my energy flagged. He told me stories to keep my spirits up: how the holiday celebrated the season of planting. He showed me boxes of barley seed that people place by their front door at start of festivities. The size of the shoots at the festival's end predicts how good the harvest will be in the coming year. We stopped in a small town, where he left me in the shade of a pipal tree.

"We have tins, but get fresh food when can."

I heard him going around the village calling out for food to buy. I didn't know what he was asking for, but he came back with half a dozen eggs, four limes, and small package of red and green lentils. "It for soup. Good for you." He was tucking the package in his backpack. A half hour later, we got to a small field where the others had stopped for lunch. I lay down right away. Pemba went to talk with Noonie, the cook. George bent over me.

"Glad to see you made it. How're you doing?" he asked as Leon peered over his shoulder. I lied about feeling a little better.

"That's good news," Leon chimed in between gulps of tea. "Sorry I was so far ahead."

George interrupted him to ask me about cramps or diarrhea.

"Just cramps now and then."

He slipped a thermometer into my mouth, told me to lie there and he'd be back in a few minutes. "Let her rest," he told Leon.

I was glad to be left alone. The heat of the sun spread like a blanket over me, helping reduce the chill I'd begun to feel. Just as I'd drifted off, I felt George removing the thermometer from my mouth.

"Well?" I said without moving or opening my eyes. His voice came like a god's from beyond the mountains.

"About a hundred."

I asked if that was bad.

"The start of something, maybe."

Whatever it was, my insides told me it had already started. He wondered if I'd eaten anything I wasn't suppose to. Did he mean last night's duck à l'orange? I asked.

"Don't be a wiseass. I'm just doing my job. Take these for nausea."

He shooed Leon away, saying I needed rest. "I'll get someone to bring you tea to help wash them down."

He pressed two blue Compazines into my open palm. When I awoke a little later, the pills were where George had left them. Pru was holding a cup of tea. A short distance away, I saw Nawang and George in what seemed to be a conversation of few words and many gestures. I hoped it wasn't about me. Pru was following my gaze.

"Beware, you've got the experts conferring."

I told her they needn't bother, that I was going to be all right.

"Of course you will. But don't spoil George's fun by feeling better too soon. He loves emergencies."

Nawang and George were looking directly at me now. I waved, gave George a thumbs-up and swallowed the pills. Pemba came and crouched beside me. In his hand, he held a bowl of thin vegetable stew.

"Noonie make it. For stomach." He smiled and held the spoon out to me. I couldn't refuse, even if it threatened to send my insides to my throat. While Pemba watched, I spooned it down in small doses. "Always work," he said.

I don't know whether it was the soup or the blue pills, but by the time George came around with Nawang, I was feeling somewhat better.

"I'm okay," I said, getting to my feet. They looked at me skeptically.

"It's four more hours of hiking until dinner," George warned. I told him I had no choice. I couldn't just stay where I was. He had the sympathetic look of a doctor before he says you need surgery.

"You could always head back," George said quietly. I told him he was crazy and I wasn't going back. He suggested Pru might accompany me.

"Pru? No, George," I said. "That's not going to happen."

He looked at me and grunted. "Have it your way."

Nawang interposed, "Pemba watch her. Tonight see."

By this time, the group had gathered around me and was listening.

"I'm not letting you out of my sight this afternoon, sweetheart," Libby said. "We're going to be like Siamese twins. You stop, I stop. You go, I go." Libby grabbed me around the waist. Leon asked if that left any room for him.

"Sure. We can be triplets. You take one side, I'll take the other." The group was all smiles now. Even George managed a thin grin, emptying some more blue pills into Libby's hand.

"Give her this in three hours if the nausea returns." He was all business. "Send Pemba up the trail to tell me if she feels worse. Nawang and I are going ahead to make sure the camp's set up before she gets there."

"Don't worry. We'll carry her if we have to, won't we?" Libby looked around as everyone nodded.

"It makes walking all the more appealing," I said. I picked up my stick and waited for someone to take my arm. The afternoon proved more bearable than the morning, at least the first part of it. All of us walking together. Libby was full of funny stories about her life before Howard. The singles weekends at resorts. The telephone calls from nerds. She'd pretend they had the wrong number: "No have Libby here. Have moo goo gai pan. You want order?"

Leon said it sounded like marriage was the solution to a pretty screwed-up life.

"It wasn't screwed up, it was different, that's all," Libby retorted.

Paul asked if married life was as interesting. "After a while don't you know what Howard's going to say before he says it?"

Howard, behind us, tugged at Libby's backpack and asked if he was really so predictable.

"I'm afraid so, dear. But that's all right." She stopped to take his hand. "You're the sturdy perennial in my garden." She gave him a wink and a kiss.

Leon declared he was a city boy and didn't know from gardens.

Libby nodded. "It's time to learn about them, Leon. The right woman. A row of beans."

I reminded him of the time we tried to grow tomatoes on our fire escape. Hard green things that never ripened. I came home one day and they were suddenly red and looked ready to eat. I went to pick one and found they'd been painted.

"Henry Eskin photographed them, remember? Sold them for a lot of money," Leon said, and suggested that we try growing them again with better fertilizer and more sun. He put his arm around me. It felt like a vise. I loosened his grip by turning toward Pemba.

"Do you think about marrying?" I asked.

"Maybe uncle arrange. Then go to astrologer to see if good match."

We were crossing a narrow river. The water was shallow at this point but the current swift, the water icy. We searched for the river's bottom with our walking sticks as we picked our way from stone to stone. Pemba, going ahead, turned and reached for Libby's hand to guide her. But she didn't move from the bank, looking at him with astonishment.

"Marry someone you don't know?" she asked.

Pemba replied his friend had met his bride a few times at her parents' house before the ceremony. He added that the couple would need to be pleasing to one another and to their families. Marriage didn't seem something he wanted to talk about. When we reached the other side, Pemba suddenly pointed.

"Look there!" he whispered. "Under tree. Snowcock. We very lucky. They usually higher up mountain and hard to see."

He turned his back to me so I could dig my binoculars out of the pack he was carrying for me. As I did so, he moved his head from side to side as if to work out a kink. I was tempted to massage the taut muscles around his vertebrae, to dab the perspiration from his shining skin.

Once I had my field glasses, he directed my gaze by standing close behind me and pointing over my shoulder. Under the lowest branch of a juniper sat a large pheasant-like bird. Its head was white with dark streaks that ran down its neck. It had a bluish-gray collar and what seemed like stippled black-and-orange feathers on its wing. I asked Pemba if he thought it nested nearby. Before he could answer, Libby interrupted.

"How do you know you will fall in love with her?"

I had handed my binoculars to Pemba, who was looking through them. He passed them on to Libby, saying, "Look at bird! She go soon."

"Is it that big thing?"

"Yes." Pemba was standing just behind Libby now. He described the sharp, curved bill that was good for digging roots. Libby studied the bird with a worried expression.

"Where's its mate?"

Pemba said it might be near or perhaps had been caught by an eagle. Libby had lost interest in the bird and was handing the glasses back to Pemba.

"Don't you want to get know her first? Make sure you love her? You two could be very different."

"Love not something need to marry. Grow with man and woman when live together, have children, when eat from same plate."

I knew that eating from the same plate was part of the Nepalese marriage ceremony, like sharing the wedding cake at ours. But I remembered from my Asia Society visit just how complicated getting married was. There was still a caste system in Nepal. Pemba would have to find someone of the laboring class like himself. Negotiations between the two families would take place through an appointed mediator. If the families reached an agreement, Pemba and his relatives would bring gifts of food, nuts, sweets and fruit to his bride's family: luxuries they'd be hard-pressed to afford. In addition, the bride's mother would have to be compensated for the time she spent suckling her daughter.

Pemba elaborated on what I already knew as we passed the

binoculars back and forth. While the bride-to-be accepted gifts at her home, a procession of friends and relatives accompanied by a band would start from Pemba's house toward hers. He would not be part of the parade, but his relatives would celebrate with the bride and her family. When the bride finally came to Pemba's house the next morning, Pemba's aunt would wash the girl's feet in holy water. Aunty would present the bride with a key to the house in which she was to live with Pemba and his family.

"Wife have to take orders from aunt, if we stay in village. Better to go to Kathmandu," he laughed, "or stay and chew nuts." He explained that eating the right nuts would make you high enough to not mind aunty and kill your tapeworms as well.

I took one last look at the bird and the field into which it had flown. Hard brown poppy pods stood atop sturdy stalks like musical notes on a green page. Pemba picked one and put it to my ear. The dull rattle of seeds. "When shake these, sends prayer to heaven."

He ran his finger over the rough roof of the pod and showed us its tiny pores. He and I studied the surface, our heads almost touching. "This how seeds get free," he said, turning the pod upside down and shaking it hard. Tiny black specks filled the air and floated downward. "If lucky, seeds find home and marry ground."

While I still blow about, I thought. Relationships arranged, ceremonies that sealed them, the certainty of home and family. It seemed appealing.

"I've never liked big ceremonies," Libby said suddenly. "Howard had one for his first wedding. We just went to a justice of the peace."

Leon said marriage was a crapshoot under any conditions. Pemba wanted to know what a crapshoot was as the bird suddenly took flight.

We must have gone another half mile with Leon explaining the game before Pemba understood it enough to say, "I see, marriage like game of luck."

"You got it, kid." Leon patted Pemba on the back.

Pemba shrugged. "Life crapshoot too."

We walked for a while in silence. Each of us, I suppose, thinking about those times when we were young and thought we knew what was best for us.

"Museum school in Chicago?" my father asked. "Isn't there a decent place in New York to study? I'd like you nearer." His hand was cool from the gin and tonic he had set down to touch the back of my neck. "That way I could keep an eye on you." He looked at me over his glasses. "Although I needn't worry. Girls who go to museum school don't go out much."

It was nonsense, of course, and irritating. He said it of any woman with ambition. As if wanting something for yourself prevented you from being loved by someone else. But he had been right about me so far. And about Chicago too. The school turned out to be a disappointment. The professor I had planned to work with got sick. I didn't get along with his replacement. It wasn't clear if another MFA program would accept me. The process of applying and interviewing began once more, before finally landing me at NYU.

And here I was again, uncertain of my future. I didn't think I wanted Leon, and what I thought I could have had with Frank wasn't in the cards. Is it a matter of chance how things work out, or is it choice?

CHAPTER THIRTEEN
THE CROSSING

The sun beat down hard as we walked. The heat made me dizzy. I took off my straw hat to fan myself and noticed it was discolored by sweat. "I'm not feeling well," I told Pemba. "It's a crapshoot whether I can make it to Gokyo."

"No one control Nature, but you have own will also." He took my arm. "Ready to walk?"

It was about an hour later that I first saw the plume, jutting up from behind a nearer mountain, the white triangle calmly piercing a bright blue sky. "Sagarmatha?" I whispered to him. He nodded.

"We must think good thoughts, so she be kind to climbers."

Bobby came up behind us. "That's it, isn't it?" He was almost yelling with excitement. "Wow, look at all that snow blowing off it."

Pemba said the winds blew around the mountain night and day.

Leon asked Pemba if Sagarmatha had a will. If those climbers died in an avalanche, was that her will? The Holocaust? Had that been God's will too? His words flew out like pebbles from a speeding car. They stung, and the group moved away from him.

"We not always know." Pemba looked confused. "But what is Holocaust?"

We groaned. Libby shook her head. "You don't want to know. Not here, you don't."

But Leon put his arm on Pemba's shoulder, saying he would explain, and then Pemba could tell him if it was God's will. Pemba spent the rest of the afternoon with Leon, learning in excruciating detail the horrors of the Holocaust. He checked back with me once or twice, but seeing I was in good hands, hurried up the trail to rejoin a war that had been fought before he was born. The others took their turn hiking with me. Like nurses on duty, they patiently cheered me up the trail. Libby held my shoulders when I vomited the first time.

"It must have been the lunch. Greasy canned fish and heavy naan," she said. "It's a wonder we all aren't sick." I reminded her I'd had only tea and Pemba's lentil stew.

"I guess that didn't help like it was supposed to." She was wiping my forehead with a tissue. Her kindly face floated in front of me. "Now, close your eyes."

I remained standing while she patted the perspiration from around my eyes and then from my upper lip and chin. How good it felt to be nursed by a friend. I stood very still as Libby continued to gently run a wet tissue around my forehead and neck. For once, she was silent, allowing me to take in her touch, a mother's touch from a childless woman.

When I wasn't sweating, I was cold and asked for a sweater, even though the sun was blazing. I felt dizzy, but I was determined to go on. Bobby, looking worried, volunteered to stay close. I thanked him and asked how much farther it was to camp.

"I'll go find out." He scampered away, relieved to have an errand.

The next hour seemed like four. Friends came and went like figures in a dream. They made sure someone was always with me. I stopped frequently to catch my breath. All I wanted was for the sun to stop beating and for my intestines to stop twisting. And for my friends to stop talking. Talking because there was nothing else they could do for me and because sickness and silence are a frightening combination.

How was I doing? they asked. Was I still queasy? A hand on my forehead. Another taking my pulse. A bottle of water pushed toward me by Pru while Howard warned against drinking too much. While they argued about how much liquid I should take, I threw up a second time. Worried, they tried to distract themselves and me from the thought of serious illness. The camp, they said, wasn't too far now. They joked and told stories: Pru about getting drunk in college, Paul about Zoe's first day at preschool. I tried to join in, but their attempts to cheer me up reminded me of my mother's nurses and I began suffer from their efforts.

❧ ❧ ❧

The nurses had been all smiles after her surgery, had dragged her like a rag doll up and down the hospital corridor. They filled her silence and covered her pain with their well-worn phrases.

"There you go, dear. Getting the strength back in your legs. You'll be able to race your little girl down the hall in no time." They had held her tight as her knees buckled. "That's right. Regain your balance. We'll try you with a walker this afternoon."

They coaxed and cajoled her, got angry with her and then apologized. But she never did walk again, not really. At first, when she got home, she'd force herself from bed to toilet, sometimes to her vanity to apply rouge before my father came home. Toward the end, the makeup made her look like a clown, irregular red patches on a face as white as the wall.

* * *

Paul walked with me for a while. His expressed concern over my sickness bled into wondering if things were okay back home and whether his patient "Mrs. K" was all right. He thought she was just crazy enough to come to Nepal. "It's unlikely she'll know where on the trail to find you," I said.

I felt suddenly envious of Mrs. K as well as sorry for her. Just a comfortable poolside neurotic, I thought, feeling unhappy because her analyst was away and her drink hadn't arrived. But I had to give Mrs. K credit, and Frank's Ursula too. They'd never find themselves in my situation. Those two gals had something I didn't—staying power, the ability to become some man's prolonged preoccupation. When later I confided my feelings of inadequacy to Libby, she seemed baffled.

"Do you think it's because you slept with them too soon? I kept Howard waiting until he'd proposed." I told her it was not about when you sleep with a man.

"How do you know? The only thing that preoccupies most men is dicky dunkin'."

Her tone suggested she was heading toward another verbal meltdown, her anxiety about me fueling it. I sent her off to ask Howard if what she said was true.

"I'll ask. But men don't tell the truth unless they have to."

My head was aching and I couldn't get the acid taste of my insides out of my mouth. I heard Howard's answer coming from up the trail, surprised and defensive.

"That's not why I married you."

Bobby had not returned, but Pemba came to say we were almost there—just to the bottom of the hill and then across the river—another twenty minutes. But comfort, like the horizon, seemed a place I could never get to. A blister on my right foot made me wince. My hands were cold even in gloves. There were only two sounds I was aware of: my labored breathing and the low incessant rumble of the Dudh Khosi ahead. Pemba walked with me, his face full of worry—surprised, I suppose, at how much worse I felt. But he seemed concerned about something else as well.

"You Jewish too? Like Leon? Family die in Holocaust?" When I told him I wasn't and they didn't, he smiled and looked relieved.

"Body sickness. It be fixed. But for some . . ." He shook his head sadly.

Blotches of color growing larger. Dashes of yellow and blue on a green canvas. Tents. The porters, relieved of their day's burden, gathering like withering leaves around an autmn tree. Noonie, our cook, was holding a chicken by its legs. It flapped weakly, giving out short startled calls. Only twenty yards separated me now from camp. Between it and me, the river had narrowed, digging itself deep into the tough flesh of the mountainside. A swift, icy current tumbled over jagged stones, trying to pry them loose. Two cedar logs loosely lashed together by vines and fraying rope spanned the river's steep banks.

"Nothing to hold on to?" I asked.

Pemba shook his head, saying he would cross first and guide me from the far bank.

"Look to me," he called. "Just me."

I began to cross slowly. My whole being fastening itself completely into each step so that it seemed impossible for me to loosen my foot and take another. I locked my eyes onto his, his gaze a rope slowly drawing me in. Suddenly the porters began to hoot and laugh. I looked away and saw a headless chicken scuttling in the grass, blood spurting from its neck. I let out a long, low moan before tilting first to one side of the bridge, then the other. Involuntarily I began to flap my arms, trying not to fall. My arm met the broad brim of my straw hat and pushed it forward on my face, blocking my vision. My fingers grabbed at the air as a blind woman might.

Pemba's voice: "Come on, missy. You make it. Fix hat. Look at me."

I heard him but couldn't move. Panic surged in me like the river below, threatening to sweep me away. I bent my knees and tried to sit on the logs.

"Listen, missy. No sit down. Make hat straight." Pemba's words were raising a wall around me, but I was afraid to lean against them.

"I'm so—"

"No talk!" he called impatiently. "Just do what I say. *Hat!*"

His tone wounded me. I wanted to tell him I was going to die now on the bridge or, later, off it. Did it matter when? I hated his youthful arrogance, with his *missy* reserved for foreigners. As if he knew what was best for me and could cure me of my terror.

"Hat!" he shouted again. I did as he told me and met his eyes. "Come!" he commanded, beckoning me slowly.

When I got closer, he extended his walking stick and, with a sudden yank, pulled me to the bank and into his steadying arms. Hoots and clapping rose around me. Even the porters joined in. Bobby put his arm around me. "That a way, Hannah. You aced the bridge."

"Not exactly," I replied, bending over to catch my breath.

"Yes, exactly," said Libby. "Look, you're here."

I was eager to lie down, to get away from embarrassing compliments and from Pemba's hand on my arm. He pointed to my tent. "Thanks. I think I can make it now," I said.

George had already opened my duffel and inflated my air mattress. I crawled into the tent, shoving the mattress under me. Every part of me was in pain. The constant dull ache of overused muscle was punctuated by attacks of sudden, sharp, staccato-like stomach pains. The streaks and patches of dried mud on the tent walls were like the map of my body, a suddenly unfamiliar territory that I studied with uncertainty. Then Bobby's voice from the next tent.

"I thought Hannah was going to take a dive, didn't you?"

Silence.

"Pemba talked her off of it, though."

No response.

Undaunted, Bobby asked if his stepfather had seen "that old guy" on the trail wearing bells and a big knife on his belt. "His hat had earflaps. Crazy! Like Genghis Khan or somebody."

Paul finally answered: no, he hadn't seen him. Bobby seemed doubtful, insisting that Paul must have seen him, that George had and so had Libby.

"Bobby. I just don't remember right now. I'm really tired and need to lie down. Maybe I did see him, I don't know."

"How can you not remember what you saw?" Bobby asked.

Bobby with his stepfather made me think about my own father, about my body and about seeing.

White tub. Water rising. Steam drawing a gray curtain over the window and mirror. Naked, I hang a red towel on the metal hook behind the door, then sit waiting for the tub to fill. The rim feels cold on my ass. Father opens the door and looks in. "Sorry," he says, but doesn't close the door right away. For just a second, he stands there looking. It seems like a lifetime. I don't move, just listen to the bathwater running. It gets louder and louder, pressing against my eardrums. I feel dizzy. "I just wanted to make sure you were all right," he says, shutting the door. In the tub, I let my face sink below the warm water and wonder what it's like to drown.

I open my eyes to the blue surface of the tent. Mountain ranges and vast deserts stare back at me from the mud stains on its surface. They resembled the craters of the moon. Grimaldi, Goclenius, Landau, Larmor. The names remembered from planetarium shows I saw when I was a child. The auditorium dark. Father next to me. The amazing images from the moon fought with my urge to be outside, in the daylight where people move about and talk. Now it was Libby's voice.

"Just a nip. It's getting chilly."

Howard saying she should wait till dinner, and Libby asking why. I stayed very still, like I was as a girl hearing my parents argue in another room: Pretending not to listen, pretending to be deaf. But I am not deaf. I am eight years old, sitting at a Steinway upright, and they are arguing again. Then I begin to pick out "Three Blind Mice" with a single finger as loudly as I can. *See how we run?* Pink roses on the wallpaper behind a piano. The living room rug *ice blue,* according to my mother.

"Follow the ice until it turns to sky. Then we will be there." Where will we be? So many days of trekking. Twelve? Fourteen? Each morning, like my mother's face: pale, unflinching, demanding that I face it. "Why are you dying?" I cried. "I want to be with you."

"You are," she said, and looked away.

CHAPTER FOURTEEN
DINNER

Outside, metal stakes were being pounded into the resistant earth for a dining tent. I had no appetite, but had to appear. Otherwise, they'd think I couldn't go on. Then the sound of the dinner bell. I changed into a heavy sweater and ran a tissue over my face, rubbed my neck and hands with another. Brushed my hair without the help of a mirror. It must have taken me longer than I thought. Voices were coming from the tent as I approached.

"She has to go back," George was saying. Leon wanted to know why.

"Where is she anyway?" Libby interjected.

"Here," I said, opening the flap of the tent to the silence that followed. Everyone was seated. The tent was long and narrow, with just enough room for Noonie to squeeze around. A variety of crates, serving as seats, had been placed around two rough wooden planks set end to end. The table legs were stacks of plastic storage containers. Two kerosene lanterns, giving off smoke and an acrid smell, hung over the table. Small gusts of wind played with the thin nylon walls, setting the lamps swinging. The light from them flared and died, brightening then darkening the faces turned toward me. On the table: candles stuck in used tins, a stack of aluminum bowls and mugs, piles of cheap aluminum silverware and a large pot with a ladle.

I sat on a crate between Paul and Libby. She asked how I was. Paul bent to listen. I shrugged, glancing at the faces around me. Serious, troubled looks. Libby nodded and pushed a bowl and spoon in my direction. She ladled out thin liquid. I didn't want it or the *dahl bat* Noonie announced was coming. So I took my time spreading the thin paper napkin over my lap, then blew on the soup, pretending it was still too hot. Everyone was staring. Howard shot a worried smile.

"Take your time, Hannah," he said as he continued passing the soup. I touched the liquid to my mouth and then returned it to my bowl. Leon leaned toward me from across the table.

"You're going to have to turn around," he said gently. "We think you're too sick." He went on: it would only get harder from here.

We were at nine thousand feet with five more to get to Gokyo.

Libby suggested we stop for a day and let me rest. George vetoed the idea. There wouldn't be time to get to Gokyo and back for our flight home. "Besides, I've got surgeries scheduled."

Paul asked whether getting to Gokyo was really that important. "Only a few small stone houses, right?" he said, looking to George. "Used in the summer and empty this time of year."

George's jaw tightened. He stared into his hands, which lay on the table. "Every time I whip Paul's ass at squash, which is most of the time, he starts with this shit. 'It's not winning,' he tells me, 'it's the way you play the game.' "

"That's only after you've started cursing over a missed shot," Paul replied. George's face grew redder.

"Bullshit!" He turned to the group. "And every time I tell him he's right. It's the way you play the game—and I play it better." Pru placed a warning hand on his arm, but he shook it off. He pointed his spoon at Paul. "Look, buster, I didn't bring myself and your sad ass all this way to sit around. If you want to play nursemaid, that's your business."

"George!" Pru cut in sharply. "Hannah's our friend, for God's sake."

George looked at his wife. He reached across the table and took my hand. I didn't stir.

"You are," he said gently. But he insisted that a day of rest wouldn't make a difference, that I was sick and shouldn't fool myself. We were nowhere near help if I got sicker. There were good doctors in Kathmandu who could care of me.

"What about you and Paul? Aren't you doctors enough?" Libby asked.

George shook his head. "Whatever she's got, we don't have enough drugs to treat it."

Howard asked if it could be altitude sickness. George replied that going down was the only cure for that. He looked me straight in the eye.

"It's likely dysentery. Salmonella? Shigella? Giardia? Who

knows what bug or how you got it."

But I needed to be tested and treated. I took my hand away. He said it was because he cared about me. I knew he did and I also knew his heart was set on Gokyo. I didn't blame him, not really.

Noonie set two pots of rice on the table and a large bowl of dung-colored lentils in which I saw pieces of what I supposed had been the chicken.

Leon began helping himself then stopped, holding a spoonful of rice above his plate. "Look, she's not going back right now. It's nighttime." He suggested seeing how I felt in the morning. He talked about how some might stay behind with me and catch up later. He looked to George for a reply.

George just shrugged and stared at his plate, picked up a fork and began to eat. The silence was broken only by the clatter of utensils against metal plates.

"He doesn't beat me all the time, just mostly," Paul said, finally. "His form is for shit, but he's all over the court."

"Have you tried lessons?" Howard asked sympathetically.

George looked up, saying lessons wouldn't help, that Paul just didn't have the killer instinct. It wasn't something you can learn. "Every time he has the chance to put it away, he muffs it."

A pained expression crossed Paul's face. He began rearranging the silverware in front of him. I felt sorry for him, attracted to killers like George and Mrs. K. I wanted to help him.

"But he beats you sometimes," I said.

George reddened and fixed his gaze on me. "One more day, Hannah." He was pointing his fork at me. "I'll give you one. If you aren't better, you go back." He looked around at the group for assent. Everyone nodded but Libby.

"Tomorrow, we pass a monastery Pemba told me about," Libby said. "We'll get you blessed, honey. That could help."

Libby turned to Nawang, who was clearing some of the dishes. "Isn't that right?"

Perhaps the Sherpa didn't understand or was pretending not

to. He didn't answer. George asked if Libby was planning to dawdle her way to Gokyo. His tone was demeaning, the one he uses when surgical residents close too slowly.

"I do win once in a while," Paul said quietly.

I got up from the table, tired of being talked about. "A good night's sleep will help," I said.

CHAPTER FIFTEEN
A CONVERSATION

And it did. In the morning I woke to the steady hum of voices too indistinct to understand. My stomach was still in trouble, but settled a bit after morning tea and Kaopectate. My temperature, according to George, "above normal." He handed me two enteric-coated aspirin. A headache was developing that I said nothing about.

"I'm better," I told Howard, who inquired through the tent wall. I struggled into a shirt and jeans, wiped my face, threw a wool cap on my head, then crawled outside to sit and look into the merciless dawn. Pemba had been waiting to pack up my tent. I wanted to crawl back into it before it disappeared. Leon was already giving my sleeping bag to a porter. I glanced at my watch: seven o'clock and I was already tired.

Leon came over, saying, "We're set." I held out my hand and he pulled me to my feet. He didn't let go as we began to trek.

I don't know how far we went that morning. The group was more silent than usual and sticking together. I was bringing up the rear, moving slowly enough to count all the mouse holes along the trail. Pemba spotted a Bengal fox, but I wasn't quick enough to see it. I did see a lark and a flock of what Pru said were rosefinches. Mostly, I studied the trail at my feet. I stopped only once to relieve myself. What I saw wasn't reassuring— tiny streaks of bright blood and strands of greenish mucus. There was no use telling anyone. The news wasn't going to make the distances any shorter or my progress any speedier. I only hoped the antibiotics that George had started me on that morning would work.

When I had headed for the bushes to relieve myself, Leon waited for me. I insisted he go on. If he'd stayed, he'd have wanted to look at my stool. When I stood, a bout of dizziness caught me. I stumbled back onto the trail, feeling that I'd emptied more than my bowels. It was as though my will had leaked away. I steadied myself, took a drink from my canteen and began to walk, hoping the world would stop turning. I saw Pru speeding downhill toward me.

"Is anything wrong?" she asked. "Leon said you stopped."

"Ladies' room." I saw worry in Pru's face. She touched my forehead, saying I had a fever. I said it was due to exertion and asked her not to make a fuss. If we walked together, I'd be okay. She looked doubtful but I insisted I was feeling better already, now that she was with me. She took my arm.

"We'll just pretend it's Broadway. Remember when we walked all the way from Seventy-Second down to the Village?" It had been for a drink at McSorley's. I reminded Pru that after the whisky sours, she had been ready to walk back uptown. She laughed. "Oh, I just said that. I was glad enough for the bus."

Getting short of breath, I said I wished a bus would come along now. Pru agreed and imagined us viewing the mountains from an open-top double-decker that that came up Fifth Avenue and then cut to Riverside Drive. She regretted those buses having been sold to some South American country. It was part of things changing—and not always for the better. She longed for those days when we could roam freely.

"No children, no men."

I told her she'd forgotten our loneliness. I hesitated for a moment.

"There was blood when I went," I blurted out.

She stopped and stared at me. "Well, then, you'll have to go back to Kathmandu, won't you? As quick as you can." She was sure one of them would go back and stay with me until I was better. I asked her who that would be. She reminded me George would be happy if she went, now that others were along. "I'm the blister on his happy soul—excuse the pun!"

He's probably sorry he invited me," I said, grimacing.

Pru reassured me that George had always wanted me to come, but he just couldn't abide anything or anyone that stood in his way. She was being harsh, I told her. Being determined made him a good surgeon and a decent guide. Pru looked me in the eye. "Do you really want to keep talking about George?" she asked.

Maybe the thought of having to go back made me want to make things better between them before I went. I looked at my friend, at the way she hadn't combed her hair, and wore a sweater with moth holes. It was easier to take back home when I saw her once a week, at most. Now it was every day.

"He's not so bad, you know. You're not very generous about him."

Pru quickened her pace. "You think I shouldn't mind?"

My heart began to race as I tried to keep up with her. I knew what was coming and tried to dodge it. "It happens sometimes with very successful men," I said.

Pru had turned back and was staring at me. "Do you forgive Frank?"

Her plain face, with its chipmunk cheeks and tiny nose, had hardened into rock. Only the small mouth moved. Didn't I know by now how it made her feel, his screwing around and everybody aware of it? Paul probably knew the most, hanging around in locker rooms with him.

"He wants to be like George, that's what his involvement with Mrs. K is all about. Only, he isn't George, is he?" she said.

If only the nausea would go away. I leaned heavily on my walking stick and wiped my forehead with my gloved hand.

"You don't want to end up alone. Take it from me," I said.

Pru asked how I knew what she wanted. But she had told me many times why she stayed. The kids. The money. What work would she do if she left, she asked, while reminding me I had a profession. She'd tell me how raising money for a cancer cure or an end to heart disease was what she did. And she did it well. But she couldn't turn volunteer work into a paying job. George didn't want the consequences of divorce, in any case. Staying married made affairs simpler. Women knew what they were getting.

"Not always," I said, thinking of my mother who, I knew, had hoped for more than she got from my father. Fooling myself into thinking Frank could give me more than he did. I sat down at the side of the trail, saying I couldn't talk anymore. I told her that right now, being in anyone's bed, even George's, seemed better than being alone. Pru sat down beside me, placing her hand on my knee. She said she was sorry, that her complaints about George must seem heartless. But I was her friend and who else did she have to talk to? She smiled and said I could have George if I were really desperate, though he wasn't my type. She might feel better if he chose women like me. She held out her hand and hauled me to my feet.

Pru was in front of me now with a Kleenex, her voice gentler. She told me I'd never really wanted to get caught, just thought I did. She thought my mother's death had frightened me about getting too attached. Or was it my father's manner, his way of being a bit too interested and not interested enough?

"If you do have to go back, who would you like to go with?" she asked.

"You need to stay. Otherwise things between you will unravel more."

She nodded, saying there was always Leon. Or there might be Paul, who wouldn't be averse to going back. Bobby could go on with the group.

I stood still and closed my eyes. The sun warmed my face. "You go on. We can talk later." Pru wouldn't budge until Pemba arrived to help me.

"Okay, now I'm off," she said, picking up her walking stick. "Catch you later."

CHAPTER SIXTEEN
THE MONASTERY

"The monastery is coming up. We can rest and get a blessing too," Libby said. I joked that last rites would be more appropriate. Libby looked worried. "Maybe starting out on Saturday wasn't a good idea," she said.

The compound consisted of a stone temple, a cinder-block dormitory for half a dozen monks and a separate two-room wooden house in which the lama slept and received visitors. He must have been fifty or so, more muscular and robust-looking than I thought appropriate to his vocation. He sat cross-legged on a Hunzinger-type couch upholstered in heavy blue brocade. His scarlet robe seemed right. But the gold-rimmed aviator sunglasses and Accutron with silver expansion band took me by surprise. The walls were covered with thangkas from which a thousand Buddhas smiled at us. A roughly woven rug, red as blood, spilled across the wooden floor. The lama nodded a greeting to each of us as we crowded into his study. He silently accepted our gifts: long white scarves of cheap gauze bought before entering—scarves in which it was suggested we place cash donations. The lama blessed each scarf while he deftly extracted the money. He hung the empty strips back around our necks.

"English?" he inquired through his interpreter, who gave a whispered reply. "Ah, American. Far from home." He smiled and then launched into what appeared to be a set piece about the founding of the monastery, the chores of the monks and the number of visitors each year. He left no room for questions.

It reminded me of a fund-raiser the Albrights had given for Eugene McCarthy in 1968. I had looked forward to meeting Gene, the only candidate I could trust. But the man I met was already dead, drained of any human response by too many talks in too many places. A meaningless smile was lacquered onto his face, like the work of an expert undertaker. After the round of cursory handshakes with people he wouldn't remember, he took an obligatory sip of punch and bit into a cookie. Then after ten minutes of promises that were as stale as last week's bread, he was gone. I voted for him anyway.

Leon, of course, wasn't about to settle for just a blessing. He asked how men might learn to live in peace, earnestly searching the lama's face for an answer.

"This monastery is dedicated to peace. There are five monks living here in peace." The guru was repeating himself. As usual, Leon was looking skeptical, wanting something more.

"Is he saying if we all became like monks, there would be peace?" he asked the interpreter. The aide whispered in the lama's ear. The guru looked perplexed and glanced at his Accutron.

"Applications to stay are carefully considered. The last person to stay any length of time was Mr. Pearson in 1951, the year Nepal was opened to foreigners. He was here three months and four days."

I told Leon it was no use, but he ignored me and moved closer to the lama.

"I mean, what I want to know is, do you think the Buddha is more of the way than Jesus or Muhammad or Adonai?"

The lama glanced at his watch again. He leaned back to indicate the audience was coming to an end. He smiled at Leon and folded his hands in his lap. "Travelers of many faiths come this way. Last year twenty-three Protestants, sixteen Catholics, three Jewish people and a Witness for Jehovah."

The interpreter rose from where he had been sitting beside the guru. Bowing, he said, "Please sign the book as you leave and indicate your nationality and faith. Our master says 'Namaste. Come again.' "

The lama nodded. Through a window the plume of Everest was visible. Outside, a group of young monks were taking pictures of one another with a Polaroid camera.

"Well, little hope of salvation there." Leon turned an accusing eye toward Pemba. The young man's reply surprised me.

"Salvation come when poor people don't have to sell things at side of road."

Stung, Leon became belligerent. Didn't Pemba believe in a free market economy, he asked? Was he a communist? Was he in favor of the road from China to Kathmandu that was being considered?

It would be like Haussmann's boulevards in Paris. Built for troops to march on. It would mean the end of Nepal's sovereignty. Is that what he wanted?

Pemba looked at the ground and shrugged. He said he had never heard of Haussmann but China and Nepal needed to be connected by more than roads.

Leon was a dog with a bone. Even though the lama had said "Come again," he was sure the welcome didn't extend as far as Beijing. "The communists will have the lama for lunch. And maybe you too."

Pemba remained calm, looking at Leon with something like pity. Leon made one more attempt at mastery. He put his hand on my ass. "*Come again?* Like get off, again and again? Is that what he meant?" I felt a squeeze.

"Don't!" I exclaimed, and shoved his hand away.

Pemba stood very still, wishing, no doubt, he were somewhere else. After a while, he said to me, "We have way to go."

"How far?" Leon demanded.

I signaled to him to keep his mouth shut. He could tell I was unhappy about his ass grab. He put his hands in a prayerful position, as though asking forgiveness. I turned away, ignoring his facetious apology. I'd been groped more than once by one of the Baudry's trustees. When I complained to Harrington, he shrugged. "Like to put their hands on more than money sometimes."

When I asked if that was all he had to say, he added that I had a good job and hoped I would keep it.

Leon picked up his stick and was heading for the trail. I waited for him to disappear before starting.

"He gets a little crazy sometimes," I murmured.

"Need balance with self." He shifted his weight nimbly from one foot to the other, arms extended like a dancer. He became a small beautiful bird ready for flight. "Mind and body one; need to hold them even. Leon heavy on one side. He want some other lama. Mistake. No balance. Make him ready to fight."

When I said he had really no one to fight with but himself,

Pemba replied, “Angry water buffalo charge at clouds.”

“You out of balance too,” he continued. “Don’t fight with body. Give in to what it say.”

Around us, firebush plants, their thick branches broken by the mountain wind. Above us, a hawk circling. I tied the flimsy gauze scarf around my neck, hoping the lama’s blessing would do some good. It may have helped. Or I gained some strength from knowing Pemba was right. My continuing cramps and fever told me I would have to go back. Now that I realized the need, it became all the more urgent. I asked Pemba how long it would take to get to Kathmandu. “Few days,” he replied.

Before long, Leon was back again, all solicitude.

“I’ll do that,” he said to Pemba, taking his place at my side. Pemba left me with Leon the rest of the afternoon. I couldn’t head back until it was determined at camp that evening who among the porters, now scattered along the trail, would also return. I watched Pemba stopping to talk with hardscrabble farmers and disappearing into villages we passed.

“Don’t be like that, please,” I pleaded.

“Like what?” Leon took my fanny pack.

“The way you are with Pemba.”

He said we wouldn’t need him anymore. We were going back, the two of us. I asked why he would ruin his trek.

“You’ll need help with doctors, with the embassy in case you have to go home. “Guides aren’t up to that.”

“Pemba knows more than you think,” I countered.

Leon wasn’t in the mood to argue over Pemba. His mind was made up. He couldn’t see leaving me. He still wanted to work things out between us because I was the reason he came. I told him it wasn’t my reason.

“Not yet,” he replied.

“Besides, we’ll need someone like Pemba to translate, help us find a doctor, a pharmacy.”

Leon thought the hotel could do that. He was sure they were

used to people getting sick. I supposed he was right, but the idea of being without Pemba made me feel more alone.

"We need to give him some money if he doesn't come with us."

Leon didn't respond at first. Only held me tighter. Then he kissed me on the forehead. "Sure, baby. We'll give him something, but I'm not sure what you see in him. He's a peasant with peasant ideas."

I said he was kind and easy to talk to.

"Strangers on a train going nowhere makes it easy."

I told him he was being cruel. Pemba was smart and being a peasant wasn't his fault. Besides, did Leon really know where he was going?

"To Kathmandu with you. And maybe Pemba, if you insist."

The conversation tired me and made me go slower. Leon was having a hard time with my snail-like progress. "Let's not stop, Hannah, till we get to that tree." Then, "Keep going until that hut."

"Go ahead, already," I said. "I can't stand any more encouragement."

He looked apologetic and said there was an airport at Lukla where we might catch a plane. "Let me check with George."

He bounded up the trail, stopped for a moment, then yelled "Stay with her" to Pemba, who suddenly appeared behind me.

"He strong man," Pemba remarked, watching Leon increase the distance between him and us. "Very determined, no balance."

"Determined to get away from a slowpoke."

"Not far," Pemba replied.

I slipped my arm under his and leaned hard against his shoulder as we walked. I said it wasn't easy to drag an anchor over dry land. When I explained what an anchor was, he nodded but seemed preoccupied.

"What?" I asked.

"Many things attend to."

"You've been disappearing on and off all day." Pemba didn't

answer. "Leon can be difficult. I know, I lived with him for three years." Silence. "It didn't work after a while, but now he wants me to reconsider." He still said nothing. "You see how complicated it is. I can't figure anything out, the distance from home is just too great."

Speaking left me breathless. I had to stop and lean on my stick. But there was more I needed to say. I told him how the trek makes every minute more intense, magnifying things you like about your friends and things you don't.

"You can't get away from them or yourself," I said. I told him how my thoughts had begun to lose logic, had no beginning or end. "They just keep going like a car that lost its brakes."

I felt ashamed of babbling, for having told Pemba about Leon and me. How could he possibly understand what had happened between us? Yet I wanted him to. I felt spoiled and sick, and sick of myself.

"You okay?" Pemba turned to me.

"No! That's what I'm telling you."

All my weariness and confusion descended on me and I began to cry. The tears just kept coming like a soaking rain. Pemba put his arm around me and looked at the ground. And I kept crying. After God knows how long, when I'd run out of tears, I took a couple of deep breaths and gave him a wan smile. "You didn't know what you were in for, did you?"

"Easier to climb hundred mountains than know own heart." He held my arm as we began to walk, trying to match his stride to mine.

"If you go back with us, what will you do in Kathmandu?"

He would wait and see how I was, and if I was better he would wait for Nawang and the group to return. He was hired for the length of the trek.

He is a stranger doing his duty, I thought. A young man who had to be told about the Holocaust, who could never imagine a city like New York, who'd never been to a ball game. He seemed smart to stick with what he knew. He wasn't like Nawang, who started to hint at being invited to America on our dime. Or like those young Nepalese who walked around in Grateful Dead T-shirts and Yankees baseball hats. Or like me, stranded in a place beyond my imagining.

CHAPTER SEVENTEEN
THE DECISION

Without thinking, I put my hand on Pemba's shoulder as we walked. His muscles danced under it. Sensing when I needed to stop, he showed me the footprints of a vole and told me how he and his father had hunted deer in the mountains and how wolves sometimes came into the villages. He told me how little the government did for his people while King Birendra and his friends grew rich.

"They hunt tigers in India. People here hunt food." Birendra, he said, was also hunting America's favor. "More luck than with tigers."

He pointed to where a farmer had set out a tin cup of milk and rice to appease a snake that lived near his house. "They afraid to kill it. Afraid mate seek revenge." He told me how the Hindus believed that a dying man should try to hold on to the tail of a cow. And while he talked, I wished it were just the two of us going back to the city. No personal history to sort out. Only the history of Nepal. Instead, we were slowly climbing toward Namche Bazaar, a trading town on the crest of a mountain, eleven thousand feet above the sea.

After Leon had spread the word that he was going with me, the group headed back toward me.

"I'm so relieved," cried Libby as she embraced me. "You don't know how worried I've been."

"Leon. Take good care of her," Pru said in a warning tone.

"Of course he will," Howard chimed in.

Bobby almost knocked me over with his hug. "I'll miss you, Hannah. Send me a postcard."

George pushed forward from the group. "You'll fly back from Lukla. It's a day's trek from here." Once I was back in the city, the Sherpa cooperative could deal with getting me on a plane to the States, if need be. Otherwise, I should wait for them to return.

"There'll be a lot to do around Kathmandu when you're better," George said.

At camp that evening, the same routine: the blue mess tent

set up again while the porters sat together on the ground, some distance from us, plates in hand. Noonie always fed them first. Then they disappeared to sleep or drink. The dinner, however, proved rather festive, fueled by relief at being rid of me soon.

George was full of plans for the next day. "Most of us will have hit the trail early. Pemba knows the way to Lukla, so you can leave later, if you want."

Howard gave advice on what to see in Kathmandu. Bobby asked me to buy him another flute. Libby wanted to make sure Leon got me a good room at the Bodnath.

"Back where I started."

"Not really," Libby answered, eyeing Leon appreciatively. "It's huge, his deciding to go back with you."

After dinner, Paul stopped me. "So, it's good-bye for a little while." He asked about my going back with Leon. I told him it hadn't been my decision, exactly. He eyed me skeptically. I assured him I could take care of myself and that he should focus on Bobby. "But who will I talk to?" he asked.

"Your son," I replied. "Stop thinking about her and think about him." Bobby was the way teenagers were. Didn't he remember what he was like at that age?

"Not like him. I did what my parents wanted. Wasn't thinking about getting high all the time."

I told him everyone has some escape in mind. For Bobby, it was the Holy Ganesh Bakery. For me, art. "For you, Mrs. K, is it?"

With a stern look he told me it wasn't an escape but a "possibility." I said that oxygen deprivation was clouding his judgment. Mrs. K was the kind that ruined careers. Where would he be when she got tired of the game? God only knew what rumors she'd already been spreading about the two of them. She'd get him kicked out of the Institute sooner or later.

"They would be only rumors, wouldn't they?" He assured me nothing had happened yet.

Then how could she have gotten a notion of where to find him?

He blushed. "Like I said, in case of an emergency." He asked me to try to find out if she was in Kathmandu, his face turning as crimson as the Virgin's robe.

"And if she is, what?" I asked.

He shrugged. "Just tell her you don't know when I'll be back."

"Don't try to compete with George," I told him. "You'll lose again, only big this time." Paul turned away. I dug myself into my tent.

The next morning I felt too weak to walk very far. "She'll have to be carried," George told Nawang.

There were no stretchers, of course, so one was improvised. Large, sturdy straw mats strung between bamboo poles. Leon did not trust the porters with the job, so it was he on one end and Pemba at the other. Their difference in height meant I was frequently gripping the sides of the stretcher to keep myself from sliding toward one or the other. I was afraid that the ties would not hold and I'd be suddenly pitched to the ground. The swaying of the mat, the sudden stops and starts, the men setting me down and picking me up increased my nausea as well as my guilt. I was a parcel of shortcomings that others had to deal with.

The effort of carrying me made Leon irritable. He took to giving a stream of commands as we crept along: "Easy, Pemba." "Slow down now!" "Hold your end higher, can't you?"

Pemba never answered. When we stopped to rest, I sat up while Leon rubbed bacitracin on his hand where the pressure of the poles had formed and then broken a blister. Pemba watched silently. He pointed to where a finch had made its nest and later to a skink hiding in the shadows.

Lukla, when we arrived the next day, was not what I expected. The town had nothing to recommend it but a few scrawny guesthouses and a magnificent view of the mountains from its rutted streets. Only a few people actually lived in Lukla. The majority were on their way to someplace else. They'd finished their climb or were about to begin one.

The airport, named for Tenzing and Hillary, was a rutted pasture about the length of a football field that ran downward to a cliff edge.

"Add to speed," Pemba said. "Help take off." He motioned upward.

Around the field, the rusting carcasses of planes lay like dead animals. Opposite the airfield, the grim granite face of a mountain peered down at us. Its angry surface looked like the school bully searching for his victim. Planes, twelve-seaters, bumped along the ground and, once airborne, immediately banked sharply to the right to avoid crashing into the opposing mountain. Landing was just as dangerous. More than one plane had missed the narrow field trying to land in foggy conditions.

"Will be first ride on airplane," Pemba said.

Leon replied that it might be his last, adding that the Lukla airport was thought the most dangerous in the world. The hut that served as a terminal was crowded with trekkers waiting to fly out. Strong winds had put flights on hold. An air of anger, impatience and fatigue permeated the place. Hikers crowded around the one hapless clerk at a makeshift desk, besieging him with questions for which he had no answers. We picked our way toward him through scattered mounds of baggage; Leon led the way, Pemba helped me walk. When we neared the desk, I sat on someone's duffel while Leon elbowed his way forward. I heard his raised voice.

"I don't care. I've got a very sick person here. She has to leave on the next plane."

I heard Pemba murmuring to the clerk, perhaps trying to bribe him. Leon again: "No, she can't go alone. People have to go with her. No, not just one. Two!"

The clerk seemed to be pleading with them, but Leon wouldn't listen. "If she dies, we'll sue. . . . No, she can't afford medevac."

I would have given any amount to stop the arguing.

"I can wait," I called.

"No you can't! . . . Get us on the next plane, okay?"

They did, once flights resumed. There was a single row of six hard plastic seats on either side of a narrow aisle. Pemba sat across from me and Leon behind. The other passengers were part of an Italian trekking group who shouted excitedly to one another over the whine of the engine. The plane bumped and shook as it tried to gain speed. I thought it might fall apart before we even got off the ground. As we lifted off, the plane's wings dipped sharply as we veered right. I reached for Pemba's arm across the aisle, but he was unresponsive, engrossed in looking out the window. The trip from nine thousand feet was bumpy and my stomach surged, bringing bitter stuff to my mouth. From my window I looked down on the narrow ribbon of trail we had trekked. What had taken thirteen days to cover, we flew over in forty-five minutes. Leon kept pestering me with questions about how I was feeling while Pemba continued to gaze at his country.

After landing, while we were waiting for our backpacks, I noticed Pemba seemed unhappy. When I asked him about it, he said he never felt comfortable except when trekking. "Kathmandu, too many people. Temples instead of mountains." He looked at his watch. "Too late for hospital today."

Leon protested, wanting to go there right away. "She's sick, man."

"No doctor there now." He picked up my backpack and headed for the door. Leon followed, still arguing, leaving me to limp after him. Pemba found a bicycle rickshaw into which we all squeezed, gear on our laps. The exhaust from taxis and buses, the stop and go of afternoon traffic set my head spinning.

Pemba left us at our hotel, saying he would be back in the morning. While I sat in the lobby, head in my hands, Leon talked with the man at the desk, going over with him the wisdom of waiting until morning to get to a hospital. He was finally convinced, and a porter helped me to my room, which was crowded with useless things. One twin bed too many, three folding chairs lined up by the window as though I were expecting guests, a standing lamp, a wooden desk and a large metal wastebasket. I pushed my soiled duffel onto a bed and stripped off my clothes to shower. I held on to the blue tiled wall while the hot water poured over me. Washing myself slowly, I was surprised how much bone rose to meet my wandering hands.

CHAPTER EIGHTEEN
HOSPITAL

I had a terrible night, stomach pains, fever, most of all fear of what was going to happen next. I couldn't get comfortable, shifting positions and pillows. Pushing off the thin polyester blanket when I was sweating, pulling it tight around me when I felt chilled. I thought of how my mother had asked the health aides to keep adjusting the hospital bed that had been set up in our living room. Lying flat, she had trouble breathing. Sitting up, her back ached. Every five minutes she asked to be shifted from one position to the other. She finally turned away from everyone and didn't ask for anything. Useless to us as we were to her. Now it seemed my turn. Past and present collided. Voices in the hotel hall became those of my parents. A door slammed, as startling as those of childhood.

"She has to go away. I don't want her to know," my mother said.

My father said he couldn't do that. I was their daughter. I'd find out sooner or later. My mother persisted. "She can go to Dana Hall."

"They don't take girls her age," my father retorted.

Then I could go live with Dad's sister. "Because I'm not sick, Jim, I'm dying. I don't want her to remember me this way." She began to cry and asked over and over who would take care of me. When Dad said he would, she began to scream. "You? You don't know how." He won in the end. A Pyrrhic victory. I stayed and watched her die.

After a while, she couldn't get up for dinner. Later, when friends got tired of bringing casseroles, my father and I ate cold cereal or a scrambled egg while Mother drank liquids from an IV. Sometimes, if he thought of it, he'd bring home a pizza or a bucket of Kentucky Fried. All the time, I felt her wanting me away from her.

"Why not the Bir?" Leon asked Pemba as the three of us bumped along in a taxi the next morning. He'd been told that government officials went there for treatment. His tone was aggressive and unwelcome. "I want her at the Bir."

All I wanted was help and I didn't care where it came from.

"Government not know what best," Pemba replied sourly. "We go to Panchu."

Pemba's choice didn't look promising. A small one-story stucco building with a large circular driveway that surrounded a large statue in a small, untended garden.

"Who's that?" Leon demanded. "The Virgin Mary?"

Queen Victoria eyed Leon with Anglican disdain.

"Was private hospital for English. Now Nepalese," Pemba replied.

Dr. Panchu was a short, heavyset man with steel-rimmed glasses and a white Nehru jacket. He pressed his dark hands together in greeting and bowed, then motioned me to a seat at his desk. He spoke to Pemba in Nepali. Pemba nodded and escorted a protesting Leon from the room. The doctor asked me how I liked Nepal. I said very much until I got sick. I told him about the bloody diarrhea. He listened with his arms folded over a protruding stomach.

"Cramps and nausea," I added. He rose from his desk, checked my pulse, listened to my heart through my shirt and tapped my chest with short hammer-like fingers. He motioned me to an examining table, pressed on my stomach in places that hurt. Helping me up, he told me the plan: a stool sample, IV antibiotics, bed rest. I asked how long I would be in the hospital. He shrugged, saying Pemba could bring me anything I needed. Friends could visit anytime. There were books he could lend me to pass the time. I said I couldn't read Nepali. He suggested Balzac or Stendhal. Did I read French? If not, he could get ahold of some English translations. "I studied in Paris," he said simply.

A nurse waiting in the hall showed me to a bed. Pemba and Leon trailed behind. Leon wanted to know right away what Panchu had said. I told him.

"But you were in there for only ten minutes," Leon protested.

Pemba said Panchu was a very good doctor who treated the poor for free. Leon said we weren't looking for charity and if he was so good why wasn't he at the Bir. When I told him Panchu had studied in Paris, Leon shut up.

We entered a large ward with ten steel-framed beds lining either side of a central aisle that mushroomed into a glass solarium. Women on one side, men on the other. Small windows punctuated the stained green walls, and there was an odd smell of disinfectant and cooked vegetables. The place felt more like a train station than a hospital. People filed in and out with pots of food and strange-looking plants. A monk chanted softly at the bedside of an elderly woman. We passed a young girl with facial bandages. Her relatives were mashing leaves into a foul-smelling paste. Two young men, bedded side by side, talked quietly to one another. One had casts on both legs. The other, a bandage on his chest where a tube drained pink liquid into a bottle on the floor. Families were moving in, spreading blankets on empty beds and storing belongings under them. Others were placing mosquito netting over their prostrate loved one.

"This place smells like everybody's shit in their pants," Leon announced. Pemba reiterated that Panchu was a good doctor who believed if families took care of their loved ones, they recovered more quickly.

"Sterile conditions? Hospital infections? What about that?" Leon inquired.

Pemba responded that patients wanted a place like home. Home, I thought. Where is that? My stomach ached and Leon's remarks weren't helping.

"I'm contacting the embassy for a recommendation," he said, getting up to leave.

"Rich get sick, go first to Bir then to Delhi, then maybe cemetery. Better here," Pemba explained. He said there were things I would need: towels, soap, and a bowl for washing, maybe a bedpan. He would get them if I was okay here.

"Fine," I replied, eager to be left alone.

"Ask for nurse if need help," Pemba suggested. I reminded him I couldn't speak the language.

"Everyone understand suffering. Make face and signs with hands.

Dr. Panchu came by with a collection of stories in English by

Colette. He took my pulse, palpated my stomach again and asked how I felt.

"Like a stranger in a strange land." I sighed.

Panchu reiterated that I wouldn't be in the hospital for long, maybe a week if all went well. My nurse, Comrade Magar, would come soon with antibiotics.

"Comrade? Is that what you call your nurses?"

He nodded and asked if that was all right with me. Afraid to offend, I said it was his hospital but that it sounded ominous. "Rather like Russian-style medicine."

He laughed, saying that all good medicine is the same, even in Russia. "We are all comrades in fighting disease."

I raised a weak fist and whispered, *"Aux armes!"*

He smiled and said I would indeed need my "armes" for the IVs.

After I was plugged into antibiotics by Comrade Magar, a young, rather timid girl, I spent the afternoon watching a woman rub liniment into an emaciated girl who I imagined was her daughter. It was an intimacy I'd never known. Later, they carried her away in a blanket. No one spoke to me although a few smiled and bowed as they passed my bed, their faces filled with curiosity. The room was hot and I felt nauseated. Thirsty too. I was hoping Comrade Magar would come so I could ask for bottled water. But neither she nor Leon nor Pemba appeared. Instead, a skinny man arrived with a barrel strapped to his back and began spraying the room with what smelled like DDT. Huge clouds of pesticide hung in the air. I began to choke, then cough, waving him away as he approached my bed. My lungs burned and I tried holding my breath as long as I could. My cells were already beginning a strange dance while I imagined my bone marrow turning orange. I had to get out of there, so when Pemba returned, setting up everything I needed on the dented metal table beside me, I asked him for pen and paper. He disappeared, and after what seemed like an eternity, returned with a ballpoint and several sheets of lined paper. I dug in my fanny pack where I kept my wallet and pulled out a crumpled note. It had the name and address of Grace and Jeremy Butler, Australian cultural attachés. It was the only time I felt grateful to Harrington. On hearing (no doubt with joy) that I was taking an extended vacation, he had scribbled something on a pad that bore his name and position, lest anyone forget.

"Here you go," he had said, handing me the note. "Besides knowing about flowers and that sort of thing, they're quite avid collectors of indigenous art." He had met them years ago, God knows where. Christmas cards ever since. He asked me to send his greetings to them. With that, he picked up his phone, motioning me out.

I handed Pemba Harrington's note with the Butlers' address. He stared at the paper. I gave him a gentle push. "Tell them to come fast."

He insisted I would be okay, that many people came to see Panchu.

"It's just not what I'm used to."

He smiled and said I was used to fancy. I told him I wasn't interested in fancy, just in feeling safe.

"Where no one called *comrade*?"

"Where no one sprays DDT. You're my only comrade, Pemba." I clutched his arm and pointed to my note. "Do it for me."

Leon bustled in. "The fuckin' hotel doctor wouldn't come without being paid first. The more I told him about you, the higher his price got. I told him if he didn't come by seven tonight I was going to report him to the Nepalese Medical Association."

Pemba smiled. "He not like this place. He rich. Now head of Nepalese Medical Association."

Fortunately, the Butlers dispatched their personal physician as soon as they read my note. It must have been close to ten at night when Dr. Percy appeared. He was one of those trim Australians full of confidence and good cheer. He spent a long time taking my history and then examined me carefully. Then he sat on the edge of the bed and patted my hand.

"First thing we'll do, Miss Avery, is change your bed sheets and get you into new nightwear. I see the pesticide man beat me to you. Panchu insists he shouldn't come, but he comes anyway.

Some kind of government job. Excellent man, Panchu, in his own way. This place is surprisingly good, given what he has to deal with. Not Western, of course, but there is more than one way to skin a cat, eh? Not much government funding. A bit too far to the left for most people's taste."

He held one knee in his hands and rocked back on my bed. "You didn't expect anything like this, I imagine. Everything points to dysentery and they've begun antibiotics." He turned to Pemba, who was standing at a respectful distance.

"Pretty common around here. Wouldn't you say?" Percy continued, "along with TB, hepatitis, sepsis—the list goes on. Not things for you to worry about. First things first: Compazine for nausea, keep you hydrated, and keep the IVs going to chase away the bugs. You'll be feeling a bit weak in the knees for a while. You'll need to rest and regain your strength slowly. You got to see some of the Himalayas, at any rate. How much longer are you planning on staying?"

"About three weeks more," Leon interjected, nudging himself between Percy and Pemba.

"Plenty of time, then," Percy said, outlining a plan in which I would feel better in five or six days, and then could go about slowly for another seven. He asked where I was staying. When Leon told him Hotel Bodnath, Percy looked displeased.

"One of the better ones," he admitted, "but not very comfortable when you're sick. And the food . . ." He shrugged. "Well, they do try. No, I'm afraid Grace won't hear of it."

Leon protested that he could take care of me himself, studying the IV bottle as though he knew something about it.

"If you want to go toe to toe with Grace Butler, be my guest," Percy said rising. She will come in the morning.

"Be warned," the doctor went on, "she's planning to spirit you away to her garden. Convinced of its healing powers. She's writing a book called *Planting Health* that she says will put us quacks out of business. You're not the first 'broken bloom' she's tried to revive."

Leon reasserted that I was going with him. I closed my eyes against the headache that was forming behind them. My stomach felt like I'd swallowed a rock. My feet were cold while the rest of me felt feverish. I just wanted to live or die without arguments. Concern for me brought out intransigence in Leon that I didn't want to deal with. Neither did Percy. He ignored him.

"I keep telling her to start a vegetable patch if she wants to do some good, but she won't hear of it. Doesn't want celery stalks crowding her dahlias. And she assures me her roses would wilt at the sight of a potato. Of course, she does good in lots of ways."

Percy reported she was serious about preservation of old buildings, raised quite a bit of money for the art museum, and was active in the local Red Cross. She would never forgive him if he didn't hand me over, and he didn't want to be crossed off her list of dinner guests. "A consummate cook." He turned to Leon. "Of course you can try if you want, old man, but I don't think you'll get very far."

Meanwhile, Pemba had vanished. When I asked where he had gone, Leon answered with evident disinterest, "Sherpa meeting of some sort. I imagine he'll check in with us soon enough. Try to get some sleep." He bent and kissed me on the forehead as though he were planting a flag on the moon. Without looking at Percy, he told me he'd be back in the morning.

CHAPTER NINETEEN
NIGHT VISITOR

I did sleep, and when I woke in the middle of the night, I found Pemba lying on the floor beside my bed. I reached down and shook him.

"What are you doing here?" I whispered. He rolled over on his back and stared up at me.

"Like you. Trying to sleep." Confused and not fully awake, I asked hadn't he gone somewhere?

"Yes and come back."

I said I couldn't sleep knowing he was on the floor. He sounded impatient, telling me it happened every night somewhere. "Some in beds. Some on ground. Go to sleep."

He turned over. I lay awake, comforted by his presence; disturbed by it as well. I couldn't offer to share my bed with him. I'd done that often enough with friends, but he was a Sherpa and a stranger. Besides, I was too sick for company of any kind. His breathing began to take on a steady rhythm. In it I heard the sleep of my first lover. He was a Trinity College junior. I pictured his hairless chest rising and falling, his nipples small pink boats bobbing in a milky sea. He had been eager, gentle and brief. Where was he now? I wondered. With what kind of woman?

At the end of the ward, a bare bulb cast a dim and eerie light in my direction. I turned onto my side. My sudden movement pressed the needle into my flesh, spreading pain like an electric current up my arm. There was no sense waking Pemba about it. I lay in the semidarkness feeling how strange it all was. The different men who'd entered my life—Pemba, Leon and Frank, and that first, unsatisfying boy. They all would go on, whatever happened to me. For the first time, I knew how my mother felt before she died. Her pain and suffering hadn't made a difference. She would die and my father would go on. When I did fall asleep, I dreamt of her, something I don't remember.

In the morning, to my surprise, I felt a little better. My arm ached and appeared slightly swollen, but the cramping had been replaced by a dull and tolerable ache. When I looked over the side of the bed, the floor was empty, leaving me to wonder if I'd dreamt Pemba there. A woman came to give me a sponge bath. The water was cold and the washcloth rough. There was no modesty to be had, but I didn't care. I would never be here again. Magar came and switched off the IV, pressed the swollen area, and made motions suggesting the needle would need to be reinserted in the other arm. Pemba came a little later with clean sheets. I sat on the opposite bed while he stripped mine.

"You were here last night, weren't you? It wasn't a dream."

"All night," he said, not looking at me.

Yet waking was what seemed like a dream: people coming and going, cooking at bedsides, cries of pleasure and pain. Comrade Magar made several more visits, taking away the bedpan, setting up the IV, bringing bottled water. Leon appeared with tea in a carafe, and a fruit salad and rolls on a tray covered with a hotel napkin.

"Room service." He set the tray down and kissed my cheek. "Not easy in a rickshaw with this stuff. Sleep okay?"

"Well enough." I glanced at Pemba, who was fussing with a pillowcase. "But I think I should stick to tea for now."

Leon poured tea for me and himself. He apologized to Pemba for not having an additional cup, explaining that he didn't think the guide would come so early. His tone was demeaning. He waved the carafe in Pemba's direction. "Have some if you can scrounge something to drink from."

Pemba bowed slightly and said he'd already had breakfast, but Leon persisted. "Fruit salad? Where might an extra fork be?"

"He's told you he's eaten. What's the point?"

Ignoring me, Leon extended a basket to Pemba. "You might like a roll."

"I go now," Pemba said as Leon settled into the chair beside my bed.

"You didn't have to do that."

"What?" he replied.

I turned away and refused to speak to him until Grace Butler arrived. A tall, angular woman striding down the long line of beds as though she were a colonel reviewing the regiment. She wore a print dress of large purple and pink clematis, a broad-brimmed straw hat with a band that matched, and white sneakers. She carried a huge bunch of flowers.

"It's Birnam Wood!" Leon muttered as Grace came toward us waving a free hand.

"I knew it must be you—the only lily among these dusky roses." She extended her hand to me from what appeared a great height. "Percy gave me a full report. I expect he'll be around to see you later."

I thanked her for coming and squeezed the hand she'd proffered. I introduced Leon. Grace took her hand from mine, offering it to Leon as he rose.

"Very pleased to meet you, Mr. Kaminsky. Polish, isn't it?" She took the seat beside my bed that Leon had occupied.

"Before the war. Polish-American now."

She turned back to me. "Of course, you mustn't stay here long," she said matter-of-factly. I glanced at Leon and saw his jaw tightening.

"Would you be good enough to find something to put these in?" She handed him the bouquet.

Leon took the flowers but made no move to go. Instead, he told Grace of his plan to move me back to the Bodnath within the week. She stared at him without expression. "Under Dr. Percy's care, of course," he added.

I closed my eyes. Maybe all of life was just people pushing and pulling one another.

"We'll see what's best for Miss Avery," Grace answered. When I opened my eyes, her long, narrow face was leaning over me, blocking out everything else. She asked how I was feeling.

"A little better, thank you."

She leaned back with a satisfied look, calling Percy a "good man." She folded her arms and stretched her long legs so that her feet were somewhere under my bed. "The Musée Baudry, isn't it?

I do what I can to help the museum here along. Harrington's still with you, I gather. He told us of the rose garden there."

Her talk was making my dizziness return. I nodded, saying that the roses didn't get the attention they deserved.

"They rarely do," she sighed.

I must try to do something about that when I return, I thought. "I promise to take better care of them," I said, wondering if I would.

Leon stood behind her, bouquet in both hands, looking like a jealous bridesmaid waiting for the ceremony to end. But Grace persisted. "And what brought you to this part of the world?"

I shrugged and said it was a place I'd never been. She looked at me dolefully while removing her straw hat and setting it on the bed. It seemed she was planning to stay awhile.

She said in her experience people come to Nepal for two reasons: "Either for love or the lack of it." She twisted herself around to talk with Leon. "Mr. Kaminsky," she said, pointing to the flowers, "my girls are getting thirsty. Could you help them out?"

Leon reddened. "Sure thing," he said, looking around for assistance. As there was none, he was forced to wander off in search of a vase.

"Jewish, I gather," Grace said.

I nodded. I wasn't going there with her, so I asked what had brought her to Nepal.

"Not a what, but a who. Mr. Butler. But that's a long story." She smoothed her skirt.

I could go back to the Bodnath, but she wouldn't advise it. It was not very comfortable, for one. And secondly—she leaned closer—"Judging from his treatment of my girls, I don't think Mr. Kaminsky would take good enough care of you." She suggested I come to her. She sat back. "I suppose he will mind," she mused.

I knew he would and said so. They could fight it out for all I cared, but the match looked uneven so far.

"I do hope he's found some water. They haven't had a drink since they left home. Nor have I for that matter." She searched her purse for a large silver flask. "Only water," she said, holding it aloft. Then, leaning forward in her chair, she asked if Percy had mentioned her garden.

"In some detail. Said it was magical," I lied, hoping to stave off a description.

She reported that Percy didn't know a dahlia from a daisy and that there was nothing magical about it. "Just nature taking its course, with a little help from Jeremy and me." She smoothed her graying hair, which ended in a bun at her neck.

Leon returned with the flowers stuffed into a metal pail. Grace Butler grabbed the bucket from him. "My goodness, what have you done?" She began to lay the blossoms on the blanket that covered me. "They can't be crowded together higgledy-piggledy!"

When all the flowers were out of the pail, she began to put them back again, one by one. First the gladioli, red as arterial blood, then bright yellow snapdragons, followed by snowy daisies and then lilies, amber and scarlet. "There," she said as she put in the last flower.

I was amazed by her work, the whole arrangement coming to life, a breathing, living creature. I touched the edges of the blossoms. "It's beautiful."

She smiled and brushed my cheek with her still-damp hand. "I'll drop by tomorrow." She extended her hand to Leon. "Thank you for your assistance."

"Don't mention it," Leon replied, not letting go of her hand. "I hope these will last until we get to the hotel. Come visit. We can sit by the pool."

A look of distress clouded Grace's face. She asked if he really planned to sit me amidst all that chlorine and crabgrass. Proof, she thought, that he was not cut out for nursing. She asked if he would kindly give her back her hand. "It's the one I count upon for spreading manure."

Leon dropped it, turning a shade of red that Grace's gladioli might have envied. She turned and strode away, straw hat in hand.

"That woman needs pruning," he muttered.

"And I need sleep." I reached up to touch his hand. "Go away for a while."

Sometime later I was awakened by a gentle pat on the shoulder. "Sorry, old girl, but the IV has infiltrated again. Arm a bit swollen. Best to keep it elevated." Percy tucked a pillow under it. "It does mean we'll have to use a foot this time." He pulled the needle from my arm and wheeled the IV around to the other side of the bed. "Grace has already reported on her visit," he said as he massaged my foot to find a vein. He looked up and smiled. "Rather likes you, I think."

I was in the hospital for another five days. The cramps slowly subsided and the diarrhea stopped. I still had little appetite, but I could walk to the solarium. I sat there, staring at an empty stretch of untended lawn until my strength wore out. Every day seemed like the one before: Percy came and went, Panchu stopped by, Leon brought room service that I didn't eat, and Grace appeared with yet another bouquet. And every night, without their knowing it, Pemba slept on the floor beside me. He came late, after the others had gone, bringing with him small strange fruits and special tea.

"Where shall I go, Pemba?" I asked one night as he sat opposite me on an empty bed he refused to sleep in.

"Where heart wish."

What would happen if I moved to the hotel? Could he still visit at night?

"It raise questions."

"For whom?" I felt suddenly resentful. "For you, because you might have other things to do once I'm out of here."

Pemba said yes, there were people he needed to meet and no, he couldn't tell me where to go.

In the end, I decided to go with Grace Butler. The path of least resistance? Maybe. It would have taken more strength than I had to oppose Grace's plan, which Dr. Percy supported. I knew she'd care for me in her own peculiar way. In the hospital she visited every day at teatime, followed by a servant carrying a large straw hamper. From it she unloaded a half dozen issues of the *Gardeners' Chronicle*, a china tea service, and gentle treats that she had made herself. Lemon curd and freshly baked crumpets, cucumber-and-watercress sandwiches cut into precise squares that filled my mouth perfectly.

"I know your stomach is still a bit skittish, but you must try a little of this," she'd say. She'd spread a linen napkin over my lap and hand me a small round wafer spread with butter and wild-berry jam.

She told Leon, "You've been very kind, but I think we can dispense with room service."

Her manner with everyone but Dr. Percy was peremptory. There was a roughness in the way she plumped my pillow or straightened the covers. When she walked me to the solarium, I felt not so much helped as marched. Yet I also felt an almost desperate need for her touch, for mothering in whatever form it might come.

My decision to go with Grace infuriated Leon. He fought back in ways that made me miserable. He appeared at the hospital with Dr. Pataman, a tall, heavyset man with straight, shiny black hair plastered in a circle around his skull. He wore a blue short-sleeved shirt with dark buttons that strained against his belly before disappearing into neatly pressed pants. I could see he had been handsome once. Now his face was a bloated brown balloon floating above an immense azure sea. He didn't examine me, but like a schoolboy reciting a text, told me that the Bodnath was "a fine establishment" where I could recuperate very happily.

"There are many beneficial things about hotel life. There is availability of our room service that I gather you've already tried as well as our lovely ground floor restaurant with nourishing foods." Leon was nodding. "There is the pool area where you can take the air and, when you are stronger, there is a bar for a little restorative should you wish." Then there was the medical coverage to consider, provided twenty-four hours a day to all guests by Dr. Pataman himself, who was always "just a bicycle ride away."

Leon grabbed my hand, smiled and raised his eyebrows in expectation of consent. He had other ploys as well. He tried to make me feel guilty about his having paid the hotel in advance for my new stay. When I looked skeptical, he admitted to offering to paint "something" in the restaurant's lavatories in return for a free room. An offer that was politely declined. He was merciless in his persecution of Grace's bouquets. Every chance he got, he snapped a stem or crushed a petal when he thought I wasn't looking.

"What has happened here?" Grace would almost shout as she arrived. She would immediately set about trying to revive her offering, splinting broken stems with hairpins and pruning mutilated blossoms. "It's Big Foot's doing, isn't it?" Her new name for Leon. Once, she turned to me accusingly and hissed, "You saw him do it, didn't you?" I tried to look puzzled by her question, but she'd have none of it.

"Just because you lie with a man doesn't mean you have to lie for him," she said. I told her I wasn't sleeping with him. How could I in my condition?

"But you have, I can tell." I didn't answer. "He touches you in ways that only a lover would." I could feel my color rising. I told her it was none of her concern. Her concern, she insisted, was that nothing impede my getting better. She put a hand on my cheek and looked at me with an intensity that was frightening. "Be careful of Big Foot. He could hurt you like he has these flowers." Her hand felt like a hot brand pressed against my cheek.

I pulled the covers tighter around me, a shield against Grace's words. I needed Leon, I told her. "And Pemba too."

"Pemba? He's not like Leon, who is a friend, or tries to be. Pemba is a suitable guide, nothing more." She sat down in the chair beside my bed, stroking the stem of a blue cornflower in her lap. "If you are thinking of Pemba as your friend, you are making a mistake. What have you in common to be friends about? There are women who come to Nepal looking for someone or something. It rarely ends well."

And what did I know of him anyway, other than that he had been good at doing the job he was hired for? With Big Foot, there was at least a shared Western culture, "if Poland counts." She replaced the cornflower in the vase. "I know you think I am meddling and prejudiced. Perhaps I am. But you must be careful. Kathmandu is a small town, really. One gets to know everyone sooner or later. When you suggest Pemba is a friend, I fear for you."

That night when Pemba was lying on the floor beside my bed, with the sweet smell of his body rising, I asked him why Grace didn't want us to be friends. He answered with silence. I persisted, "So I wondered if there was more about her I should know."

"Her or me?" he said, finally. I reached down and brushed his cheek with my hand.

"I feel I've known you since I was a child. How can that be?"

He sat up and leaned against the neighboring cot. I turned on my side to face him. His arms were resting on his knees, staring at his fingers, which were interlocked in front of him. In the dim light, his black hair glistened. He raised his face to reveal its toughened skin and the dark eyes that I couldn't read. A young man not particularly handsome, but at that moment, he seemed to hold the world. His rutted face contained the mountains I'd climbed, the rivers, however terrifying, I'd crossed. I saw in him, too, the things I'd missed, that I'd not had the strength to face.

He told me that Grace was part of the crowd that hung about the king. "Some say she was in love with his father, Mahendra." In the past, the kings of Nepal had more than one wife, he said. That time had passed, though there were still mistresses. The queen was suspicious of Grace, and the ministers disliked her attempt to influence the king. "She always afraid China take over Nepal. Want Maoists in jail." I asked what he thought the country needed.

"Change." His tone was sharp. I had heard that the Maoist faction, while small, was slowly growing stronger. They wanted to overthrow the government, by force if necessary. There had been Communist-backed *bandhs*—general strikes. Roads had been blocked, fires set. There had been attempted assassinations and bombings. I wanted to ask more but Pemba grew silent and just said, "Mrs. Butler not like me much."

The sudden idea of going to the Butlers' and not seeing him frightened me. I depended on his presence, on telling him of the day's meager events, my physical discomforts, my history. His breathing underneath me had been the engine that drove my talk, and in the dark I unfolded like a night-blooming flower. I asked if he could still come to me. It was a silly question. Was Grace going let him sleep on her floor? Set up a bed for him in my room?

Pemba laughed at my question. "Over wall at night?"

"If you can't, I won't stay with her." I was surprised by my own conviction. I took his hand. The skin was rough and callused. "I don't know why, but I need you." A look of consternation crossed his face. He lay down again where I couldn't see him.

"We very different. Different things have to do. That separate us, not Grace." I became tearful.

"I have nothing I have to do." And I felt the sad truth of it. The world I inhabited seemed small and empty. This bed. That chair. A few old paintings to look after. I didn't want to die, but in truth had nothing to live for. No husband, no lover, no child. No flowers except my tulips and the ones Grace brought. Who was there to miss me? At the Baudry, Harrington would be happy to replace me with a recent graduate hungry for work and eager to accept half my salary. This sudden trip might, in fact, give him a chance to get rid of me. If I died, there would be a few tears shed and then they'd all get on with it. Whatever their *it* was.

Pemba read my thoughts. "You have idea if someone loved you, everything be all right."

I told him it would be a start.

"Not so simple."

I felt a sudden panic, as though an elevator had stopped between floors. I saw my mother's sick face, no longer smiling, just staring at me with nothing more to give.

"You don't want to be my friend."

"We friends, Hannah. No changing that. At night, we together, think of each other. But in day, we think different. You think of home. I already home."

I told him I didn't think of home. I thought about where he was when he wasn't with me.

"Meet people."

I asked what people and began to be afraid of his answer without knowing why. He was silent, but finally spoke in a soft tone. "My life here, mine."

"Of course it's yours. Whose else could it be? But lives can be shared." He rolled over on the floor, his back to me, and bid me good-night.

CHAPTER TWENTY
AT THE BUTLERS'

The next morning I left the hospital before Leon arrived. Grace Butler came early, pushing a wheelchair with large rubber wheels and a rattan seat.

"Get in, dear," she commanded.

I asked if I shouldn't tell someone I was leaving.

"Percy will take care of that." She was stuffing my belongings into a large straw bag. "Pemba can fetch whatever you've left."

She had parked her jeep at the hospital entrance despite signs not to do so. "It's supposed to be for ambulances and hearses, but families bring the sick themselves and leave with them, dead or alive. So there's really no reason," she said, abandoning the wheel chair with a push toward the entrance and opening the passenger door. "We'll be home in a jiffy."

I rolled down the window and breathed the fresh morning air. I felt abducted from a world of disinfectant and dark faces. It reminded me of my mother being ill and my aunt coming to take me out for a hot fudge sundae every Saturday. We'd drive to Teaneck, have our treat, then shop for the few things she claimed I needed. A new notebook, a barrette. Sometimes a blouse or a sweater. All afternoon, as we went from place to place, I tasted the sweetness of chocolate and felt the bitterness of betrayal.

Home for the Butlers was a spacious wooden bungalow in Kirtipur, a short distance from Kathmandu. Its large windows and wide doors were designed to capture any summer breeze. The vine-covered porch that wound around the front and sides was filled with wicker chairs and small wooden tables, each with its vase of flowers. Grace took me through the large rooms with their high ceilings and slowly churning fans. The polished teak floors were covered with Tibetan rugs. Bookcases displayed tattered volumes on Asian art. Interspersed on the shelves were ancient pots, brass figures and an antique silver-and-lapis brooch pinned to a black velvet board. On pale-yellow plaster walls, precise drawings of Himalayan flowers hung in ornate frames.

"Some of the better ones, Jeremy did himself," Grace proudly announced. "When you're stronger, there's the dining room. But for now you'll be most comfortable in the garden."

She opened French doors that led into a bright afternoon sun that blinded for a moment. The garden was more modest in size than I had imagined, but was like Giverny in its bounty and array of color. It stretched perhaps fifteen yards in each direction before its arms began circling the house like a mother in a bright dress enfolding her child. A high brick wall enclosed the space allowing only mountaintops to be visible. A small greenhouse stood at the far end of the garden, its insides ablaze with unfamiliar blossoms. There was a small pond in which pink and white lilies floated like small moons. Under a chinaberry tree, Grace had placed a wicker chaise with a worn brown pad and green canvas hood that could be raised and lowered by leather handles. A cream-colored afghan was thrown across it. A low rattan table held a pitcher of iced tea, a silver bell, and back issues of *Amateur Gardening.*

"Now, just settle yourself. The servants have off till dinner, so no one will disturb you. Rest is part of the cure. After tea, we'll move you to a sunnier spot. Each part of the garden has its own particular effect. You must visit them all."

As I lay down, Grace disappeared into the house. Somewhere beyond the garden wall, the sound of temple bells, a mother calling to a child, the song of an unfamiliar bird. I fell asleep and awoke some time later to Grace rummaging around in a flower bed in a corner of the garden. She made no effort to engage me.

"I suppose you made this afghan. It's beautiful," I called.

Grace didn't answer. I wondered if she'd heard me, but decided not to try again. I thumbed through a magazine and glanced at the garden wall, and pondered if Pemba could scale it or if he would even want to. And if he did, how would I know he had come? Could I sneak out to meet him without Grace knowing? I hardly felt the tranquility she had prescribed. Anxiety dogged me and my head began to hurt. Where was he anyway? He hadn't yet come with my things. How many servants did Grace have and where were they at night? I raised the hood of the chaise as though to protect my thoughts from Grace's knowing them. Trying to concentrate on something other than my concerns about Pemba, I studied the narrow strip of garden in front of me. Gentians as blue as veins ran in long rows and stout chrysanthemums paraded like kings. But my mind was elsewhere. I wondered if Leon would come and try to claim me before I saw Pemba again.

"When do you think he'll come with my things?" I asked. Grace answered this time, without raising her head.

"Pemba? There's nothing you need from him."

She was digging vigorously, uprooting stubborn weeds. She explained from a nearby rhododendron that the restorative power of flowers is not enhanced by conversation.

Left alone, I noticed my mind wandering, focusing first on an unfamiliar flower, then on Pru and Libby being somewhere I'd never see, and then wondering what happened to Leon, then back to Pemba again. I'd been hurt when he said his life was his own. Why wasn't his life my concern? Don't friends care about each other's lives? Why did he have to keep day and night so separate? Maybe he had a girlfriend, a wife, a gambling or drug habit that he was hiding.

Grace got up to leave. She wiped her hands on her smock then bent to pick up her basket of tools. "If you want anything, ring the bell."

Her manner had turned surgical, leaving me feeling deserted. Even the last of the summer asters blooming with all their might couldn't console me. Toward teatime, Grace appeared with a large tray and a copy of the *Himalayan Times.* "Mr. Kaminsky called with his apologies," she said. He would see me later.

"And my things?"

"Not a word from your Sherpa. They're always so helpful when they are around, it makes you think them reliable. What I am saying is for your own good. Don't end up trying to use Pemba or being used by him."

When I was better she would drive me around to see the sights. "Then you'll go back to New York," she said firmly.

"Use him? How?" I asked, offended.

She set the tray down beside me and pulled up a chair. "Shall we have tea?" Jeremy would be along in a few minutes and was dying to meet me. It was clear she didn't think it wise to dispense any more advice, and I didn't want to hear any.

"Dr. Percy mentioned you've been here awhile," I said.

"Is fifteen years awhile? Jeremy was sent out here to the Australian Embassy. Cultural attaché at first, then kept on as majordomo to order supplies, ensure repairs, general upkeep. I'd not thought of settling here, amidst the dirt and disease. Certainly no place to raise a child. But Jeremy was committed to the country and we were looked upon favorably by some."

She was adding honey to my cup when her husband arrived. Jeremy was a large, affable man with a hawklike face and eyes alert to any movement about him. His white hair was as thick and smooth as feathers.

"Ah, the American transplant. Welcome." He kissed my hand. He took off his jacket and loosened his tie. "Has Grace made you comfortable?"

It was hardly a question. His short sleeves revealed flabby white arms. His belt seemed about to be buried by his belly. He studied my face, saying he'd heard so much about me. "Lying here, you could be Puccini's Mimi or perhaps Violetta in *Traviata*. Don't you think so, Grace?" Before she could answer, he hastened to assure me my ending would be much happier. "My wife does wonders." He glanced at the headlines in the newspaper lying beside me. "Unrest at the university again." Then he picked it up. "Students arrested. A policeman badly injured."

Grace shook her head. "Maoists, I suppose."

Jeremy read aloud from the paper about the demonstration against the monarchy being the largest yet. He turned to me. "There are some who favor communism, but a Chinese takeover is unlikely."

"That's what the French thought about Vietnam. Now Ho Chi Minh is in Hanoi," Grace said, "and Maoists are in Kathmandu."

When I said there were also demonstrations in the U.S., against our involvement in Vietnam, Grace took umbrage.

"It's not the same. You're not trying to overthrow the government like they are here. Do you think Nepal would be better off with peasants running things? In Jhapa last year, plantation owners were murdered." Grace pushed at the folds in her skirt. I asked about economic inequality. People seemed so very poor and a few so rich. Jeremy leaned forward.

"Of course they're poor, held back by illiteracy and disease. Violence is inevitable when the disparity between the rich and poor is so great." Jeremy held out his teacup for Grace to fill.

"Pemba said—" I began, but Jeremy cut me off.

"Of course, the government is trying," he said.

Grace looked disgusted. "The few who aren't corrupt or incompetent." She added that King Birendra was a good man, but weak. "Not like his father." Unfortunately, the Himalayas had been no barrier to radical ideas. "Outlawing dissent," she said, "has had little effect." She passed a plate of wafers to me, saying there was no excuse for murder. "I'm glad I'm as old as I am, with less to have to live through," she concluded.

Jeremy rose, with apologies for having to look over some orders. He handed his cup to Grace, asking if there were dinner guests expected other than me.

"None. I thought *thukpa* and a vegetable curry would do." She had made the guest room up for me already, but he might fetch a few extra towels. They would eat after I was settled for the night. I watched this ritual of man and wife. The inquiries and the replies. Everyday questions and ordinary answers. Is this what I was missing?

It seemed odd to be in the Butlers' garden while people were under arrest for wanting a little more of what I already had. I wondered how much someone like Pemba had and what he wanted. I imagined him walking in the crowded streets, eating at the teahouse where Leon and I had stopped, studying maps for his next trek. I wondered where he slept and who his friends were. Was he making love to someone? Would he come tonight? Grace, noticing my preoccupation, asked if I was all right.

"Just a little light-headed. This spot is so magical, I think I would recover even more quickly if I slept out here."

Grace could hardly contain her excitement. "I'd thought of that, but wondered if it might be too much for you all alone. Perhaps I should stay with you. Jeremy won't mind."

I said I couldn't put her out like that and I promised to wake her if anything bothered me.

"I could ask one of the servants to stay with you." They usually went home after supper, she explained.

"I'd really rather be alone."

* * *

Before dinner a cot had been set up under a mulberry with mosquito netting draped from its branches. Leon called to say he would come in the morning. His voice was thick with excitement. "There's something I've got to tell you." I told him to tell me now. He said he couldn't and he had to go.

When I reported the interchange to Grace, she replied, "He's not a man to be counted on under any circumstances."

The three of us sat in the garden as darkness crept over the far wall. Grace lit a lantern. She and Jeremy sipped sherry while I stuck to soup and sweet tea. The talk was inconsequential, flitting from one topic to another, memories like hummingbirds darting about at twilight. Jeremy spoke of his time in Africa before coming to Kathmandu, Grace of her childhood in New Zealand. The warmth of the liquor and the sweetness of the night bathed them in a river of abandoned desires. After a while, making sure I had everything I needed, including a bedpan borrowed from the hospital, they bid me good night.

It took awhile before the house was dark. Each stirring of the breeze, each rustle of a leaf made me start in expectation. The night grew colder. I pulled Grace's afghan tight around me. A half-moon rose in a cloudless sky, casting ominous shadows. The croaking of frogs and the mole crickets' incessant song only made the garden more desolate. Perhaps Pemba had a wife. But why stay with me at night, then? Did he consider it his job? Was he told to do it? He could have come today for just an hour to check up on me. And why did he and Grace dislike one another? He was a peasant. That was probably reason enough for her, but she must have seen how bright he was. And what was Leon so mysterious about? I fell asleep, exhausted from trying to figure things out. A dream, like an angry mongrel off its chain, followed me until dawn.

I am expected at a party. I'm in a rental car. There is a bouquet on the seat beside me. I drive pass MOMA, then the Baudry, where a young man sits in the street. In Central Park: speeding cyclists and galloping horses, roller skaters and joggers, Boy Scouts picking up trash. It's hard to find a way out. At a dilapidated brick warehouse by the East River, I climb three flights of stairs to a door with flowers on it. A man who looks like Pemba asks for my ID. I can't find my driver's license.

"Your passport will do."

"I don't have it with me."

"Then you can't come in," he says, and shuts the door.

In the morning, Grace placed my chaise by the pond. "You look tired. How did you sleep?"

"Bad dreams."

She commiserated, asserting that the first night in a new place is rarely easy. She pointed out how the water lilies floated lightly upon the surface, never betraying their connection to deeper things. "Wellness is the ability to float," she stated with conviction.

"I'm afraid I've never been good at that."

Grace looked displeased, claiming it was something people could learn to do and asked if I was ready for breakfast. She had eaten and had to leave but Jeremy was still about. Struggling out of the cot, I replied that I wasn't really up for eating.

"You should at least try," she said, smiling and holding out her hand. She helped me into the bathroom, where I could wash my face and brush my teeth with bottled water. I was combing my hair when I heard a knock followed by Jeremy's voice through the bathroom door.

"Breakfast. Won't you join me?" When I repeated that I couldn't eat anything, he suggested I talk to him while he did. I came out to face him. He looked as sheepish as a boy at his first high school dance. "Unless you're not feeling up to it."

The table was set with a cloth with a pattern of leafy vines and purple grapes, matching napkins, and crystal glasses. In reaching for water, I knocked over a china cup, the handle breaking as it hit the ground.

"I'm so sorry." I bent to pick up the pieces and set them on the table.

"These things happen." He turned the remains of the teacup over. "It has a number. Grace can send away for a replacement." When I offered to pay for it, he looked bemused. "Don't be silly, my girl. It's only a cup." He gazed at the mountains piercing the clouds. "But a broken heart, that can't be written away for."

He didn't say any more and I wasn't about to ask. A servant silently replaced the broken cup. Jeremy held up a silver coffeepot. I shook my head.

"You won't mind then if I do?" He didn't wait for an answer and, filling his cup, leaned back in his chair. "Did you sleep well?" I told him I hadn't. He nodded. "When we first came here, Grace and I, we hardly slept at all. The excitement of a new place, so much to see, to learn."

I asked if it was still that way for them.

"Not quite." Jeremy eyed me carefully. "The whole country, what we saw and learned, seemed only the backdrop to our intensely private romance. A painted set in front of which actors perform." He took a sip of coffee. "That performance ended for us some time ago." He looked at me, his pale blue eyes searching my face for something like understanding. "When you've been together a long time, things change. Passion for one another becomes a passion for other things—like plants or politics." I looked down at my empty plate.

"I suppose so. I wouldn't know."

"Why is that, Miss Avery?" He turned toward a servant who was bringing a tray of melon slices before I could summon an answer.

"Ah, there you are, Dep." He rose and took the plate from the servant's tray. "Do try a slice." I studied his offering while trying to find an appropriate reply to his question. It seemed as though everyone felt free to ask about to the love life of an unmarried woman. I took the smallest slice I could find.

I placed the melon on my plate and began to vigorously slice it into pieces. But Jeremy, seating himself again, repeated his question. "Why is that?" he asked. Dep presented me with a poached egg and toast.

I avoided looking at Jeremy and stared instead at the garden—the row of blue asters, so carefully spaced, the tangled branches of wisteria that had lost their blooms, daisies beginning to curl in on themselves. But no tulips. Nothing to remind me of my lived life. I felt useless, a scrap of foreign newspaper that had been blown over the wall. I heard Jeremy's voice pulling me back to him. "You do have choices, you know."

I was silent for a while, trying to free myself from the past and focus on what he was saying. Had I choices, really? About my mother's cancer? About how my father was? About how the Baudry was run? What might be sold off in my absence? What stolen? The Rembrandt landscape taken from the Montreal Museum of Fine Arts was still missing. Our own *Mistress and Maid* could disappear anytime and no amount of insurance money could replace it.

"Choices?" I asked. "I have to work, if I still have a job. Or I could quit, try to find another position, which is unlikely. There's younger and cheaper than me. Collect food stamps? Join the lady at the Seventy-Second Street subway?" Jeremy looked puzzled. "She's crazy. Homeless."

He tore a piece from the roll on his plate. He said the craziest thing of all was love and asked if that entered the picture.

"The man I lived with left me." I took another bite from the melon. It was cool and sweet but ended with an unexpected sharp bite and acrid aftertaste. "My personal life is hardly worth your time," I said, avoiding his gaze and flattening the napkin on my lap.

When I looked up, Jeremy was putting a small bit of bread in his mouth while still staring at me intently. "Worth my time?" His smile was thin and sardonic. I tried a different tack.

"You and Grace have been a great help." But Jeremy wouldn't

be put off.

"There's a choice you haven't mentioned." He pushed his egg around his plate without looking up and said, "You could stay."

"Here?"

He nodded to Dep. "You'll have another, won't you? Poached, they are rather easy on the insides. It's become somewhat of a morning ritual for Grace and me."

Dep went to the kitchen.

"Not stay with us necessarily. But in Kathmandu for a while." I asked what for. He shrugged. "For the sake of it." He thought there'd be some kind of work for me here. He and Grace had connections. "The museum here is in somewhat deplorable shape, despite Grace's enormous efforts." He reported that it was difficult to know the origin of most of the statuary, as they were catalogued only as "Shiva" or "Tara," without dates or provenance. He thought the collection a rather odd one, with its beautiful thangkas, Tibetan muskets with leather decorations, and a portrait of Prince Albert. "It is a collection in search of a curator," he concluded.

I said it was very sweet of him but it didn't make much sense. Dep was back with the eggs. Yellow eyes stared up at me from the tray. I took one.

"Pemba will be disappointed," Jeremy said matter-of-factly.

"Pemba?" I felt my chest tighten. "What has he got to do with it?"

Jeremy studied the eggs being offered and pointed to one without lifting his gaze from the tray. Dep skillfully slid it onto his plate.

"He was hoping to show you around, be of some help were you to stay longer." Had he seen and talked with him? "Kathmandu is not very big," he answered.

I asked Jeremy how well he knew Pemba.

"Well enough." He and Grace had met him four or five years ago when Pemba was about twenty. He couldn't recall where. Had it been at a lecture or some reception? He doubted it could have been the latter. "He's not invited to many. An intelligent man with too many interesting ideas." Jeremy described him as determined to make things better for his people, ready to make whatever sacrifice was necessary. His dedication was "unusual and not always welcome."

It seemed to me Jeremy knew him well. He poked at the yolk of his egg.

"As well as one can know anyone here. I run into him quite often, in the street, at the markets." He was hinting at something. I felt a kind of fear that a Bosch painting induces, turning me upside down into free fall. I looked toward the greenhouse, where a stampede of unfamiliar flowers pushed against one another to get at the sun. I wished someone else were with me, protection from whatever was coming.

"She never told me you see him."

"You have to understand, Grace is complicated. Rather like a cook who gives you the recipe with all but one ingredient. This time it's Pemba."

"You shouldn't be talking about him." Grace's voice was raised. Neither of us had noticed her arrival. She repeated herself while she flung a hand toward Dep, indicating he should leave. "You shouldn't be talking about him with her." She turned toward me. "Excuse Jeremy. We've had such little company of late that he's lost the art of meaningless conversation." Her hands, held stiffly by her side, had curled into fists. "What has he told you?"

"Nothing, really." My stomach began to churn and I felt I might have an accident. "I'm really not quite right," I said. Impatient, Grace turned to her husband.

"What did you tell her?" Jeremy stared intently at his wife, his cup in midair. He answered slowly and with emphasis.

"Only that we might help her if she decides to stay."

"Stay?" She turned to me in surprise. "There's nothing here for you."

The sharpness of her tone caught me unprepared. I felt breathless and dizzy. I pushed against the table to rise.

"Stay where you are," Grace commanded. "You've asked about Pemba more than once. Do you know why he hasn't visited?

Because he's been in jail. And he'd be there still if Jeremy hadn't bailed him out. Do you think that helps us here? Sympathizing with a protester?" She turned toward her husband. "What were you thinking, Jeremy? It will be in the newspapers." She turned back to me. "These so-called student protests that the newspaper describes. Students are involved, yes. But many, like Pemba, are not students. They are troublemakers. Socialists, Maoists, anarchists." She asked me if those were the people I wanted to befriend. In a strident voice she told me to go home before I got caught up in things I didn't know anything about.

In contrast, Jeremy spoke in a low, clear voice. "Pemba wants to change things and why shouldn't he?" He said he and Grace had seen enough poverty and illness, enough corruption and graft, to know things needed changing.

"You make him sound like a saint. The man is a murderer. He has plotted with Maoists. He has probably helped plan the murder of the landowners. He believes in violent overthrow." Grace was jabbing the table.

"Nonsense," Jeremy said calmly. "You believe everything you hear at embassy picnics."

Grace said Pemba was organizing peasants in the countryside while he was out on treks. That was the reason he'd taken the job. She told me he acted the willing guide when needed, but he was out there to stir up trouble. "You only see the side he wants to show you, my dear. Don't be fooled."

I asked Grace what she thought Pemba wanted from me. He hadn't touched me, I told her. Furthermore, it had never occurred to me that Pemba or anything in Nepal would be worth staying for. Even as I spoke, I pictured Pemba lying on the hospital floor. I felt him smiling. But I remembered how often he'd looked troubled and preoccupied. When he'd be vague about whereabouts, I felt I hadn't the right to pry.

"Grace, nothing's happened. I hardly know him."

Jeremy sipped his tea. "My wife suspects anyone who isn't royalty. She fears 'revolutionaries' will trample her flowers and make . . ."

Grace interrupted. "I'm more afraid of you trampling on our life. How will we continue to live here if it gets in the papers?"

Jeremy said he had merely suggested to the police that they'd be better off following Pemba than keeping him in jail.

"And what if he leads them here? He's not to come here. Do you hear me?" Jeremy suspected that Pemba had better things to do. Grace was adamant. "Whatever he does, I don't want it done around here."

Pemba was to give Big Foot my things. I told Grace she needn't worry. There was nothing I needed, and I wasn't expecting visitors.

"Given your choice of friends," she said, "I'd say it's a blessing. But, unfortunately, your Leon phoned to say he would be over after breakfast."

"So, where is Pemba?" I tried to appear casual, but Grace was irritated.

"Why do you still bother so about him? It's like asking the whereabouts of a wildflower. It grows where it will, not where you want." A servant appeared in the doorway. Grace nodded toward him. "I think Leon has come," she said.

I went into the garden and back to the chaise. Jeremy said he had to leave for work.

CHAPTER TWENTY-ONE
AN ARRIVAL

Grace seemed reluctant to leave after Leon arrived. She kept up a stream of nervous chatter about the building of their bungalow, the Hotel Bodnath's history, its guests, its bad restaurant. I knew it was Pemba's release that worried her and that she was staying for a reason. After a while, she asked casually if Leon had seen yesterday's newspaper. "Not even today's," he answered. Had he run into Pemba, by any chance? He had not. He'd eaten breakfast at the hotel and then come to see Hannah.

Relieved, she rattled on. "Have you had their *Chicken Gordon Blur*? If they can do that to the French language, Mr. Kaminsky, imagine what they've done to the chicken." The only place to eat, she said, was the Yak and Yeti, run by the Russian Boris Lissanevitch. Leon nodded patiently. "Boris is a remarkable man. Came here about the time we did. Arrested once on the king's orders. Some financial misunderstanding that landed him in trouble."

Grace described how Boris had been raised by a family that bred horses for the czar. He had fled the revolution to become a dancer in Diaghilev's Paris ballet company, later settling in Calcutta, where he had opened the 330 Club—the favorite of British governors and Indian rajas. When it was clear British rule was ending, he moved to Kathmandu, opened a brewery that failed. He was the first European ever to be jailed in Nepal. "You have to be careful to make the right friends here. They were able to get him out," she said.

Evidently, a criminal record hadn't prevented Boris from catering King Mahendra's coronation in 1955. Grace sat straighter when she described the event. "Fifty-seven cooks and one hundred and fifty trained servants from India. Six thousand live chickens and God knows how many guinea fowl. Even the ice had to be imported, tons of it." She turned toward Leon. "I could go on, Mr. Kaminsky, but you mentioned on the phone something important had come up." She asked if he was in any trouble. "You have to be careful what you say in public."

Leon confessed complete ignorance about the political situation in Nepal. He had not known there was rioting. No, he did not know where Pemba was. It was clear he wanted Grace to leave.

"The Bodnath's okay. Their scrambled eggs aren't bad," he noted laconically. He shifted uneasily in his chair and looked around. "It's like the Brooklyn Botanic here, only smaller." Grace acknowledged that she had never been to Brooklyn and wondered if she should pay it a visit.

"As soon as you can," Leon said, looking her straight in the face, a weight behind every word. There was a long, awkward silence.

"Manners are not your strong suit, Mr. Kaminsky," Grace said as she rose to leave.

Leon leaned toward me. "It's Mrs. K. She claims it's only about friendship, but to come all this way? Who's she kidding?" He went on to say she'd arrived two days ago; that Paul would be in for some surprise. Leon began to look out at the garden. "You don't think Grace is lurking behind those bushes, do you? She could ruin him."

"She doesn't care about Paul. Hasn't ever met him. She's worried about her own ruin now. What's her name?"

"Martha Klingman." Had I heard of the Klingman Pavilion at Presbyterian? That was her—her former husband, actually, who was rich as Croesus. Leon had told Martha about my being sick. She offered to make an appointment for me with her doctor when I got home.

I emptied my tea, grown old in its cup, onto the ground. I asked what she had offered to do for him. Leon blushed. "Nothing yet, but she told me the Pavilion walls were pretty bare."

"What does she want from you beside paintings?"

"Wait a minute!"

He put his hand on my arm, explaining that she was at the hotel desk when he went to see if they could store my things. They were taking up a lot of space in his room. She was ahead of him, inquiring if her room could be changed. Wanted something larger facing the pool. Couldn't believe they didn't have suites. Her outfit had New York written all over it, "designer stuff with names." She turned and excused herself for taking so long. Told him she'd come to meet a friend who hadn't arrived yet and she didn't know a thing about Kathmandu. Her travel agent had suggested the Bodnath, but she wondered if there was a better place.

"I told her the Bodnath was okay if you don't expect too much. Suggested she test out the bar. Over drinks, she told me her friend was Dr. Paul Levin, with the emphasis on *doctor*. Wanted to know all about him, but I didn't say much. I told her who I was and about you. She wants to meet you and anyone Paul knows."

I told him I had no wish to meet her and he should stay away from her himself. "This is a mess that only Paul can clean up," I stressed.

"I wouldn't say she's a mess. Pretty, lots of dark hair and . . ." He held his hands in front of his chest, palms upward, and shook them gently. He leaned back and smiled. "Don't go prude on me now. You might like her. She knows about art."

"The art of troublemaking."

But it was clear Leon was intrigued by her, explaining how Mrs. K was very understanding when, at breakfast, he told her she couldn't meet me until he'd asked me.

"Breakfast? And what did you do between breakfast and drinks last night?"

A quick dinner, a walk around town.

"What? You don't have a leg to stand on, Hannah. Choosing Grace." He leaned closer. "She has a crush on you, I think."

I turned away from him. "Don't say such things."

Leon put his hand on my forehead. I pushed it away. "I don't have a fever, damn it. Paul off where no one can reach him. You with Klingman. Grace here giving advice I don't ask for. And Pemba never shows his face."

"Ah, Pemba!" He leaned back so that the front legs of his chair were off the ground. "The boy's left us, or should I say, left you. Miss him, do you?" He stood up and began a slow circle around the pond examining the water lilies, hands behind his back. When he returned, he stood with the sun behind him. I had to shade my eyes to see his face.

"Tell her to go home," I said.

Leon shook his head. She wasn't going anywhere until she saw Paul, he said. Then he reiterated that all he wanted was to go home with me. "When you're better, we'll look around a bit and then fly back to where we belong."

"Going home together? To what? What is it you really want, Leon?"

He sat down. "What you don't, evidently. Do you ever?"

"Don't go there! I tried. Now you expect me to try again while you're hanging out with someone else?"

Leon insisted I was being ridiculous. I could have chosen "hanging out" with him at the hotel but didn't. I was with Grace. He insisted he had no interest in Martha. Besides, the woman was obsessed with Paul. He was all she could talk about. And if she liked his paintings and could be of help . . . hell yes, he would be nice to her. Besides, it wasn't that hard. He grasped my hand. "This isn't about her. It's about you and me. That night? I was trying to make things happen again for us—weren't you?"

"I don't know what I was doing. Pretending something was happening, maybe thinking it was."

My head hurt and the garden's perfume was cloying. In the sick room where my mother lay dying, the aides had sprayed air freshener to sweeten the smell of death. "She's looking better today," they'd say to me, smiling brightly, their hand on my head. I had wanted someone to either tell me the truth or leave me alone. I had the same feeling now. Could I trust what Leon was saying? How serious was he? Serious enough to marry me, to consider our having a child? And did I want us to reach that point? I wished I could talk to Pru or Pemba or ask Jeremy more questions.

Leon got up, looming over me like a dark cloud. "Hannah, I'll forget about this conversation. We'll talk when you're feeling better. You can't pick up people and put them down when it suits you."

"Isn't that what you did? Go away! Go be with her, get laid. You'll be doing yourself and Paul a favor."

I was bone-tired even though it was not yet noon. It was an effort to pour more tea and bring the cup to my lips. It was all so crazy. I felt unhinged myself. Leon hadn't moved. We stayed silent, each of us wanting something from the other, the assurance we wouldn't be left all alone. That we could still be loved even if we behaved badly. I stared at the bare clematis vine on the wall and wondered where Pemba was. Thinking you knew people and finding out you didn't. And when you discovered what you hadn't known, it made matters worse. Somewhere Paul was toiling up a mountain of worry, while Mrs. K sat by the pool and Miriam took care of Zoe. It seemed a vast game of hide-and-seek that never ended.

When I looked back, Leon was gone. Grace reappeared and asked what Leon had to say.

"Nothing, really." I said he'd run into someone who knew one of our trekkers.

Grace eyed me with suspicion. "That doesn't sound important."

"I don't know what's important anymore," I said.

CHAPTER TWENTY-TWO
AT NIGHT

I must have passed out. When I came to, it was dusk. Grace was placing a bowl of soup beside me. "That man exhausted you. You slept all afternoon. He called a little while ago wanting to speak with you. When I wouldn't wake you, he became as fierce as a thornbush and about as likeable, if you ask me."

"He wants to live with me."

"Men always want something, regardless of the consequences."

"What does Jeremy want?"

"He got what he wanted and I got a garden and charity work. Of course, the museum here is worth supporting and the Red Cross is very much needed, but was it a fair trade?" She shrugged. "I couldn't have a child here and he couldn't leave."

"One can have a child anywhere."

"But then you haven't, have you?"

"I could with Leon."

"Do you really think so? Of course, biologically it is doable, though a bit risky at your age. Do you really think Big Foot could tolerate a child for long? And could you? How can one be sure?"

I didn't want to argue. Maybe she was right. Perhaps I was more like Grace than I knew, distrusting motherhood.

Dinner brought Jeremy home. With him came talk of China's wish to build a highway into Nepal.

"And what will happen when Chinese tanks roll over it?" Grace asked.

Jeremy reminded her that the king had said if that happened he would inform the United States. We all laughed. "But the country does need a better infrastructure and they cannot afford it on their own," Jeremy added.

"What they can't afford is a Communist takeover," Grace insisted. Jeremy acknowledged that they would turn her garden into a cabbage patch. It went on like that, back and forth. I sat there, invisible.

Later I lay in the garden feeling, hoping maybe, the darkness would swallow me up. There was no moon. Thick clouds hid the stars and the air grew colder. I stared into the night for a long time. It was nearing dawn when I heard Pemba's voice close to me. "I'm sorry, Hannah," he murmured. Surprised, I instinctively reached out, grasping his arm before finding his hand.

"I didn't think you were ever coming."

He was a shadow, dark on dark. "Delayed."

"In jail."

He stretched out on the ground beside the cot. "There are things . . ."

I was fully awake, my heart beating fast. "What kind of things?"

"Best for both of us you not know."

My hand went to his face. Its pockmarked surface seemed like craters of the moon, distant and unsettling. "Who are you?" I peered down at him while my hand rested on his cheek.

He looked at me steadily though the cool graying light that precedes the sun. Then he got up and lay beside me on the cot. I could feel the warmth of his body, his breath on my face. I tried to move so as to give him room, but there was no place to go. We were squeezed together: I on my back, Pemba on his side facing me. He was so close that I could not fully look at him.

"You've helped me so much. Thank you," I whispered.

There was a long silence. I didn't know what more to say. It was easier in the hospital when there was no chance of his coming into my bed. All I was aware of now was how strange it was to have him beside me and yet how much I wanted him to stay.

"When sick needed me. Now maybe not want me."

"Is it any clearer for you?"

"Yes," he said simply. "I want be with you, but things . . ."

I grasped his hand and gazed at a wisp of cloud suspended in the morning light. "If you have a wife or a girlfriend, tell me now."

"Why you mock me, Hannah?"

I struggled to sit up. "It's been known to happen."

He grabbed my arm and pulled me toward him. "I not like others. I want be with you." The force he exerted frightened me. There was steeliness in his voice that was new. He held on to my arm. I tried to wrench it free.

"What does that mean? Sleep with me?"

"Yes, sleep with you, talk with you, eat with you, walk with you." I asked for how long.

"For as long as it good." I asked again how long that would be. He smiled without answering. I asked why me. Said he hardly knew me.

"Why flower want sun? To grow, to live. You kind, gentle, good. We make world larger for each other. We different, but see world same. Have same sorrows. Same wish be happy with someone." He said he understood how I was afraid to love him, to live far away from friends, in a strange country.

"Lie down, so we talk," he whispered.

I did, stiff and unmoving, staring straight into the lightening sky.

"What do you do when you're not with me?"

"I do things you not like." He sought my hand.

"Things others don't like?"

He was silent.

"Violent things? Things that could jail you, kill you?" No answer. "I can't be with someone who has secrets."

"All have secrets. If I tell you, might be trouble for you. For me, if you tell someone."

"Do you kill people?"

Silence, then "People die in revolution."

"Does Jeremy know what you do? He agrees with you, doesn't he? Grace was right. You go on treks to organize peasants, to stir up revolt."

"People poor, often sick. Not enough to eat. Babies die."

"Those police who were killed also died."

"Everyone die."

"But not everyone is killed. Some of them, I'm sure, had wives and children, and parents."

"And we the same. Our people killed by corrupt system."

"You can't justify—"

"Not to you, Hannah. Woman from a different place."

"What does that mean? Killing is killing."

"To kill system, need kill people sometimes. People are system."

"There are other ways, public pressure, strikes, voting."

"Not enough. Government strong and rich, peasants weak and poor. In Nepal, we tie up buffalo, tiger come to eat, then rich tourists shoot it. Money buy power. People have no money. Are like animals to sacrifice. We have to use what can."

"Terror."

"You not know terror of poverty, be hungry, no have work, be invisible. They not see us as men. Only work animals to sacrifice, breed for profit and beat so we obey." His hands were fists; his dark eyes menacing. "You have same. Negroes without future. Poor whites without work. People use drugs. It easy. Changing things hard.

"You're a Maoist."

"I am a man."

"A Maoist man."

"If you like. But you not like."

"Could you kill me?"

"You afraid of me?"

"Could you?"

"Never."

"But what if I told you I was going to report you. What would you do then?"

"Why you torture me with questions? It is you who kill. Kill what possible. Kill life. You like this beautiful garden where things grow, but nothing happen. Leave that. I take care of you. You get better quicker." I pointed to the flowers brightening with the first light and told him that beauty happened here. Things grew and blossomed. Didn't he see it?

"I see lot of money wasted. These plants not feed people. Only beautiful if people not hungry." I turned away and told him I couldn't go anywhere with him if he was still doing those things.

"Then stay here." He got up. The shadows cast by the mountains were retreating as the sun rose.

"You're so very young," I said. He smiled.

"And you already too old." I reached for his hand. "Maybe so, but I don't think I can do it. Will you come back anyway?" He bent down and kissed me, a kiss that would linger on my lips all morning.

"Tonight," he said, and left before the Butlers awoke.

Breakfast was a confusing affair. Jeremy looked like the Cheshire cat while Grace seemed fidgety and upset. "You've a bit of color this morning. Feeling better?" Jeremy asked, smiling over his breakfast plate.

"I think so," I said, helping myself to the poached eggs that Dep offered.

Grace asked if I had been woken in the night. Reaching for a roll, I said I hadn't.

"Someone or something seems to have stepped on my viburnum plicatum. You didn't hear anything?"

"I slept soundly for a change."

"Strange." She eyed me suspiciously. "I will speak to the servants. Not that they ever admit to anything."

"I'm always careful where I step," I protested.

"I'm sure you are," Jeremy interrupted. "No real harm done. Grace can fix anything. You're an example. Much better already. Feel up for a short walk? First venture out?"

I agreed, saved from Grace's suspicions.

"Good," said Jeremy, slapping his knee. He went to fetch a

walking stick. We went slowly, Jeremy using the stick while I took his arm. The sun was out now, the hills were green. There was the sound of a stream nearby and the short calls of tree pipits.

"Beautiful, isn't it?" Jeremy said, breathing in the cool, clean air. "It's why I can't leave." I asked if there were other things that kept him in Nepal. He gestured toward the mountains. "Not reason enough? Of course," he added, "there have been roots set down, connections made. Not time enough to start over now." I stopped and faced him. "Revolutionary roots?"

He turned to face me. "You mean Pemba? Yes, we see things the same way. I have tried to help him when I could. Grace knows about it. A dangerous family secret, if you will. She has tried more than once to break the bond. Believe it or not, her political views, expressed so often, are a combination of her convictions and her love for me."

"You know he came last night."

"He told me he would try. I marked the wall where it was best to climb. Grace suspects, but it's safer to blame Dep for the viburnum."

I asked if he knew exactly what Pemba had done.

"I have a good idea and so does Grace, but we say nothing to anyone. Grace tells me not to see him and doesn't want to hear about him. Afraid we will all get in real trouble. In Nepal, it is better not to know too much."

I asked if it bothered him, what Pemba did.

"Of course it does. But when you have lived in this country and seen the violence done to the people day in and day out, while the king sits on a golden throne, so to speak, it becomes more understandable."

"But innocent people."

"No one is innocent. We are all implicated. Doing nothing is a form of violence. But he does not expect you to be involved. For reasons I can quite understand, he has fallen for you. Something he hardly wanted. It does complicate things, but when is love simple?"

"He is so young."

"Living here ages you quickly."

I said it couldn't last.

"That means you have considered it?"

"Not really."

He smiled. "I see—like a painting in a museum that, for a moment, you consider stealing, but decide it's not worth the consequences."

I told him I did not want to own anyone or anything.

"But you told me about your tulips. Not one, but two paintings you own. So much of nature comes in pairs."

"You think I should stay, don't you?"

"It would make Pemba very happy. And you might be too."

I asked him what he thought I had to offer.

"That you don't know is your problem, always has been, I suspect." He added that Pemba was going to Pokhara in a few days. If I felt strong enough, I could see that part of Nepal.

We turned back and walked in silence, Jeremy shading his eyes to catch the flight of a bird. I told him Pemba planned to come again that night.

"I'll tell him to watch where he walks."

The next day Grace had no complaints. Pemba came over the wall where there were no clematis vines or night-blooming jasmine in the way. A cloudless night and a waxing moon made him more visible.

"Hello." He bent and kissed my forehead.

"Hello, yourself." I got up from the cot and put my hand on his cheek. He kissed me again.

"You're going to Pokhara."

"Thursday."

"To organize a demonstration."

He shrugged. "See friends."

"Comrades."

"If you like better." He took me in his arms.

"I don't like. But I do like you, though it's crazy."

"Never crazy to love."

I said that was not my experience and asked him if he had loved someone before.

He nodded. I asked what had happened. She had married someone else.

"And you?"

"Sad, but no sorry."

"I'm always sorry."

He asked me to come with him, that we would go slowly. He would tell me about his country as we went.

"But maybe I won't sleep with you."

He shrugged again, looking straight into my eyes. "Be sorry, but not sad. We together." My lips ran over his cheeks and found his lips, rougher and less pliant than I was used to. Only his tongue in my mouth was soft, as were the two words that followed. "Trust, Hannah."

CHAPTER TWENTY-THREE
SAYING NO

Leon came early the next day while we were finishing breakfast. He sat down uninvited and signaled Dep by bringing an imaginary cup to his lips.

"I think our guest would like coffee," Grace said.

"Black, please."

"He doesn't trust milk," I explained.

"He shouldn't. Brucellosis is common enough."

"Grace insists on powdered milk and filtered boiled water," Jeremy interjected.

"Any eggs left?" Leon asked, eyeing my plate.

"Dep!" Jeremy ordered, and eggs were brought.

Having gulped down his breakfast and drained his cup, Leon sat back and began. In six days everyone would be back. They would fly from Lukla as we had. He hoped they wouldn't have to wait for a flight. It would eat into the time they'd planned to rest up and tour the Kathmandu Valley. Leon went on to say that Martha seemed confused by the trail maps he showed her. She didn't understand why they wanted to trek. Not big on outdoor exercise.

"More the spa type. Can't get the hang of this place."

"There's not much hang to get," Grace said. "And that's from someone who has been here for years."

"I don't believe that," I said, thinking of what I'd already learned about Nepal from Pemba.

"Believe what you like," Grace replied, turning toward Leon. "Mr. Kaminsky, what *is* your friend doing with herself?" That was the problem, Leon said. He described her as "a dependent type," always asking him to take her places: to the temples, the outdoor markets and restaurants she'd been told about. She didn't like eating alone so she didn't mind paying. Sensing my discomfort, he turned his attention to me, put his hand on mine and asked if I was feeling better. I described briefly the walk I'd taken with Jeremy the morning before.

"I'm surprised you didn't run into their pesky, roving cows," Grace said.

"Nothing's sacred with Grace unless she's planted it," Jeremy said, raising his cup toward her.

"But you can't predict what nature will do, can you?" Leon said, tilting back in his chair.

"What is predictable, Mr. Kaminsky, is that you are about to break my dining room chair."

Leon swung forward. "Sorry. I guess I've been living alone too long."

"From what I can see, you are likely to continue that way."

"Unless Hannah agrees."

Grace said she knew he wanted to live with me, but hadn't he tried that already? He answered that people, like plants, needed time to grow. "Only in the right climate," Grace retorted.

Leon said he could make things warm enough. He gave Grace a broad, charming smile and asked, "Why don't you like me, Mrs. B?"

"Because you are likely to break not only my chair, but also a woman's heart." Leon thought I could take care of myself. "Can she? How has she done so far?"

Jeremy tried in vain to steer us to another topic. "Trouble still with the viburnum, dear? Or is it the unrest in the city?" Jeremy patted my hand. "She's like this when there's a cloud over Eden."

But Grace was a dog with a bone. She insisted she just wanted to help me make the right choice. It would be terrible to be stuck in something one can't easily get out of. And a baby would only make it worse.

"Who's talking babies?" Leon asked. "We aren't even together yet. And if she wants a baby, as long as it's mine."

"Possession is not the same as loving a child," Grace replied.

I stood up. "Listen to yourselves! Talking as though I weren't here."

I excused myself and I headed toward the garden. Leon followed me.

"You have to leave," he whispered. He had checked with the hotel, but it was fully booked. There might have been a room if Martha hadn't taken two rooms next to one another on the second floor. She slept in one and sat in the other, where, at her request, the bed was replaced with a comfortable chair and reading lamp from the lobby. And she didn't like having to go up and down stairs.

"If she stays long enough, she's likely to donate money for an elevator."

"Martha?" I stared at him.

"What do you want me to call her? I can't call her Mrs. Klingman all day."

"Why not?"

He told me I was as crazy as Grace. Of course they were on a first-name basis. Didn't I understand they were both waiting? He took me into his arms. "She for Paul, me for you. Okay?"

"Would you want a baby?" I asked.

"What's all this about babies?"

"Would you?"

"As long as we don't have to move. I like my place. You did too. Is it a baby you want?"

I said I didn't know.

"Then why are you asking?"

"Just in case."

He said he didn't want to be an "in case" husband or father. "You've got to want *me.*"

"Grace never had a child and it's made her bitter."

"That's not an answer and besides, she couldn't have handled one."

"How do you know?"

He said he had been with enough women to know. She was like Martha. They liked to be in control. And kids get out of control. But, in the end, Martha would probably have one because it was expected of her. "Just pray it isn't Paul's."

"Why do you want to be with me?"

"Again? You ask me again? Because of *love.*" Did I know what that was? Because he'd never met anyone as interesting and intelligent as me. Because I understood what he was trying to do in painting. He put his hands on my ass. "Because you can be so loving when you want to."

I stepped back. "I don't want to."

"When you're better."

I said I didn't know what I'd want then.

"You've never known what you wanted."

I told him that wasn't true; that I had been in love with him.

Leon looked skeptical. He wondered whether I'd loved *him* or the man she hoped to make loveable.

"Make better. That's what lovers do for one another," I said.

Hadn't their night at the Bodnath proved just that? Leon asked. That they could be better to and for one another?

"One night tells you that?" I shook my head in wonderment.

"It's not one night. It's remembering all the good nights and wanting them back again."

"The Bodnath hasn't worked for me the way it did for you."

"Come stay with me at the hotel. Maybe a bigger room will open up." He suddenly kissed me, opening his mouth for my tongue. I didn't give it to him. "Come on. It could be good again."

"With Martha down the hall?"

He pulled back. "She's on *your* mind, not mine."

She wasn't really, not that much. It was Pemba I'd been thinking of.

"I'm sorry." I put my hand on his chest. "I just don't trust men anymore. Not since Frank."

"What made you think you could trust him in the first place?"

"I thought I knew him."

"But you didn't. And I don't think you know me."

I agreed, saying I was good at judging paintings only because they stayed the same. "I did have an idea of how you should be. Now I've no idea," I said.

"We can find out together."

I said I didn't want to take the chance.

CHAPTER TWENTY-FOUR
POKHARA

But then why did I take the chance with Pemba two days later? Not telling Grace, not even leaving a note for Leon. Just going before I changed my mind. I later learned that when Grace found I'd left, she was furious, while Jeremy pretended to be mystified. Leon checked other hotels, then went to the Sherpa cooperative, where he found that "Miss Avery has scheduled a solo trek around Pokhara with Pemba Golu as guide."

It was a short flight to Pokhara. One of Pemba's friends met us at the airport with his motorbike. He insisted we have it while we were in Pokhara. He would take the bus back to town. Pemba rode me to Baidam, on the southeastern shore of Lake Phewa, where another friend owned a small guesthouse. Baidam, the starting point of the Pokhara-Jomsom trek, contained an endless array of lakefront lodgings, cheek to jowl with bars, restaurants, souvenir stalls and shops filled with travel guides and hiking equipment. I was surprised to find the town bursting with boisterous college students starting on a trail that for centuries had quietly moved people and goods between Pokhara and Tibet. Rice, sugar and kerosene had been hauled over the mountains to be exchanged for Tibetan wool and salt. Nepalese tour guides were now trading the beauty of their country for money.

We bought samosas and drank tea where a reflection of snow-covered Machhapuchare rippled in the green water. We visited Tal Barahi, a simple two-story pagoda in the middle of the lake, dedicated to the Hindu goddess Durga. Praying there helps ensure a happy conjugal life, Pemba told me. Worshippers, both Hindu and Buddhist, released their gift of doves. White wings, nature's prayer flags, fluttered about in the temple and crowded the sky, making it seem like whole island might take flight.

We sat by the water while Pemba told me, "People believe Vishnu come some day. Put end to no justice. People will tell only truth, will not pray for more money. Women be equal to man. Maybe that time soon. Not from Vishnu but from change in who rules country."

I didn't argue. I envied that he could believe in any solution for mankind. And I loved him for trying, even if his way was dangerous and misguided. And I couldn't forget how I felt on a moonlight boat ride we'd taken the night before, when we heard the rustle of monkeys in the trees and the hoot of a brown fish owl as we snuggled in a chill wind.

Pemba made sure to show me a crowded camp where some of Tibetan's twenty thousand refugees lived. They had fled to Nepal when their country was "liberated" by China in 1958. Vacant-eyed women and scrawny children sat in a large shed making trinkets and weaving shawls while dispirited fathers carved trumpeting elephants and enlightened Buddhas.

"No one want them. Have no rights in Nepal. Cannot own house or business or even to work. Only this government-controlled workhouse," Pemba said.

It made me sad for all of us—Pemba, me, these Tibetans—longing for a better tomorrow. Only Pemba had an idea of how that could come about. I bought as much as I could from the refugees, things that were light and easy to carry. Shawls for Pru and Libby, a small Buddha for Harrington that I knew he would stick in a drawer.

When we began to walk into the mountains, it was "teahouse trekking." We walked only a mile or so each day and stopped often at food stalls and small cafés that dotted the landscape. Pemba carried everything. The trail toward Jomsom was a living thing, filled with animals, trekkers and locals. Herds of goats descended upon us, guided by their owners wielding long staves. The animals' long hair had been colored fuchsia or ocher, branding and decorating them at the same time. More than once, huge black bullocks edged us to the side of the trail. Their massive bodies, their wild eyes and dangerous horns frightened me. Pemba told me how farmers tied them up so as to poke a sharpened stick through their nostrils.

"Make hole. Put iron ring there," he explained. "Our people like angry animals also led around." He made a ring of thumb and forefinger and held it to his nose.

The more we walked, the more I understood Pemba's politics. He read me the government's lies about how quickly things were improving: increased foreign investment, better health care. But

I saw with my own eyes how hard people struggled to keep themselves alive, how little they could count on government help, how many infants died, how many old had no teeth, how many young bones were bent. We never got very far, stopped by too many funerals and a few weddings. Villagers would flock around Pemba, touching him, asking favors of him, offering him food, giving him small presents that he passed on to others.

We spent a few nights in the huts of his friends. Slept on their earthen floors, inhaled the smoke from their fires. Pemba brought them food and gave them money. He had packed medicines they needed and vitamins for when they hadn't enough to eat. I contributed all the money I'd brought. It felt good to be of some use, but I also found it hard, all of it—the ground we slept on, the climbs and steep descents, the different kinds of food, the daily confrontation with poverty and need, the strain on my muscles and mind. It was the life Pemba lived and wanted me to understand and join.

Pemba sensed my physical discomfort. In the larger villages, he insisted we stay at inns instead of camping. My stomach could manage the modest dinners of dal bhat or cabbage-stuffed potato pancake. It felt good have an appetite and bad to satisfy it.

"I feel guilty eating," I told Pemba, "when others don't have enough."

Pemba smiled. "You get better, then you make others better. Just make today good," he said, taking my plate to wash it.

He seemed to always know what I needed, the kind of tea that would make me stronger, another that could help me sleep, the spices in dal that I could tolerate. I would be lulled to sleep by the voices of the innkeeper and Pemba talking quietly over mugs of chaang, a home-brewed beer made from fermented barley or rice. I never asked what the conversations were about, but the next morning Pemba would give what I suspected was an edited report of what was going on in the village.

He was talkative on the trail, and I realized how much freer he seemed than when he trekked with our group. He told me about the lives of his friends, like Dharma Ratna Yami in Kathmandu. Yami had come from a rich family whose lands had been taken from them by the ruling Rana family before they were overthrown in

1951. He became a rebel, not to recover his family's property but to help all who were deprived of land and rights. Yami wanted to overthrow the government by any means and he wasn't shy about it. He spoke out against government corruption and the caste system. He hired an untouchable to be his cook. His subversive activities led to years in prison. Yet Yami also later served in the cabinet at the insistence of the king, who had hoped to appease revolutionaries by this appointment. It hadn't worked. Yami's recommendations as minister were ignored. Violent demonstrations continued, and left-wing political parties were ultimately banned.

Pemba told me who lived in the villages we visited and what they did. He introduced me to the man with a sewing machine in one village, to a mother who carried rocks to Pokhara, where gravel was made. He told me about the Brahmin widow who refused to be seen in public. He loved recounting the fables he'd learned as a child.

"Was a king mouse. He want daughter to marry most powerful man in universe. So he go to Sun god and ask him to marry daughter. Sun god flattered but admit he not most powerful. 'Cloud come between the earth and me,' say Sun god. 'Nothing I can do. He more powerful.'

"So Mouse-king go to Cloud with daughter. 'But I not most powerful,' Cloud say. Wind blow me where he want.'

"So Mouse-king go to Wind, and daughter go too. 'But I do nothing against Mountain,' Wind say. 'He blunt my force. Nothing shake him.' So Mouse-king say to great Mountain, 'You most powerful. Take daughter.' Mountain say, 'She very beautiful. Is true I can stop Wind, but can do nothing against you. Mouse dig holes in my side, bring in air and slowly make me weak. Bring me down.'

"So Mouse-king learn about own strength and marry daughter to one in own village. Fairy tale good for children. Children feel weak, but can be strong. We tell them we all mouse—can bring down Mountain of the rich and make all equal."

"I'd be that mouse, undermining you," I told Pemba. "I can live the way you do now, for a week or so, but not more. I couldn't keep up. And then you would be away a lot on your own. I'd be alone and always afraid for you."

"Are who you are. That enough." He kissed me.

There were only kisses in the beginning. Pemba was careful, offering a hug at night, a hand to help me in the morning. I snuggled closer to him after we'd zipped our sleeping bags together. He responded gently, at first rubbing my back and legs through my pajamas. "Silk?" he asked.

"Rayon, I'm afraid."

I found myself wishing that his hands were firmer, stayed longer. I turned on my back and put his hand on my breast. I felt his hands run over by body while he kissed me, first lips, then cheek and neck. Then he stopped, looked into my eyes and said, "Later."

"Why not now?" I asked.

"Good things come slow," he answered, rolling over with his back to me.

What was slow were the passing hours. I turned one way and the other, sat up, then lay down again. Wanted to wake him but didn't. The next morning, he brought tea to our tent. Neither of us spoke much.

When we had finished, he began to undress me—first my top, his hardened fingers playing with nipples that swelled to his touch, then my pajama bottoms, sliding them down and spreading my legs.

"Don't keep me waiting again." I whispered, clinging to him.

"No. No cook curry two times. Once increase appetite."

"It's mean."

"Sorry. I make it nice now."

I quivered as he found where I was most responsive. His penis was hooded and unfamiliar to me. The skin was soft and easily pulled back. Then the careful entry, the first long, slow thrusts, so tender, so vivid, familiar, yet so new. His cheek hard against mine, then the rough lips on my neck and breast while the muscles of his back, under my hands, seemed like tumbling rocks that could bury me. It was missionary all the way. No tossing one another about, like with Leon, no finger up my ass like Frank, just the on-going movement toward unbearable desire and release. Neither of us spoke, each focusing on the steady rhythms of love.

That day, neither of us mentioned what had happened. Just repeated it with more variation and more ardor that evening. And to my surprise, there was nothing about it I wanted to discuss. We journeyed on, the sun hot by noon. Often we sought shade at midday and, despite the heat, lay in each other's arms. I hadn't had a period since I'd been ill and was thankful for that. So it surprised me when I began to bleed. Not very much, but enough.

"How you feel?" Pemba asked.

"Okay. Just some discomfort."

"A woman's blessing."

"We call it *the curse.*"

"In tree, sap run so fruit can grow."

"It's not at all the same. Trees don't need tampons."

The blood seemed not to bother him as it does some men. He said that putting women away during their menses was backward and unkind. Women who were isolated had died when they fell ill in the huts or when temperatures dropped to freezing. Or maybe they'd just died of the shame that they were supposed to feel. He was just as eager to be with me as ever, but gentler. He said he liked the smell "of life" and proceeded to paint our faces with my blood.

"Stop it!" I cried. I'd never liked blood, my own or anyone else's. Even the drops on Christ's body in the paintings of Giotto made me uneasy.

He said it was only nature. I rubbed the blood from my face and told him nature wasn't always pretty. He said I was.

We climbed hills, crossed streams, stopped at teahouses where people knew him. Sometimes, in a village, he would ask me to wait for him by a wall or under a tree. He had "things" to do.

"How long will you be?"

"As long as takes."

"But how long?"

He'd shrug. "If not back, someone come for you."

He always returned. Sometimes in an hour; sometimes half a day. In one village, Pemba's friends showed me how they allowed a calf to nurse and then pulled it from its mother's udder so they could collect the milk for themselves. In another, I spent the morning watching villagers at a water tap. Men came to wash, stripping off their shirts, rubbing their arms and legs and dipping their heads under the tap. Women came to scrub metal pots, chattering to one another as they worked. Children filled plastic jugs to lug home. I was beyond their pale, a figure in the shadows of their lives. I had a hard time imagining them with guns, ready for revolution. What did Pemba say to them? Had any of them killed or set fires?

Pemba's absences also gave me time to remember. It was odd, the more we walked away from my life, the more it seemed to return when Pemba left me. Sudden unbidden images of life back home: grilled cheese sandwiches on a green plate at Miriam's, the taste of cherry cheesecake that I treated myself to at Tip Toe Inn, the weary line at Zabar's on Sunday mornings, walking along Riverside Drive to Grant's Tomb when the sun shone on the Hudson. Frank, flabby and naked with a small eager prick. Leon's paintings under the bed; the broken cups he kept. Mother, broken by cancer, kept around too long; her face as white as the restaurant-supply dishes Leon hated so much. Plates thrown in the garbage. I retrieved them, left his apartment with them, and use them still. These memories faded like negatives exposed to bright light when Pemba returned.

Pemba's presence seemed the medicine I needed. He appeared unafraid of death, his own or anyone's. He'd seen plenty of it, much more than I, and yet he was not diminished by it. Willing to kill, even. He wasn't hard or cruel, just matter-of-fact about what eventually happens to all of us and what needed to happen sooner to some. It was the death of children that affected him most, murdered by TB, cholera or Japanese encephalitis. He struck back with the only force he thought effective.

"Was anyone hurt?" I would ask when Pemba returned.

Silence.

"I feel like a Mafia wife."

"What is Mafia?"

So I had to explain it. In the end, he thought it the result of capitalism.

"It's not just about capitalism. It's the ugly part of human nature. Our greed, the desire for power, our built-in aggression. Freud and the death instinct."

"What is Freud?"

Another hundred yards of explanation that left me winded and worried. What was I doing with him? He was a youth, only a decade older than Bobby. Like Miriam's boy, he understood nothing of the world. He was crazy with his talk of revolution, and in the end he would be killed, maybe with good reason. But he was also gentle and kind and loved me. When I asked him why, he said, "You bring different view of world. That what lovers do."

But I countered that lovers needed to share as well. I asked what world we shared.

"Bodies, feelings, stories tell each other." When I wondered if that were enough, Pemba looked puzzled. "What else to want?"

"A common culture, a common vocabulary, having childhoods we can imagine."

"We both know loss," he said.

But our losses had been very different. He had told me of carrying his mother back to the village after she died.

"My mother didn't want to be touched."

He nodded. "Both still gone."

"I'm more like her than I knew."

He said that all children start by copying their parents, then begin to change into themselves. I told him he didn't know anything about how or where I had grown up.

"I see you in tall building. Many neighbors. All together. Walk on cement to get to school, like in Moscow."

"But it wasn't at all like that! I lived in the suburbs, in a house. We didn't know our neighbors except to say hello. When they heard my mother was dying, they left casseroles on the doorstep for a couple of weeks."

"What is casserole?"

"That's exactly what I mean!"

He laughed and took me in his arms. "You tell me about casserole. I tell you about kukri." He whispered in my ear, "Kukri always find sheath to fit." He squeezed my hand as we began walking.

"There is story about Uttis Tree almost not marry beautiful Rhododendron. Proud Uttis Tree fall in love with Rhododendron when first meet her. Ask her marry him. But then not want her when meet again. She change, not flower like he remember. She say, 'You imagine you know me. Have to marry what not know too.' He agree."

In my mind's eye, I saw the stretch of rhododendron forest we'd passed through, a forest that had finished blossoming months before. I thought of George, always eager for a new flower; of Pru, hardened over time. I thought of the choices we make and how they shape us.

I wondered how I would live in Kathmandu. In what kind of house? Maybe just some rooms, maybe only one. How much would my savings translate into if I stayed? What would happen when that money ran out? Pemba didn't make anything to speak of and didn't care to. Maybe that would change, but I doubted it. Organizing in the city would be more dangerous, and I couldn't live in a village with a community tap. If a bomb went off, if police were killed, how could I bear it? Even if Pemba had told me it wasn't him, could I believe him? Even if he weren't responsible, maybe his friend was. I would always be afraid of a terrorist attack, not as a victim, but as one who knew the perpetrators. Could I live with that, even if the cause seemed right? What if Pemba were killed or both of us ended up in jail for a long time?

Jeremy had talked of a job at the museum, but museums seemed like musty places now. And what would I be going back home to—the Baudry and Harrington? To lonely tulips on an apartment wall. I might carry a sign again in antiwar marches through Central Park, but never dare arrest. I would undoubtedly run into Frank sometime. There was no way I would live with Leon, not for a while, if ever. We'd probably settle for what we could have: dinners out, visiting galleries, gossip over drinks, and sex sometimes, that naked attempt to make us feel a little more alive.

After a while, Leon would meet another art student to help fight the holocaust within him. I wouldn't find anyone else. Men my age with their complicated histories wouldn't appeal to me and younger ones without them wouldn't resemble Pemba. I didn't have the courage to think of women.

"Uttis Tree was brave," I told Pemba. "He was taking on a strong woman."

"Need be brave to learn. And learn by love," Pemba replied.

Because people loved Pemba, they took me into their homes, showed me how to heat fresh milk until the liquid evaporated, then add flour to make a dough. They taught me to shape the dough into small round balls, fry them and then roll them in a hot sugar syrup. When I made Pemba taste what I'd made, he said, "Good! But can't eat it all day."

I laughed and told him he was afraid of becoming bourgeois, that it was his secret wish. He smiled and kissed me. He said there was not enough *lalmohan* in all Nepal to change him. He taught me to make a delicious vegetable curry instead. "Better for you," he said. It is one I still serve.

"You are so strict with yourself sometimes," I said one night. "It takes the fun out of baking." He disagreed. Baking was good. Good for me, good for guests. He liked sweet things too. But I needed to remember that many people here had no money for sugar. I sighed and told him that, of course, he was right. But his politics didn't make for fun parties.

"We have party after we win."

I said I hoped it was soon. "What should we do until then?" I asked, knowing he'd have an answer in mind.

I unbuckled his jeans as his cock rose to greet me. I took the sweet tulip in my mouth. He took my head in his hands, sometime guiding, sometimes being guided toward the music of moans and sudden gasps. I loved his fullness in my mouth, the warmth of it, the possession of it. His control amazed me, even when I was at my best. After a while, he lifted my head and looked into my eyes.

"Now me." He took his time between my legs, exciting me and urging me toward him. He kissed me and I felt him enter me.

I warned him to be careful, now that I'd had a period. It's that kind of talk that turns men off. But I couldn't help it. I had always been a worrier. He said they didn't sell condoms in the mountains and asked if I wanted to stop our lovemaking.

"No. No. Just withdraw at the right time?" He asked when that was. "When you feel you are about to spill."

"That right time?" he protested. "That worst time."

"Just do it for me."

He tried, but it takes practice. Sometimes he was too late. Sometimes, too early and he had to use his fingers or tongue to help me. After seven days we had to turn back toward Pokhara. Pemba had a trek scheduled. And I had to face my friends. I knew they all would be back in Kathmandu when we got there. I dreaded having to deal with Leon or explain to Grace. I wondered how Bobby had fared. As we got closer to returning, our lovemaking grew more intense and more frequent. We clung to one another in smoky rooms at night, in the mornings in fields, under trees whose shadows deepened with the setting sun. There was no talk of a future, only the intense feeling of now. And there were times I held him tight, knowing I shouldn't, when he tried to pull out.

CHAPTER TWENTY-FIVE
FRIENDS AGAIN

We got a ride with one of Pemba's friends as far as Patna and took a bus from there. It coughed us up in front of the Bodnath at dinnertime. Pemba glanced at his Russian-made watch. "Have to leave." He gave me a quick kiss and handed me my backpack. I pulled him toward me, not caring for the moment who saw us.

"Where are you going? We just got here."

He shrugged. "Things."

I was angry that he should expect me to face everyone alone. "What should I tell them about our trip?" I asked.

"Truth."

"That we were lovers but now you have other things to do?" I let go of him. He handed me his handkerchief as I began to cry.

"Some things more important than us," he said softly, and began to turn away.

"When will I see you?" I said, following him across the lobby.

"Soon," he whispered, and disappeared though the hotel doors. The overstuffed chairs in the lobby sat like disapproving dowagers waiting too long for their tea. The pool, emptied of water, was an open grave. I made my way to the desk, my clothes dusty, hair a mess. I explained that I was part of the Albright party that had already arrived, and asked for a room.

The clerk eyed me suspiciously. "Your name?" I told him. He studied a list in front of him. "Were you expected?"

"I hope so." He smiled in that conciliatory way desk clerks do when delivering bad news. "I'm afraid we are fully engaged. Perhaps the Hotel Annapurna on Kirtipur Road?"

I said I needed to speak with Dr. Albright and asked his whereabouts.

"In the dining room, I believe." He looked me over. "But we do not allow shorts at dinnertime. Perhaps you'd like to come back later or I can take a message."

Then Bobby spotted me as he was bounding down the hotel

stairs. "Hannah!" he yelled at the top of his voice. "Hannah!" he screamed again, running toward me full tilt. He almost knocked me down with his embrace. "Hannah!" again. "Where have you been?"

"Trekking like you."

"Leon told us. But where?"

"Later. Tell me about yourself. How was it?"

Bobby looked at his feet and then into my eyes. "Sometimes you dream a really big dream and you don't ever want to wake up. It was like that."

He told me they'd reached Gokyo. There was nothing there, just the name and a few empty huts. George and he had gotten to the ridge above. "Over seventeen thousand feet high, Hannah. Way taller then the Empire State Building."

He stood on tiptoe and raised his hands above his head. The others had stayed in Gokyo, too tired to make the last ascent. George hadn't been sure he wanted Bobby to go with him because the climb was so hard. They'd have to stop every few yards to catch their breath. But Paul said it was okay.

"Hoping I'd fall off a cliff, I think, but I didn't. I'm back, Hannah." He turned in a circle.

"So I see."

"But I'm not waking up," he whispered. And then, over his shoulder, I saw them all standing at the restaurant door. There was a rush across the tiled floor, fingers touching me—my face, back, hair—while my arms were pinned by George's hug. I was propelled toward the restaurant by hands that pulled and shoved, by a cacophony of cheers and questions and exclamations about my weight and my looks. They drowned out the protests of the desk clerk. Chairs scraping, waiters summoned. Everyone asking questions at the same time. How was I feeling? Where had I been? Where was Pemba?

"Get her a drink!" Libby insisted as she squeezed herself beside me. She studied the cocktail menu as though she hadn't already seen it.

George stood up at the end of the table. "Hannah, we're glad to see you."

His tone was warm and generous. He knew there would be a lot of questions, but he thought we should order first and then talk. Libby chose a chicken dish and martinis for both of us. She motioned to Howard to hand her the one she was already working on.

It was then I noticed a woman in a peach tracksuit on the other side of Paul. She looked as uncomfortable as one of the chairs in the lobby. She gave an awkward little wave, then leaned in front of Paul.

"Heard so much about you. And here you are, at last. I'm Martha Klingman, Paul's friend." She held out her hand. There was nothing to do but take it.

"Only good things, I hope," I replied. Leon, sitting across from her, was staring into space. Paul was leaning back, looking glum.

"Of course." Martha's smile was as bright as stainless steel.

As soon as menus were put down, George began. "Hannah, tell us about it."

Everyone leaned toward me. Pemba had said to tell the truth. The thought made me anxious. It seemed like the time in grade school when I was supposed to recite a poem. The best orator was to be awarded a special commendation from the principal, who visited each class for the performances. But after the first lines, *O Captain! my Captain! our fearful trip is done,* I felt dizzy.

"Are you sick?" Mrs. Oliver asked. "Or just a bit of nerves?"

Classmates began to titter as Mrs. Oliver told me to take a deep breath and try again. I did, but it was no use. I said thought I had a fever. She sent me to the school nurse, who after taking my temperature and looking down my throat, said she'd heard my mother was ill. I began to cry. It was the first time I'd admitted to anybody she was dying. My father came for me. I've never been able to get through that poem since, though I try now and then. It is always the same. I can never get to *the prize we sought is won.*

George was still smiling, though looking a little concerned. "Hannah?"

"Truth," I kept hearing Pemba say. But what was the truth and where to begin?

Somehow I couldn't tell them about Pemba, not in the restaurant. Maybe never. They would see my trip with him differently, put their dirty mouths on it, pity me and spoil it all. I wanted to tell them instead about the poem I couldn't get through and about my mother dying three weeks later. I wanted to tell them that I'd never won any prize, except maybe Pemba. But what was it I'd won, really? They'd say that it was something unsubstantial and cheap, given out at amusement parks for throwing a dart at a balloon. So I stalled, reciting words—bricks in a wall I was building between us.

"I *am* better. Still tire easily. Thought about you every day. Glad you all made it." I knew I was sounding ridiculous but couldn't stop myself. "The trip back was very hard, but Pemba was very helpful. George, I hope you will mention it to the Sherpa cooperative."

It had slipped out without my thinking. Was it to disguise my love or was it to distance myself from it? I paused while people shifted in their chairs. Suddenly aware of an omission, I added quickly, "And, of course, Leon was great too."

Everyone's eyes shifted to Leon, who remained expressionless. I went on to say how hospitable the Butlers had been and how I hoped they all would all have a chance to see Grace's garden before we left. Libby covered my hand with hers as if to quiet me. "They're a charming couple who have lived here a long time. It's a terribly poor country, but you know that. Pemba says the government should do a lot more, but there's so much corruption."

Leon interrupted to ask where Pemba was.

"He had to go somewhere."

"You were with him." George was playing with his table knife, turning it over again and again as it lay on the table. "How was that?"

Pru, who was next to him, said, "Stop fidgeting, George." She took the knife away and said, "Go on, Hannah."

I laughed. "Pemba says every kukri finds its sheath."

Silence.

"What does that mean?" Bobby finally asked. "Like there's a

place for everything?"

"Sort of," I replied. "Of course, Pemba's place is in Nepal."

"No kidding," said Paul as the others, embarrassed, played with their napkins or their fingers.

"What's wrong?" I asked. "I couldn't go alone and the Butlers don't move from their bungalow."

"We're just curious," George had taken back the knife, "about how you got on."

"I got on fine. Let's talk about your trip now."

They did, awkwardly. Going around the table reluctantly, one by one. Their descriptions were flat and colorless, their speech slow. I looked at Libby for an answer to what was happening.

"Things being over, having to go home." She signaled for the waiter.

Howard looked disapprovingly as another martini was set before her. Libby reached across the table to take his hand. "It's a poker game, honey. We're all dealt a hand and try to make the best of it. Discard this one, pick up another. Trying to win the jackpot."

"What are you talking about?" Howard asked.

"Poker."

I moved Libby's drink away from her. She moved it back and leaned toward me.

Whispering in my ear, she expounded on her imaginary poker game. George and Pru held a pair of lonely hearts, not a winning hand. Martha was bluffing, maybe. She was spending time with both Paul and Leon. George seemed to want to get in on the game. A full house, but who has the winning hand? "See what I mean?" she asked, leaning back and staring at me.

"What do you think of her?" I whispered.

Pulling me closer, she said Martha was okay in her own kooky way. "Smart, too. Used Palmer, Jackson and Lieberman for her divorce. Got a very nice settlement."

She'd told Libby she was suing the board of her co-op for not making repairs they had promised. And she was angry with her brother for some reason. She'd confessed to bad times with depression. "Says Paul is saving her life and that she loves him for it. Adds she has never met anyone as interesting as Leon. Feels coming here has freed her inner somebody."

Howard had shoved his chair back and looked ready to leave. Libby ignored him and suddenly changed the subject. "Going off suddenly without telling Leon. What was that about?"

I told her I had wanted time to myself.

"But you weren't by yourself. See what I mean?" She didn't wait for an answer. Leon thought I was having an affair, but Pru said I wasn't. It was Leon who was having the affair. "Men sometimes just fuck for revenge," Libby rambled on. And what if I did have a fling? she asked. No one was going to be angry with me about it, except Leon.

George stood up and was bending over Martha, rubbing her back while he whispered in her ear. She was smiling and nodding. He straightened up, saying the hotel was full but Martha had generously offered to give up one of her rooms so we could all be together.

Leon rose, eyeing Martha. "I left a few things there. I'll go fetch them."

"Bring a suitcase, you'll need it," Libby yelled, grinning drunkenly at everyone, all of whom sat stone-faced. "Poor us," Libby said suddenly. "Lost our sense of humor." She stared at me, her eyes watery, her hand grasping mine. She thought men were always trying to stuff their shit out of sight. She bent close to my ear, her arm tight around my shoulder. "Hubby here gave me venereal warts. Had them before we met, didn't tell me. Men, you got to love them just the same. Maybe women are the answer. Ever think of that?"

She and Pru had been talking about it. "Not about her and me, just about the topic in general. There's a solution for everything." She called across the table to Howard, who had sat down again: "Isn't that right, sweetheart?"

"Isn't what right?" he asked irritably.

"That women are a solution."

"You're pickled."

She gave him a thumbs-up and turned back to me. "But a kid from around here?" I stared at her. The drumbeat was beginning. The story that would be told over dinner tables.

Libby continued, "I mean, what can you do with him? Can't take him back. Can't stay here."

"Why not?"

"And do what? Hoe a row of beans? Or maybe he could come with you and get a job stabbing candy wrappers in Central Park."

"You know, I love you when you're sober, but you're an awful drunk."

She looked at me for a moment and then hugged me, almost collapsing into my lap, and began a drunken sob. She said she knew it. She was just worried about my choices of men and that I'd end up alone.

It would have been better if I had been. As soon as I got to my room, there was a knock on the door. It was Paul with Bobby, claiming to be the local welcome wagon. Bobby began by giving me another hug.

"Look what Dad brought." He fished a flask from Paul's back pocket. "He says I can have a sip because it's a special occasion."

I looked at Paul, who was rolling his eyes. "Just a sip, Bobby, then go see if you can find the pottery we bought. I want Hannah to have a look."

"Where'd you put it?"

Paul said it was in his backpack and not to break it.

"I'll be back," Bobby said, giving me a thumbs-up and taking the flask with him.

I told Paul how much taller and thinner Bobby seemed and how Miriam would want to fatten him up.

"Oh, she'll fuss over him for sure."

"Still on that?"

He took the only chair, leaving me to sit on the edge of my bed.

"I guess you've heard."

"And seen."

"It's a mess." He said he'd been keeping as much distance as he could from Martha, but it was hard. He made me promise not to breathe a word to Miriam. I urged him to tell Martha he couldn't continue to treat her under the circumstances. He said it wasn't that simple, that he wanted her. He knew she was crazy, but he thought she'd be better if they were together. "Says she's been flirting with Leon only because I was away. The bastard's gotten himself in the middle of it."

"Flirting? So now she's sleeping with the two of you? Don't tell me. I don't want to know."

He told me anyway, that she loved Paul but wouldn't sleep with him until he told Miriam about her. I asked if she planned to get it on with Leon until then. I told him Martha was going to squeeze his nuts till he screamed. It gave her something to live for. You didn't need to be a shrink to see that. He said I was wrong about her.

"You tell Miriam . . ." I was exasperated. "And then what?" After he realized his mistake and tried to end the affair, Martha would go after him for all he was worth. How would he explain her meeting him here?

He looked at his feet, rubbed his eyes with his hands and told me I wasn't helping. "What about you?" he said after a while. "Dumped Leon for a guide?"

"What does Martha want from Leon anyway?" I asked, not yet done with her.

"What does she want from any man? He's a well-known artist. I'm a shrink. Makes her feel important, something she never felt growing up." Paul looked worried. "Will you tell Miriam about you and Pemba?"

"Of course. She's one of my best friends."

"But what if she asks about me?"

"You! You! It's Bobby you should worry about. Who knows what he's figured out? He's very likely to mention Martha to his mother."

"She tells him she's here on business. That she's just met me and that she's attracted to Leon. Nobody says anything different. Buys him candy and stuff from the gift shop. Listens to his boring accounts of the trek."

If Miriam knew, there'd be hell to pay. Maybe more time in bed with empty coffee cups and fire department visits. And if she found out I'd known about it, our friendship would be over. I told Paul to get his head out of his ass, that Miriam loved him, only God knew why. I said he was afraid of loving anyone who might love him back.

Bobby returned, showed me an oval vase and told me what it cost. Then he spread all his souvenirs on my bed—small brass bells to wear around his neck, an imitation thangka for his bedroom, a yak pelt and a sketch of the yeti to bring to school. He held up a shiny kukri that he had pulled from its wooden cover. "Do you think Pemba would like to see it? I missed him. The other Sherpas weren't as nice."

"Good night, sweet boy." I kissed him on the cheek and let him and his father out. I had just managed to change into pajamas when Leon knocked.

"What time is it?" I asked as I opened the door. "I can't take much more." He insisted I owed him a few minutes. "I'm not sure I owe you anything," I sighed.

"You do. Leaving Grace to tell me you'd taken off." He said he knew I had "a thing" for Pemba, but he thought it was a kind of altitude sickness, that I'd get over it and come down to earth. "We were talking seriously about a future together."

"You were."

"What were you doing?"

"Trying to learn how to live, I guess."

He told me that was "fuckin' museum-speak" and that I needed to get real.

"I'm as real as I can be. How about you?"

"Sure, I have baggage. Wouldn't you if you had been through the Holocaust?"

I told him he hadn't. It was his father who had survived.

"By taking all his shit out on me and Mother. He's made his name as a painter because he survived the war. But didn't I have to survive him?"

"You have. Everyone thinks your work is fabulous."

"And don't you think that worries me? One bad review and you're suddenly gone. Look what happened to Jackson Pollock. People forgot about him after he went back to figure painting and darker colors.

I said that was only for a while and that Pollock was well regarded now. He thought "for a while" had killed him. "Drinking got worse, finally drove into a tree."

"You need Martha's admiration to protect you from feelings of insignificance."

"Okay. So what? I thought you might provide that. You're the only one who ever understood my work. You pulled them out from under the bed, made me think I had something to offer."

I said he did.

"But not to you."

"Once. Not now." I put my hand on his shoulder. "You don't want to admit how different we are." The distance from home had made him forget how he had hated all the things I tried to do to make our lives better.

"Dishes and curtains don't make life better."

"They did for me."

If that were true, he said, then why Pemba? Why a Sherpa who doesn't have a pot to piss in? I asked him not to be cruel, and admitted that Pemba might never notice the plates we ate on. And if he did, he'd remind me of those who have no food to put on them. Leon stood and pulled me out of the chair and into in his arms.

"Hannah," he whispered in my ear, "we could be better with each other. It's too hard to be alone, back into that hateful world."

I kissed him lightly on the cheek. "The hate is in you and in the world too. Your paintings change that a little, clarify things for a moment. They're beautiful. Let Martha help you. She's helped me know what I already knew. I couldn't marry you and be happy."

"You're going to be happy with Pemba. Is that the plan?"

I put my hand over his mouth. "It's strange, I know. I can't understand it any more than you. But Martha can help you. She won't let you hide if you're with her. You might even love her in the end. Though I wouldn't advise it."

"What about Paul?" he asked.

I said in the end he'd be doing him a favor.

"And you?" His eyes were soft and questioning.

"I don't know what I'll do."

"You can't stay here."

"Maybe not." I'd miss all of you, and New York too. "But I do love him, strange as that is."

Leon replied that I always loved the wrong man. I told him he had been one of them. I kissed him on the lips. "You are sweet. And I do love you, but not to live with. I'm sorry."

He looked at me sadly and shrugged. "I'm sorry too."

"You'll be fine and so will I."

CHAPTER TWENTY-SIX
DIFFERENCES

I wasn't sure if that last part was true. I spent a sleepless night, wondering where Pemba was, waiting to hear the sound of gunfire or an explosion. I avoided the group at breakfast, getting there earlier than the rest, then hiding in my room. Pemba arrived at the hotel at ten. He smiled, but his eyes were hard and distant.

"Are you all right?" I asked.

"Had talk with George. He call Sherpa co-op. Ask me come. Ask me about trip, why I agree to take you. I say that you well enough. Then he ask if we 'get it on.' I no understand. He explain what means. I say yes, we love. He say maybe I want something extra to settle things. He show me money."

"Pemba. I'm sorry."

"He say it your idea."

"No, no. I just wanted him to put in a good word for you."

"Buy me off."

I hugged him. "Never. I'd never think that. I love you."

He kept his arms by his side. "Sherpa guide again."

"You are so much more. You know that. It's all mixed up. I'll talk to George."

Pemba said I was mixed up in my mind. I let go of him. There was a long silence while Pemba studied me.

"Too hard for you to stay," he said quietly.

"Wouldn't it be for you?" I could never condone what he did. I would be frightened all the time of where he was and what he might do and what might be done to him. And would his friends accept me? Not really. Someone who didn't believe in their methods? I'd seem a threat to everyone's security. It would wear on him. I'd be this American wife who never fit in.

"Too hard to love a poor man."

"You're not poor. You're richer than me in so many ways. If you were a poor American, it would be easier. At least, there'd be common references: TV shows, movies, the names of the presidents!

But come with me. Let's try it, even if it's hard at first. There are more Nepalese in New York than there are Americans here. They will help us. It is very different, but you would like much of it. We could move out of the city, somewhere where there are mountains."

"But no revolution."

"There are poor people who need help. There's a war that needs stopping."

"Can't leave until win here."

I told him others could carry on the work. He'd done his part. Risked his life. "Don't risk love," I pleaded.

"One of us has to risk. Is work you can do here. Butlers help. What I do in U.S.? I be thinking how much there, how little here. Feel traitor. You stay here, not traitor to anything."

I began to sob. "I just can't. I have a father still, a job and friends."

CHAPTER TWENTY-SEVEN
ADVICE

"Of course you can't," Pru said sharply over lunch at the Yak and Yeti. I had sworn her to secrecy about Pemba's politics, leaving out the violence. "I'm sure it was wonderful, but you can't just walk away from your life."

"That's why you're still with George."

"Yes. You can't go tearing things up unless you've got a better plan."

"But you haven't been happy."

"I don't have a better plan, do I? That's the part that makes me angry. I'm not pretty. I don't have a career like my mother did. I left ambition to her and George." That had been a mistake, she admitted, but now it was the devil she knew. Of course, she had thought of leaving "more than once." But what would she do alone?

The same things she was doing, but with less money. She knew single women, bright, lovely people who tried to patch together an interesting life: filling lonely hours with free concerts or lectures at the New School. She reminded me that there had been a lot of good times when she and George were first married. There'd been travel they both enjoyed, reading beforehand about the places they'd visit, discussing the itinerary. They had loved watching football. Sunday afternoons in front of the TV with dinner on their laps, rooting for the Giants, knowing that sex would follow no matter who won. It had all grown stale, somehow, but there were the children who still needed her because George wasn't often around. Her two sons filled in for a lot that was missing. Besides, she didn't think she would find anyone else.

"Or worse yet, finding and failing again."

Looking for another man didn't seem worth the trouble. And women? She wondered about it, but that was all. "You're different," she went on. "Good looks. Men are interested. And you have work." It troubled her to think I would throw it all away. "Maybe Paul knows someone you could talk to."

I didn't want to talk with anyone Paul knew. I said that I was happy when I was with Pemba.

"Yes, as long as you two are trekking. The problems begin when you have to come back and make it real. Then there's sacrifice. Compromise. Times when you don't love."

"The trek, the people. They were real. I can't lose him, Pru."

"Look, let's be honest. What you don't want to lose is the dream of love. And Pemba is wonderfully caring—a great guide, maybe great in bed, but he can't look after you, really. I don't mean money. If you stay here, I guarantee no matter how much he loves you, you will feel like an abandoned child. An orphan, far from the home you once knew."

I said I felt like an orphan in New York.

"Of course you do. But at least you have friends. You have possibilities. Here there are only a limited number of people to meet." Pru signaled for the check. "I'll let you know about dinner. I think George has found a better place for us to eat than the hotel."

I wasn't coming, I said. I had an invitation from the Butlers for that evening.

* * *

"At least, back in one piece," Grace said. She inspected me as she might a bruised flower. "Tea, dear? Then perhaps you can tell us what on earth you were thinking."

"She looks like she's ready for something a bit stronger," Jeremy said. "A glass of port? What say?"

I agreed to a sherry. We sat in the garden. It was familiar, yet something about it had changed. "It's the *Tagetes erecta,* those large marigolds I put along the wall," Grace said.

Jeremy leaned forward. "I heard the trip went splendidly. Pemba told me what a scout you were."

He'd been very patient, I told them. Grace gave me a sharp look, adding that it was the way Sherpa guides were supposed to be. Jeremy asked if the trip had made me want to stay longer.

Grace put down her glass. "I don't know why you would, but Jeremy has made inquiries at the museum." They wanted to talk with me, she said, though they would offer a pittance as a salary. She thought they might better afford to pay me to return once in a while as a visiting lecturer. "They know so little about Dutch painting."

I should come back when her late-spring plantings were in their glory. She would have a party and introduce me to people who could make my visits more enjoyable.

"Unless you stay on," Jeremy interjected. "There's a lot of Nepal you haven't seen." He suggested I be their guest for a while and see how Kathmandu suited me.

"It would cost me my job."

"Of course it would," Grace interceded, "and for what?" A single American woman here would be a curiosity, she pointed out. And as for Pemba showing me more of Nepal, she thought that wouldn't be wise. He wasn't the kind of acquaintance I'd want to keep, if I were to stay. "You would not be welcome in the circles where you might feel most comfortable." But this was all nonsense, she went on. There was absolutely no reason to stay except to please Jeremy.

"Or myself?"

"Good point, Hannah," Jeremy chimed in. "If you could be happy here. And I think you could."

Dep appeared. "Pemba would like to see Miss Avery."

"I told you not to invite him here!" Grace rose, agitated.

We all got up. "My dear, he's come to accompany Hannah to the hotel," Jeremy said. "You don't need to greet him."

Jeremy walked me to the bungalow door. Grace disappeared into her garden. Pemba folded his hands in greeting before taking my hand. He smiled at Jeremy. "Soon. Yes?" Jeremy nodded, giving us a hurried wave before ducking into his house.

We walked slowly, our feet finding a joint rhythm as they had on the trail. "That okay?" Pemba asked.

I told him Grace had been a bit of a strain and that Jeremy thought I should stay.

"You not stay."

I stopped, and he dropped my hand. "I don't think so."

"I see."

"Do you? Because I don't. I'd have to go home and settle things anyway. It's not as though I could stay right away."

He said I could go back later.

"I don't know what to do. I need time to think."

"Think here. I have trek now. Back in two weeks. Told friends to meet you, make sure you okay. Jeremy can arrange."

"When do you go?"

"Tomorrow. I look for you at Butlers when come back." He stared straight at me, squeezed my hand and was gone. I looked around to see if we had been followed. The street was empty.

CHAPTER TWENTY-EIGHT
NEW YORK

I wrote a long letter to Pemba explaining my decision as best I could and delivered it to the Sherpa cooperative. I sent Grace a note. Avoided Jeremy. Then I watched my baggage being loaded on the bus for the airport. Pru reassured me that I'd made the right choice, but I felt a world collapsing within me.

"Make sure you have everything," George commanded. "We ain't coming back!"

What I did come back to was my apartment, looking drearier and smaller than ever, to the war still going on, to my neighbor having moved away, to my two tulip illustrations, to Harrington showing me the article Frank had published about the Baudrys, to dinners with my father, and to a loneliness more terrible than ever.

Of course, there was work again. When I gave Harrington his gift, he glanced at it. "Made by Tibetan refugees, huh? Interesting." Clearly, it was not. And neither was he nor the Baudry anymore, both seeming as stiff and supercilious as old ladies in ball gowns. I wondered what I had liked about the museum. It was a place filled with things no longer lived with. The objects in it had been important to their owners once. They had sat on a desk where a fine lady penned letters or adorned the wall where she dined. They had been in bedrooms, witnesses to lovemaking. Now they were packed into glass cases or hung in meaningless space. Viewers couldn't sit or lie among them, only stand and stare. They had lost life for me. They sat in my mind like discarded stuffed animals. My book on Dutch garden design hadn't been read by anybody in years. My interest in remaining a curator was sinking faster than the Titanic.

I had lunch with Miriam and told her how tired I was feeling. "You'll perk up," she said. "You've been so far from home, it's hard to get used to being back."

I asked how things were with her. "I'm glad he's here," she answered. "Bobby can't stop talking about the trek. He told me you had a boyfriend there."

"Nothing gets by that kid." I told her about Pemba. I described the jet lag that didn't end, the unease in my gut, the fear and wish that Pemba would contact me.

"Bobby told me about Martha."

My heart sank. "What about her?"

"Only that she was Leon's girlfriend and that he liked her."

I nodded and asked for more coffee.

⁂

At the next meeting of the Baudry staff, Harrington said the museum had to take a new direction. What was now "cutting edge" was photography. He had been to London and, with Board approval, had purchased a Man Ray, the cornerstone for a new Modern Photography collection. Of course, it would mean some reshuffling of priorities and perhaps selling a painting or two "if it's legal." He had lawyers working on it. I could see the handwriting on the wall. The old man would never be cleaned. And frankly, I didn't much care anymore. They would take him down soon enough to make room for a Stieglitz.

I'd left Pemba information as to where to reach me, but hadn't heard from him. But after missing a period and having a urine test that my internist told me had been positive, I contacted the Sherpa cooperative and got ahold of him.

"I'm scared," I told him.

"New life, always good news."

"Not when you're alone."

"Alone is not only choice."

"I can't," I said.

We hung up and I cried, hard bitter tears. I cried for my own limitations and for his. I cried for a life I couldn't live and he couldn't leave. I wept because the old man would end up in the basement. And because the tulips were two and I was one.

Jeremy sent me a letter of congratulations. Grace sent a telegram, recommending "termination" while there was still time. When my breasts began to swell and morning sickness plagued me, I contacted an OB that Pru recommended.

Dr. Greenfield was tall and middle-aged, with a beard, glasses and a white coat. He examined me carefully and confirmed that my uterus was enlarged. Sitting in his office, a desk between us, he asked how I felt about being pregnant. My mind, I said, hadn't yet caught up with my body. I wasn't sure how I felt beyond being frightened. He was silent.

"I suppose I've always been afraid of being a mother. Maybe this is the only way it could have happened." I went on to tell him how it had happened. He leaned back in his chair, put his hands behind his head and stared at the ceiling. "You will help me won't you? It know it's going to be hard for me and the baby, but I can't erase the love that lives in me." He sat straight, nodded and said he would see me next month.

It was hard having to explain my pregnancy to others. In 1972 being an unwed mother brought a lot more criticism than it does today. Telling people the father was a Sherpa only made things worse. Their discomfort was palpable. *Of course you want the child* was a frequent response, which was really a question.

When I told Harrington that I was pregnant, he asked me not to discuss the matter with donors or Board members. Did Frank know? he asked. He was having lunch with him in a few weeks. I told him it was none of Frank's business. His response was "I suppose you'll want maternity leave, but then, you've just been away."

He said I should think about how I would fit into the new Baudry. Younger members were no longer interested in "old stuff," beautiful as it was. "We have to keep abreast," he said. The rose garden was expensive to maintain. Using the space to enlarge the gift shop was much more economical.

I told him I wouldn't be back after my child was born. It wasn't something I planned to say. My announcement surprised both of us and made Harrington uneasy. "You've accepted another offer? In New York?"

I told him I didn't know what I was going do, but the rose garden and I would be leaving at about the same time.

"You're taking a risk," he said.

"I'm making a choice." It sounded better than I felt. All I knew was that I had to change my life.

There were those who, like my boss, were embarrassed in my company. I was, after all, the woman who couldn't find a man, who had taken advantage of a young Sherpa because she was desperate to have a child. Were they right? I knew we'd been careless during the Pokhara trip, but I would not have wanted it to be different. I must have known even then that Pemba would never agree to an abortion. And I didn't want one now. Besides, they were illegal and dangerous. I wasn't about to visit a doctor I didn't know after dark. I didn't want to see a van parked out in front of the office in case, botched and bleeding, I had to be unceremoniously dumped at an emergency room door. Pemba wrote that the baby was a gift for both of us. It didn't always seem like a gift to me, but I knew I couldn't murder the mother within me. I wept when, on delivery, I was told it was a girl.

"Your mother would be happy," my father said. I wasn't sure about that. Would she really have been happy having a Nepalese-American grandchild? I hadn't spent enough time with her to know.

* * *

My only child, May, came as the war wound down. Harrington had begrudgingly granted me a month's paid leave when she arrived.

May was a quiet, sweet infant with lots of shiny black hair and dark eyes that seemed to search for a father. My study became the nursery. Leon drew a garden on one of its walls. Libby cooed over May and said she'd wished she'd had a child. My father helped as much as he could, vacuuming the living room and tidying up the kitchen.

Paul and Miriam bought the crib. Paul came over to put it together for me.

"How are you?" I asked.

He shrugged. "Teaching at the Institute now. Working on a paper. Martha's still seeing me four times a week."

"Giving you a hard time?"

"Giving myself the hard time. Shapiro says she is my inner Circe.

I suppose that means I'm turning into a pig." He gave a pitiful oink and turned to view the scattered parts of the crib.

"And Miriam?"

"My Penelope who doesn't know I'm still away. Not yet; never, I hope," he said without looking at me.

Bobby came one afternoon to stare at May and asked what it was like to give birth. He said he wanted to write to Pemba.

"And tell him what?"

"That I want him to see what came out of your belly."

Martha sent a generous gift certificate from Saks, with a note of congratulations that included an invitation to the reception for Leon where his paintings would be unveiled in the boardroom of the hospital. She mentioned, too, how much Paul was helping her.

"You're still seeing her?" I asked Leon when I saw him next.

"She's a lovely woman."

"That doesn't sound like love."

Leon shrugged. He asked what I was going to do now that May had come. I said I didn't know. Look for a job, I supposed.

"How about a gallery?"

"Selling what?"

He shrugged again.

CHAPTER TWENTY-NINE
THE OPENING

May kept me busy with feedings every four hours. I couldn't get over her. She was my miracle. I was on holy ground. I felt like Mary in van Eyck's *The Madonna in the Church.* Only, I wasn't in Berlin, where the picture hangs, and I wasn't in a church. I loved every minute she was awake and enjoyed the silence when she slept. It gave me time to think. I thought about Pemba and our trek, about how amazing it had been and how difficult. I spent time looking at my tulips. They would be out of place in Nepal and so would I. I knew I could never leave New York. But I had changed my life with the trek. There was nothing to keep me from changing it more. I telephoned Leon and then put in a call to Harrington. He asked how May was.

"In need of a mother."

"Of course. Is that what you plan to do?"

"That, and open my own art gallery." I told him my first show would be Leon Kaminsky's new paintings. He was impressed.

"And after that?" he asked.

"I don't know."

Six months later, I was on Third and Sixty-Second. A small space, but I redid the floors and painted the walls a blistering white. Leon's paintings sold, giving me more than enough money to keep going until I found my next step. Everyone advised I continue selling contemporary art, as Leon's show had given the gallery cachet. But the only connection I had to modern painters was through him. It wasn't a direction I wanted to go in.

After Leon's show ended, I'd go to the gallery, stare at the blank walls and nurse May. I tried to think of how I could use what I already knew without going backward. Maybe not Holland but the Dutch territories. I'd come across references to Indonesian art in my research on the Old Masters, but hadn't paid it much attention. I knew the Dutch had arrived in Indonesia in 1602 and grew rich in the spice trade. They ruled the islands until the end of World War II. I'd seen some of the work of Lee Man Fong, a Chinese-born painter whose family settled in Jakarta, but that was about it.

I called colleagues in Amsterdam who put me in touch with Indonesian scholars. Over the next twelve months, while May learned to walk and talk, I immersed myself in Indonesia and its culture. I met with collectors in New York, talked with curators at the Asian Art Museum in San Francisco, gossiped by telephone with gallery owners in Paris and Berlin.

The art of Indonesia was relatively unknown to New Yorkers. That was the good news and the bad in terms of selling it. I couldn't depend on paintings alone. So it would be a gallery with a bevy of sculptures, woven baskets and textiles: valuable old ikat weavings as well as unusual modern batiks. I bought whatever and wherever I could with my savings and some funds from my dad. I couldn't leave May to go to Indonesia myself in the beginning. Instead, I commissioned colleagues and friends I trusted to buy for me. When May was older, I went myself, and once with her.

My choices aren't to everyone's taste. Harrington, for instance, circled the gallery and left quickly with a "Lovely. Good luck." George liked the textiles better than the paintings. He bought several hand-knotted rugs and an expensive bronze Buddha. Martha introduced me to her wealthy friends, some of whom became collectors.

Of course, more people travel now and buy things on their own. Art has changed from being bought for pleasure to being bought as an investment. It's harder work than being a curator, closer to being a real estate broker. I've had to move the gallery several times because of rising rents. My work provides a reason for frequent trips to Indonesia, a country I've come to love, and for travel to Amsterdam, where I meet with colleagues who still talk of tulips and ask if I am planting them in Jakarta. I've found an Indonesian Berenson to help me, met artists there I've come to love and have developed a devoted and growing clientele here. I am in the gallery most days. My hours are my own and my search for beautiful objects perpetual.

I came back from George's funeral this morning, thinking over the twenty-two years since our trek. Some things have changed, some remained the same.

I visit my father every week I'm in town. He's in a nursing home on 106th Street. I couldn't have had him live with me. He required too much care, paralyzed on one side, needing to be lifted out of bed and into a chair. His bowels not always reliable. Last year, in the nursing home, he broke his leg trying to stand when he had called for assistance and no one came. He was found moaning on the floor in his feces. Transferred to another ward. Assurances it wouldn't happen again. Suggestions he needed to learn to be patient, to wait until staff arrived with a bedpan.

When Pru asks me about Pemba, I report on the recent political changes in Nepal that Pemba helped bring about. The Communist party has official recognition and a voice in government now. He was asked to run for a seat in the Nepali Congress, but refused. He still prefers the mountains. His aunt and uncle's place is now his. His daughter and May see one another often.

It's been fifteen years since Martha left New York for a wealthy widower in California. She had a child by him who must be a teenager by now. I take it as evidence of how much Paul had helped her.

"And you still miss her?" I asked Paul.

"Not her. Just the possibility of another life."

When Leon calls, we get together—even sleep together once in a while. The sex is sweet now, if not compelling. My need for a man, in or out of bed, has diminished.

Over coffee today, Bobby told me he is dating a girl from Japan who he thinks he wants to marry. If they have a son, they've agreed to name him George Pemba Levin. When I next meet Miriam for lunch, she will tell me how much she wants to be a grandmother.

Frank has been with Ursula all these years. She wanted a child, I hear, but he didn't or couldn't. And I am alone, corresponding with former colleagues, spending time with my tulips and my gallery.

I keep in touch with Harrington, who is still at the Baudry, despite his wish to move on. He hopes to build an auditorium above the gift shop that was once the garden. His former secretary is now his wife. They have two children, young women now.

Jeremy and Grace finally left Nepal five years ago at Grace's insistence. She claimed aging in place was not an option. They are living in a retirement village near Canberra. Jeremy, after a small stroke, uses a walker. Grace runs the community garden. They want me to visit, but it's a long way. And then there's George, who always had to have his way and, to everyone's surprise, couldn't find it in the end. He helped change my life. I owe him for that, always will.

CPSIA information can be obtained
at www.ICGtesting.com
Printed in the USA
BVHW061452080419
544915BV00012B/706/P

9 781949 093094